ALL THE WAY OUT

Ingrid Sterling

Literary Wanderlust | Denver, Colorado

Published in the United States by Literary Wanderlust LLC, Denver, Colorado.

LiteraryWanderlust.com

ISBN Print: 978-1-942856-73-3
ISBN Digital: 978-1-942856-77-1

Cover design: Pozo Mitsuma

Printed in the United States of America

Dedication

The Blanket Fort, because without you both none of this happens.

Ashley for the em dashes and so much more.

The readers who loved this story along the way.

Most importantly, to the man who gave me the best love story of them all.

1

As it turned out, Grindr worked in Italy too. This little bit of information would have made the last few weeks far more interesting for Zach. He felt like the typical American tourist for not checking the app's functionality beforehand but, to be fair, it's not like he'd ever used the app for its intended purpose on either side of the Atlantic.

He'd downloaded and uninstalled the gay hook-up app more times than he could count, but eventually, guilt and common sense always reminded him that leaving Grindr on his phone was way too much of a liability. What if his girlfriend or one of his buddies happened to look through his phone and stopped to ask why he, Zachary Sugarman, starting quarterback for Northwestern University and NFL hopeful, had a Grindr profile?

He could never use the app on campus where his likeness was plastered on promotional posters all over Northwestern's suburban Chicago town and his last name was stitched into overpriced jerseys in the bookstore. The same went for road games. All it would take was one guy who was even remotely interested in college football to write some vague Tweet or post even the blurriest picture to Instagram, and Zach's hoped-for career would be destroyed. Being an out, gay football player wasn't just a serious risk, it wasn't even an option.

A few weeks earlier, Zach and the rest of the Northwestern University Football team gathered on the familiar Evanston campus to prepare for a pre-season trip to Rome. The morning of their flight, they filed into the basement of Ryan Stadium and listened to a long lecture from the school's athletic director about the rules and expectations for their trip abroad. Team building, cross-cultural experience, intense training, representing the university, yada, yada, yada—Zach couldn't be bothered with the specifics; he was too busy stifling yawns.

The general gist of the talk, though? Don't be idiots. Over the next two weeks, the team of over fifty eighteen to twenty-something young men had followed the AD's pleas for best behavior on the trip through walking tours of the Colosseum, the Pantheon, the Forum, a private visit to the Sistine Chapel, as well as a Q&A with the professional players of A.S. Roma, one of the city's professional football teams—in the European sense of the word, of course.

Zach had not thought once about trying to hook-up with some guy. His thoughts had instead been focused on the amazing travel experience.

"So, Sugarman, is it everything you'd dreamed it would be?" Wildcat head coach Tim Williams had asked Zach one afternoon as they strolled down Via Appia. Zach had turned away from where their tour guide described the Catacomb of Callixtus in her pleasantly accented English. That is when it had hit him that this trip had been molded around Zach's interests. Clearly, there were perks to being a hopeful Heisman Trophy winner and potential number one draft pick. He'd hugged Coach, hard.

Interspersed with the sightseeing were practices. They ran speed drills and passing routes in the *Stadio Olympico* under the unrelenting Roman sun, burning infinitely hotter than the one they'd left behind in northern Illinois. These interludes on the field were a reminder of what waited back home for Zach: the start of his senior year and with it, the start of his last chance to take Northwestern all the way to a National Championship title. Those expectations left Zach feeling an oppressiveness that had nothing to do with the dusty Italian heat.

On the last night of the trip as plates were being cleared from their team dinner, Coach Williams announced that there would be no curfew enforced that night, as reward for their good behavior and hard work. Zach whooped and hollered along with the rest of his team but for very different reasons.

For Zach's teammates, this bit of unexpected freedom meant an open-ended night of clubs, drinking, and *belle donne Italiane*—such revelry to honor Bacchus himself. For Zach, though, there was an instant siren's song from the phone in his pocket, from the app he knew would download in seconds and give him what was impossible pretty much anywhere else: the chance to be a nameless, faceless nobody one last time.

The whole upperclassmen crew was in high spirits, ready for a fantastic night. Their laughter echoed off old stone edifices all around them. Zach clambered down the narrow streets and up the stairway to the Airbnb where he and the other seniors had been staying for the duration of the trip.

Once inside, they turned on some pregaming tunes on Spotify and pulled out various bottles of alcohol. Christian Ruiz, an offensive lineman, located cups and shot glasses. Trey Jackson, a defensive back, began pouring strong and stomach-churning drinks for everyone, all while the group made plans to Uber to *il Campo de' Fiori*—a hot spot for nightlife—for even more alcohol consumption later.

Zach watched them for a moment, amused by their dedication to getting drunk. He was both completely at home in their company and completely alone all at once. More than purely his teammates and best friends, these men felt like brothers to Zach. They'd had his back since freshman year, on the field and off, and he knew they would one day be the groomsmen at his wedding. The same guys who one day, once they'd all suffered too many concussions and their knees had been blown out too many times, he'd call up on the weekend so they could talk about their glory days as their own kids played in the yard.

That was the dream, the future Zach had been mapping out for himself for years. But that dream would only become a reality if no one ever found out about his plans to find some anonymous guy to hook up with that night.

As the drinking began in earnest, Zach slipped unnoticed into his bedroom, pulling the door closed enough to hide himself from any curious eyes but not enough to draw attention to his absence. He opened the app that had started syncing the moment his phone connected to the apartment's WiFi and signed in.

His profile picture was old, left over from his sophomore year. He'd suffered a mild ankle sprain early in the season that year and had been forced to sit out for a week. Opening a Grindr account had been a reckless way to deal with being frustrated by his inactivity and the fact his team lost without him. The two-year-old image showed his torso, slightly angled away from the camera, offering a hint of hip bone below his well-defined abs. He'd thought it was kind of artsy at the time. It still got the point across that all the hours Zach spent in the gym had a pretty nice effect on his body.

Zach lowered himself onto the edge of his bed as he began scrolling through the matrix of pictures of men that the app deemed to be close by. It came as no surprise that most of the guys were Italian—dark hair, olive skin, showing off their bare-chests, or even more.

"24! What you doing in there?" Rick Ulrich, their placekicker, called from the other room. Zach would recognize the way Rick's Bronx accent thickened his pronunciation of the number Zach wore on the back of his jersey anywhere.

"You know what he's doing," Jackson mumbled loud enough for Zach to hear.

A chorus of high-pitched "Ooo's" and kissy sounds erupted in the other room and Zach rolled his eyes. They could be positively infantile at times.

"I'm going to FaceTime with Rebecca," Zach shouted back even as he continued to look through pictures of boys.

"Told you," Jackson retorted.

"That girl has him so whipped," Ruiz chimed in.

A louder and more authoritative voice piped up. "Don't be acting all jealous cause Zach's got a girl and all you got is your right hand."

There were further snickers as Zach got up and craned his head through the crack in the door. He waved a sweeping middle finger around the room before offering an overly courteous, "Thank you, Des," and slamming the door.

Stanley Desarmes, who went by Des for obvious reasons, was Zach's favorite wide receiver and had been his best friend since the end of middle school. Des's family had moved from Haiti to Zach's very white and very Christian suburb outside Seattle at the end of seventh grade, and the two boys had quickly bonded over their love of football. A shared sense of being the odd-one-out was what had truly solidified their friendship, as Des was only black kid and Zach was the only Jewish kid in their grade. But not even Des knew about the *other* otherness that further separated Zach from all the rest.

After a few more minutes of looking through profile pictures, one caught his attention.

Filtered in black and white, the man in the picture leaned towards the camera as he looked at something out of frame. His body was slight, and his bare shoulders were just visible in the frame. One of his hands was tucked up by his jaw, his long fingers delicately curled down. It wasn't a selfie; in fact, everything suggested that this picture had been taken by someone else, another lover perhaps. Zach thought it bold of him to share such an intimate moment.

But it was this man's face that Zach liked the most. His eyes were rimmed with long, fair lashes, his full lips pouted and beckoning, and his cheekbones looked like they had been chiseled out of Carrara marble, sculpted to perfection by some ancient master. All of that was captured under a halo of windswept, golden curls.

The profile below the picture listed his details in short bulleted points. Name: Liam, followed by Italian, French, and

American flag emojis. His age, twenty, was followed by another set of numbers. It took Zach a second to realize these were his measurements. Zach gave his phone an impressed look. Then, instead of a link to Facebook or Instagram account, there was a quote left uncredited, though Zach recognized it immediately.

"Be patient and tough; someday this pain will be useful to you."

He laughed. What kind of guys would be so pretentious that he'd quote a passage from Ovid's *Metamorphoses* on a hookup app? And why would this Liam guy choose a quote that hinted at suffering? Unless Liam was into that sort of thing. Suddenly nervous, Zach scanned through the rest of his pictures—but found no leather or whips anywhere in sight. Zach was safe.

Except he wasn't safe, because he couldn't look away. Liam was beautiful. Zach found himself imagining what it would be like to touch that perfect skin, kiss the column of that long neck. He wondered how Liam would smell. Of nicotine and designer cologne, perhaps? Would he fight against Zach's strength, using what tenacity he possessed in those bird-like limbs to resist, or would he happily submit?

Zach opened a chat window and typed.

"Nice Ovid quote."

It was the lamest pickup line Zach had ever seen, but it was the first time he'd had to flirt via text with a total stranger, so it was the best he could come up with. He bit at one thumb while the other hovered over the send button as he tried to think of anything better.

There was a knock on the door. He hit the send button and closed the app as Des entered the room.

"Everything cool?"

Zach nodded, swallowing shallowly. "Yeah, 'course. Becca's just being...well, you know how she gets." He gestured vaguely at the now black screen of his phone then slipped it into his pocket.

"It's been a long summer, man. She's probably just missing you." Des offered Zach a smile, his shoulder propped against the door frame.

If the other guys would be his groomsmen, Des would be his best man.

"You're probably right. Yeah."

Des's smile morphed, becoming toothier, and more jovial. It was the same smile Des gave Zach every time he scored a touchdown off one of Zach's perfectly thrown passes. It was a killer smile on a gorgeous guy that Zach adored, but he'd never thought of Des that way. Not even once. Not even when Zach was still a questioning teenager and the cliché thing to do would have been to fall for his straight best friend.

"Seriously though." Des gestured over his shoulder. "If you don't hurry up, we're all going to be so much drunker than you that you'll have to carry us to the club."

Zach thought of the boy with the effortless curls and the angelic face. He wished he could find out what those eyes looked like up close and in color. He wanted the chance to give in, to feel. But what he wanted didn't matter. The possibilities of a lust-filled night with Liam were slim, and here was his best friend, offering a night to remember.

—

Nights full of alcohol would be strictly off-limits once they were back on campus, so Zach downed the line of shots his buddies set up for him like it was a mission. Stoli, Jäger, coconut rum, tequila—it made for a revolting mix, but Zach barely registered the taste. He slammed the shots down in rapid order, crowing triumphantly with his fists in the air when he finished.

"Another round?" Des asked.

"Why not?" Zach's phone buzzed in his pocket. He pulled it out to see a new notification from Grindr. Liam had replied.

"Grazie. Nice abs, I guess, since that's all you're sharing." Another message buzzed immediately through. "3 Vicolo della Frusta #4 in 20 mins if you're up for it. I'll need to buzz you up."

All thoughts of more drinking with the guys quickly evaporated. His thumbs moved quickly over the glowing screen and he pressed the send button.

"On my way."

Twenty minutes. That gave him barely enough time to look up directions and walk to the address Liam sent him. Zach ran his hands through the cropped hair at the base of his skull, wishing he had time for a shower. The outfit he had on was decent enough for a night out in Evanston, but for Rome? It was going to have to do.

He hid the Google map he'd pulled up on his phone against his abdomen as Des walked over, carefully balancing two very full Jäger shots in front of him.

"To our last year and first place," Des extended one small glass towards Zach.

"You know. I'm actually going to head out for a bit."

"What? But you—"

"I've been meaning to get some pictures of the Colosseum at night."

Zach started backing towards the door as Jackson shouted over the music, "You are such a nerd, Sugarman!" His words were slurred but affectionate.

"I'm not really into the club scene tonight." Zach tried to drum up some sympathy from Des with a pathetic roll of his shoulders.

"Then I'll come with. Let me get my shoes." Des drank both shots, making a gagging sound at the back of his throat when they didn't go down as smoothly as he'd hoped.

"I don't think the other tourists looking for a romantic Roman backdrop would appreciate an onslaught of drunk college guys."

"But you're a drunk college guy," Des attempted to rationalize, but his brain was already running slow.

"I'm not nearly as drunk as you," Zach teased. He placed his hands on his friend's shoulders. "Besides, I'll be wholly less offensive on my own, charming them with my knowledge of how Emperor Vespasian built the Colosseum out of money he gained from the Jewish-Roman war."

Des's eyes glazed over. "Jackson's right. You are a fucking nerd."

Zach let go of Des, making sure his friend remained upright

when he did.

"Alright, fine," Des slurred. "Leave me with these losers as wingmen."

"Screw you, *Stanley.*" A bottle cap breezed past Des's ear and Rick howled with laughter, clearly culpable.

"Don't do anything I wouldn't do," Des said quickly before running across the room to tackle the guilty Rick.

Zach laughed as he slipped out the door. "Don't think you need to worry about that."

2

The neighborhood the team had been staying in was far away from the touristy center of Rome. The streets were lined with corner shops—fresh fruits and local meats displayed in their windows—instead of gaudy stores selling oversized I heart ROMA shirts. Even so, the neighborhood was still alive as Zach made his way to Liam's. Couples settled onto outdoor verandas enjoying an evening *apertivo*. Music selections from various apartment windows intermixed with the grumble of diesel engines and barking dogs. The late Italian summer was electric, and Zach's skin prickled with the humidity.

He walked with a purpose. The undercurrent of anticipation kept his pace steady as he checked the map on his phone and made another turn onto Liam's block. It wasn't until he pressed the large black button next to a faded placard with the number four handwritten on it that the urgency in Zach's belly turned to nerves.

Zach had always been highly self-aware. Even from a young age, he was able to express feelings and thoughts well beyond his years. He was who he was, simple as that. He hated mushrooms. He couldn't stand studying in the erratic noise of a coffee shop, preferring the quiet of his room. He would always puke if he smoked a cigarette while he was drunk.

The revelation about his sexuality had come with a similar amount of self-recognition. There was never much in the way of denial about it. During his first year of high school, his eyes had flitted from boy to girl then back to the boy and he'd asked himself if he could be. It hadn't been long before the words, "I'm gay," formed, complete and without fear, in his head. An even shorter time later, Zach repeated those words aloud in his bathroom mirror on a Saturday morning while his parents weren't home. He'd looked straight into his blue-eyed reflection and come out to himself. It was the only outing Zach had ever had.

Even at the age of fifteen, his path towards elite football had been quite clear. Zach had been savvy enough to know that his two identities—first team all-state quarterback and homosexual male—could not exist concurrently. What had followed were years of pretending. He'd started dating Rebecca during their junior year of high school and never looked back, resigning himself to living one life on the outside while knowing full well he was something completely different on the inside. To achieve what he had on the gridiron, Zach was willing to steal fleeting moments of wholeness where wanting men and wanting to play football weren't mutually exclusive.

"*Pronto.*"

The sound of Liam's voice through the intercom brought Zach back to the moment. He was immediately enamored by Liam's effortlessly rolled 'r,' the percussive stop to the 'o' at the back of his throat.

"*Si, scuzi,*" Zach mumbled, before realizing his minimal Italian was not going to get him very far. Liam had texted him in English, after all, so he switched tack. "Hi. It's, um...It's me?" Zach grimaced at his stutter. Liam's snort came through the speaker with a hint of distortion.

"Second floor. Last door on the right."

The door buzzed and the lock clicked open.

It had been nearly six months since Zach had last been with

a man. Northwestern's season had ended in a bowl game defeat, and Zach had been trying to decide whether he should declare for the draft or stay in school. His thoughts had been a scattered mess, and he'd needed something to focus on. He'd driven to Kalamazoo, Michigan, an hour-and-a-half drive that became two-and-a-half hours with the time change, where he ended up at a gay bar near the Western Michigan University campus. The man he'd gone home with that night was in his early thirties, a townie, not a student, who said he'd never watched sports in his life. It wasn't like Zach targeted guys who had no knowledge of college sports, but it certainly helped.

The hallway on the second floor of Liam's apartment building was narrow, the lights dim. The faded carpet was ornate and red-hued, giving it an ominous atmosphere. As he stepped off the elevator, he couldn't help but feel like he'd walked onto the set of *The Shining*. There was music playing softly from behind the door to Liam's place. Zach knocked and waited.

Then Liam was there, one hand braced on the frame, the other on the edge of the open door. Shirtless and with his arms spread wide, his body was on full display. His gray sweats hung so low on his narrow hips that Zach could read the brand of his dark blue boxer-briefs.

Zach was struck by how slender Liam was. He was delicate and razor-thin, but undeniably masculine, his muscles well defined like those of a runner or a diver. There was nothing soft about Liam, aside from the buoyant curls framing his face. Zach wanted to touch each one.

Meanwhile, the eyes that had been so quick to catch Zach's attention in Liam's profile picture slowly worked their way up Zach's body, scanning every dip and curve. Now in the color of reality, Zach could see that Liam's eyes were a pale blue-green, like the water of a lake, placid and soulful.

Zach's heart pounded hard in his chest as their eyes met. He did everything he could to hold Liam's immodest gaze. It lasted only a moment before Liam made an amused noise at the back of his throat and stepped out of the way.

"Come on in."

The apartment was little more than a studio, really, and not an especially nice one. The wooden floor and framing around the windows were dark wood, their varnish worn away after years of tenants. The light, low and almost hazy, came from a few shaded floor lamps and the French doors that opened out to a balcony and the city beyond.

The furniture was minimal. Two stools were tucked under the counter of a small kitchenette. Paperback books, some handwritten sheet music, and parts of a folded-up French newspaper littered the desk in the corner. There was a new MacBook open on the desk too, but its screen was blank. In the opposite corner of the apartment, a mattress lay on the floor, its sheets carelessly tucked in at the foot. A pungent, soapy smell came from the bathroom—a mix of body wash and shaving foam. The music Zach had heard in the hallway, turned low and perfectly atmospheric, played through a set of fancy Bluetooth speakers. Things were unpacked but not lived in; these were clearly temporary digs.

Liam moved into the kitchen area as Zach went to peer out onto the balcony, noting an ashtray, an empty wine bottle, and a stunning view.

"Glad to see there is a face attached to the body from your profile picture." Liam's voice drew Zach back inside. "They make a nice combination." Liam pressed his lips together prettily, and Zach blushed, the nervous energy in his belly reacting to Liam's praise.

"You don't recognize me, do you?"

Liam pulled his head back, giving himself more space to consider Zach. "Should I?"

"No. I'd be surprised if you did." Nevertheless, Zach felt himself turn away.

"You want a drink...Didn't catch your name." Liam waited for Zach's answer with his hands spread on the counter. He clearly had no issues showing off his body. Zach was used to post-game preening in locker rooms with teammates whose bodies were as muscled as his own, but Liam emanated a very different kind of power, cunning and quixotic, but equally strong.

Maybe it was thanks to the shots he'd done before he'd left his teammates or maybe it was the foreign setting. Maybe it was because Liam truly seemed to have no idea who Zach was, but he went for it and gave Liam his real name. "Sure, I'll take a beer. And it's Zachary. Zach."

Liam nodded and turned. His knees cracked as he squatted down, retrieving two Peroni out of the fridge. "American, I assume?" Liam turned back, placing the bottles on the counter. Every movement he made was effortless. He searched through a drawer for a bottle opener and cracked the caps off of the beers with an elegant arc of his wrist.

Zach nodded as he took the offered beer. "Just a tourist. I've been here for two weeks, but I head back tomorrow." The icy bottle immediately formed condensation under his fingers in Liam's non-airconditioned flat.

"You're sharing your last night with me, huh? I'm honored." Liam took a long drink of his beer, his Adam's apple pronounced on his long, pale neck. "So, how have you liked the motherland, then?"

"Motherland? You're not American?"

"One of my passports says I am, I guess." Liam gently set his beer bottle on the counter. "American parents," he explained, with the tired air of one who did this often. "Both expats, obviously. They met one summer in Sienna and decided they couldn't bear to leave each other or Italy. *Ma, sono crescuito a Firenze.* I grew up in Florence," he clarified.

Zach took a long swig of his drink as Liam switched deftly from perfect Italian to un-accented English. "Are you in Rome for school?"

Liam turned his face away, tucking it against his shoulder to hide the myriad of emotions that passed across it. He turned back, with a sardonic smile. "You could say I'm regrouping. We could all use a Roman summer once in our lives, right? The chance to be a tourist? Turns out, you and I are more alike than we knew."

With no preamble, and as if he was very much over the chit chat, Liam moved around the counter. He spun Zach on his stool and forced his legs apart, stepping into the space he'd made between Zach's thighs. It was all so suave and proficient. Liam was close enough that Zach could see the smattering of freckles on his cheekbones and nose, physical proof of summertime on his ivory skin. No other part of Liam's body had to move for him to be able to turn his wrist and cup Zach through his jeans. Zach's hips rolled, unbidden, into the touch.

"Easy there." Liam smirked as he moved in closer. Zach knew their night would be over embarrassingly quick if he let Liam continue.

Zach jumped off the stool, running his hands through his hair. He turned away to adjust himself through his jeans. "Sorry." He glanced back to see Liam's look of annoyance. "That felt really good."

"That is kind of the point of this little get-together, isn't it?"

"Mhmm, of course." Zach sounded wholly unconvinced.

Liam sighed heavily. "Look you're hot as hell, and I'm into this, but I mean..." He squeezed the bridge of his nose with two fingers, then dropped his hand dramatically to his hip. "You have done this before right?"

"No. I mean, yes. Sort of."

"Well, which is it?"

"Not through the app. But with guys? Yeah, of course."

"Good." Liam lengthened the vowels, as one might when congratulating a child. Zach didn't have time to get offended by Liam's cheek before he was speaking again. "Because I can handle a guy with a girl back home, but I don't think I have it in me to deal with a virgin. Not tonight."

"I'm not," Zach asserted, though he couldn't help but wonder if he'd answered with so much conviction that it rang false. He adjusted his tone for his next claim. "It's just been a long time."

Liam's "so what?" Shrug came as an elegant lilt of his shoulder. He began walking towards Zach, his bare feet crossing one in front of the other like a model on a catwalk. "This is meant to be fun, yes?" Liam spoke slowly. Zach swallowed. "We can still have fun. Can't we, Zachary?"

"Yes." He hated the desperation that one word held.

Liam grinned, lascivious, as he lifted his hand to touch Zach again, his fingers ghosting over the soft jersey fabric at Zach's shoulder. When Zach didn't panic, Liam shifted his soft exploration to the musculature of Zach's forearm, finishing at the fluttering pulse at Zach's wrist. Everything was safe, rated PG. It still made Zach burn.

"Do you kiss?" Liam tilted his head prettily.

Zach had been asked this question before by men he'd known intimately for one night and one night only. The answer he gave varied from night to night, man to man. Zach's eyes flitted to Liam's parted lips, pink and shapely. His answer to Liam was a simple one.

"Definitely."

Liam took another step closer and settled his hands at the small of Zach's back. Zach closed his eyes and waited for the press of Liam's mouth against his. Would it be gentle, closed-lipped, and testing? Or would Liam, sick of Zach's waffling, come at him with something rough, all-in, and commanding? Either would be fine, Zach realized, as his anticipatory heartbeats multiplied.

Liam's breath played across his mouth, teasing the moment out. Zach leaned in towards Liam but was met with nothing but air. When the moment continued to stretch on, when Zach was about to give up on Liam's baiting, when Zach felt his most helpless, liquefied, and like putty in Liam's hands, only then did Liam satisfy him with a kiss.

Their mouths slotted together like dovetail joints, something handcrafted and meant to last. The sweep of Liam's tongue went beyond Zach's mouth and into his veins, his gut, his cock, straight down to his toes, then back again. Zach's remaining nerves vaporized on the spot, and his continually repressed urges took over. He palmed Liam's ass, small like the rest of him, and erased the minimal space left between them. Liam inhaled sharply through his nose, unprepared for Zach's show of strength.

"Bed," Liam mouthed, and Zach agreed.

3

A breeze had picked up over the previous hour. It was enough to take the languid edge off the night and draw the smoke of Liam's cigarette skyward. The view of the Roman vista from his balcony was far nicer than an apartment in this price bracket should have. He would miss this city and her ancient bones when he left in little over a week's time. Liam was set to experience a new country, a new city, a new school. It was as daunting as it was liberating.

Inside, through the sheer blinds that shifted ever so slightly with the wind, Liam could make out the shape of Zach, motionless on his bed, one knee splayed to the side. Every inch of him was Hollywood perfection with softly angled cheekbones, a square jaw, and plush lips. His hair, neatly trimmed, was short on the sides. Across his brow, dark brown waves helped to highlight his aching baby blues. He had the kind of muscled chest, arms, and abs Liam didn't realize were possible without Photoshop. His defined legs stretched out from jutting hip bones and seemed to go on for days.

Liam had been sure he had Zach figured out by reading the signs on his Grindr profile. Zach provided no first name, no picture of his face. This guy was clearly closeted, probably with a girlfriend. He had assumed that Zach would arrive at Liam's place, all business and shame, and bend him over whatever surface was closest. Take him hard—with or without protection, barely any words exchanged, no kisses shared, no first name revealed—and then be done with him.

It wouldn't be the first time some self-loathing man had used Liam for a quick fix. He was petite in frame, almost feminine due to the bone structure of his face and the soft length of his hair. He filled a certain kink for a certain type of guy.

If Zach really hated himself as much as Liam assumed he did, Zach could have closed his eyes and pretended that he wasn't, you know, with a man. What did it say about Liam's mindset that he would have been fine with it if that was all Zach was offering? From Zach's first stuttered attempt at Italian over the intercom, Liam's expectations had been altered, only to be proved even wronger when Zach had blurted, "I don't wanna fuck," stilling Liam's hands on his fly.

Liam had sat back, his knees still bracketing Zach's thighs on his bed. In that heated moment, he'd need time to process the words. "You don't?"

Already shirtless and laid back on Liam's sheets, Zach had shaken his head tightly. "Everything else is okay, though."

Caught in the heat of the moment, Liam had simply sighed heavily and undone Zach's belt. "Fine." Liam had given an emphatic yank to Zach's pants, removing everything in one movement. "Hands and mouths and the power of friction it is, then, *si? Sta bene.*" Zach had grabbed Liam's face with both hands and kissed him with something that felt akin to gratitude.

It had made Liam wonder what Zach wasn't getting at home. This guy could have a different lover in his bed every night or a devoted boyfriend if he wanted, but he seemed so very alone.

Eventually, both naked, their shallow breaths falling in and out of sync, Liam had found Zach with his mouth. The noises Zach had made had been both guttural and plaintive all at once.

"I'm close," Zach had warned politely, and Liam had pulled off, aligning their bodies, chest to chest, pelvis to pelvis. Liam's fingers were long enough to encircle them both, and Zach had hissed through his teeth, his eyes tightly closed. The resulting mess had lubricated Liam's own release.

"Guess it really has been a while, huh, bud?" Liam had teased, slapping Zach's flank before quickly getting off the bed to clean up and find his cigarettes.

It had been easy for him to poke fun, but the truth was, it had been a while for Liam as well. He had spent the duration of his Roman summer bringing members of the opposite sex to his bed. He'd played at falling in love while they strolled through the dusty streets, kissing with their arms around each other late into the evening under streetlamps, then coming home and making love until the sun rose.

Liam had been romance personified, gifting them with everything they thought they wanted. After a few weeks, when big words started getting mentioned, or when he simply started to get bored, Liam would dump them with little to no afterthought, moving on to whomever caught his eye next. It wasn't like breaking their hearts felt good; he wasn't a sociopath. But it felt necessary. Like a catharsis. Like he was finally getting the return on a favor he was owed.

Zach had been Liam's first encounter with a man in at least four months. And he had to admit, it had not disappointed, even for its PG-13 rating thus far. He had missed the parity being with men brought to sexual encounters. Even when body size or experience levels were uneven, Liam loved the sameness of their anatomy, the way their voices matched, and how they got off in the same predictable way.

Liam examined the remains of his cigarette, only his sixth that day. That was some kind of progress. He extinguished the burning end against the iron balcony railing and went back inside.

Zach sat up immediately, reaching for a piece of clothing to cover himself. He muttered a quick, "Sorry. I'll, um, I'll get out of your way."

"No. Feel free to lounge across my bed in a state of total undress as long as you like. I'm not complaining." Liam cruised past his bed and went to the fridge for another beer. "You need anything? Water? Another drink?"

"I'm okay," Zach replied. He sat on the edge of the mattress with his boxers back on, his legs outstretched and hands clasped between his thighs. His head hung with what Liam hoped was bashfulness and not shame. Liam came back to the bed and felt every inch of his six-foot stature as he looked down at the top of Zach's head.

If this had been another night, with another lover, Liam would have dropped the waistband of his sweatpants and pressed Zach's face against his groin, insistent on reciprocation. Instead, he threaded his fingers through Zach's hair, scratching his scalp where the longer locks at the crown gave way to the shorter strands at the nape. Zach let out another shuttering groan.

"Only okay, huh?" Liam murmured.

Zach lifted his head, his eyes swimming. The corner of his full mouth lifted as he blushed. Adorable. "Maybe a little better than okay."

Liam gave Zach's shoulder a playful shove, and he easily fell back against the mattress. This gave Liam the room to nimbly catapult himself over Zach's body to lie next to him. As they settled side-by-side together in bed, there was something overly comfortable about this setup for two people who had met less than an hour before. Liam took a chance on the ready-made ease and lifted a finger to trace the bulges of Zach's bicep. He traversed the curve of his triceps, across his shoulder and over his collar bone before palming the entirety of Zach's pectoral. Zach twitched the muscle under Liam's hand. At Liam's surprised look, Zach flashed him a wicked grin, as if to ask, *You like that?* Liam squeezed back, twisting his thumb and forefinger around Zach's nipple as if to answer, *Of course, I like it.* Something flared in Zach's eyes then, a bit of bravery perhaps, and Liam's breath caught in his throat.

"So." Liam waved at Zach's body in general. "What do you do with all of these?"

"I play football."

Liam had grown up giving the members of *Gli Azzuri,* the Italian national football team, and their lithe, athletic bodies nice long looks, as any good European boy of his persuasion might. But the typical European football player shared nothing with Zach's muscle-bound physique.

"*American* football," Zach clarified. Liam mouthed a silent "Ahh," and propped his head up with his hand.

"Running around all day with boys in tights, smacking their asses for a job well done. What a convenient way for you to hide in plain sight."

Zach searched Liam's face. "Am I really that obvious?"

"Well, we did just ejaculate all over each other."

A rosy blush formed on Zach's cheeks again. "But the girlfriend comment from before. How did you know?"

"When you've been around the block as many times as I have—" The genuine worry on Zach's face stopped him. He restarted, not unkindly. "Look, I've figured out how to read the signs of a guy in the closet for self-protection purposes. Or self-destructive ones, as the case may be," he added grimly. "I don't think anyone who didn't have reason to know you were into guys would be able to figure you out. Certainly not by looking at you."

Zach seemed to consider Liam's comment seriously. It appeared to soothe him, and in the process, soothed Liam too.

"It's ridiculous, right?" Zach gave a self-effacing laugh. "It's 2020. It shouldn't matter anymore. But in my sport, at my level, and where I hope to play after I graduate, gay athletes don't exist. I mean, we do, obviously." He gestured at himself with a crooked smile. "But not openly."

Liam remembered how news of an English rugby player coming out had made headlines in Florence when he was a teenager. There had been conflicting thoughts on the player's choice to speak openly about his sexuality and what it meant for the game. While Liam had never lived in America, he had enough relatives to glean their puritanical squeamishness over human sexuality in general and their idolization of "manly men." It was easy for Liam to imagine how homophobic Zach's sports-centered world must be.

"There isn't, like, a secret society for gay sporty types who get together to screw each other and then talk about, I don't know, the best jockstrap brands afterward?"

Zach laughed, sincere to Liam's ears and free from any self-restraint. Liam found himself thinking that word, again: adorable.

"If there is, I haven't been asked to join."

"That's rude of them," Liam retorted quickly. "Maybe you should start one of your own?"

"Maybe I should," Zach said, with amused determination.

They lay still for a moment as their laughs faded into companionable silence.

"Where do you go to school?" Liam asked.

Zach opened his mouth, ready to answer, then seemed to think better of it. "I shouldn't say. No offense."

"None taken." Liam feigned indifference. What were the chances anyway?

"I will tell you that we're ranked in the top five pre-season in both the AP and ESPN polls. We're on everyone's prediction lists for who will make the College Football Playoffs. We missed the Championships last season by one game. I entered the National Football League combine after, but it looked like I'd go in the first round but not the top ten. So, I decided to use up my last year of eligibility and come back for my senior season. I'm hoping I can take my team all the way to a National Championship when the season starts in a few weeks."

Liam blinked at him. "I have no idea what any of what you just said means."

"It means..." Zach had Liam flat on his back and his wrists pinned to the pillow below his head before Liam knew it. Zach looked down at him with a slick smile that bordered on dangerous. His voice was deep and wicked as he spoke again. "I'm fucking good."

And there it was: the cockiness that Liam knew must be within Zach somewhere. It had clearly been hiding behind his nerves and inexperience and was finally ready to escape. Zach settled down deeper in the cradle of Liam's hips, his hardness barely contained by the fabric of his boxers.

"I'm not sure you've fully proven to me how good you are yet." Liam looked back to find Zach's eyes waiting for him. Their pale blue seemed to have become a darker mix of gusto and want.

A firm tug of Liam's waistband had his pants clear off. He closed his eyes and heard a solid inhale from somewhere down by his hip bone. Then Liam lost himself in the warm darkness of the night and Zach's mouth.

4

The first day of fall semester 2020 started like any other day for Zach during football season. His alarm went off at 5:01 a.m., nudging him into the early morning hour with a pleasant woodblock melody. If he snoozed that first wake up call, the next alarm was set to an old-school foghorn which made it sound like Armageddon was about to befall his bedroom. That alarm scared the crap out of him—and Rebecca too, when she slept over—so more often than not, Zach passed on the five extra minutes of sleep and started his day without a panic attack.

He was alone on the first day of class, so he didn't bother closing the bathroom door as he staggered in for a piss. He stripped down to nothing, then wandered to his closet to put on his workout clothes. After a banana and a PowerBar, he brushed his teeth, laced up his sneakers, and began the three-mile run to the stadium.

It sometimes felt as though he was the only person awake in the world on these early morning runs. Some days that might have even been true. Normal college students wouldn't be up so brutally early unless they were finding their bed after a crazy night out or had pulled an all-nighter. But Zach didn't mind the quiet of these empty hours. He loved the way campus looked in the pre-dawn light, the way the sidewalks were clear of congestion from slow walkers, bikes, skateboards, and those stupid electric scooters that were everywhere now.

He took the lakeside path that morning, which was longer but more scenic. If he were to run thirteen miles to the right, he'd end up in downtown Chicago. Instead, he turned left, following the coast of Lake Michigan that bordered campus on one side. The water was expansive, calm, and inky purple before the sunrise. He left his iPhone, stocked with Post Malone and Lil Nas X, in his pocket, and instead listened to the sound of his naturally accelerated breath and the rhythmic slap of his feet on the pavement.

By the time he arrived at the practice facility, the quarterback coach was already there. The man was specifically hired and paid—quite handsomely—by the university to make sure Zach was in top shape. The coach worked with Zach in the gym daily, tweaking every aspect of his technique, and helped him on the sidelines during games.

There wasn't a team sport in existence that didn't live or die on the excellence of one player's position. In baseball, it was the pitcher. In basketball, the point guard. In hockey, the goalie. In soccer, the striker. In football, it was the quarterback. Zach knew he had to be stronger, better, work harder, and be more mentally focused than his teammates. The blame for a terrible season would rest squarely on his shoulders, but so would the glory if they could win it all.

It was nearly 7 a.m. by the time he and the QB coach were finished with sprints and agility drills on the indoor track and Zach was halfway through his routine in the weight room. Many of the other elite players, including Des, had found their way into the gym and were getting in a workout before the whole team met at the stadium that evening for a three-hour practice.

"Morning, Cray-Z." Des snapped a towel at Zach's sweating bicep. Zach finished his reps and set the barbell down with a clang. He had upped his weight numbers that week, and there was a hot ache in his arms as they recovered from the strain.

Des took a seat on an empty machine next to him. "What time did you get here, man?" Des asked.

Zach wiped his face with a towel and gave himself an additional second to catch his breath. "Before your lazy ass." He threw the towel at Des, who gave him a censuring look.

"I texted you last night. Ruiz and Jackson and I were chilling. We played some Madden on the Xbox and then Ruiz's new girl came by. It would have been cool if you'd shown your face."

"I was with Rebecca."

Des gave him his patented thousand-watt smile. "Oh, I see how it is. Girlfriend's back in town so it's gonna be all, 'Best friend who?'"

Zach got up off the weight bench, leaving behind a man-shaped outline in sweat and gave Des a dry look. "What was your name again? And who, exactly, let you in here? You do know this is the team gym, right?"

Des snickered as Zach sat on the next machine to work his quads. He adjusted the weights and began, his knees bending and flexing. The burn was instant.

Rebecca had gotten back to campus the previous night. They'd cuddled. She'd complained about her connection through O'Hare. They'd made out on the couch, but then she'd left. He'd gotten Des's text, but instead of going to see his friends on their last night before school started, Zach had turned in early and looked through pictures he'd taken in Italy on his phone.

It had been hard returning to his life back in Illinois after Rome. Being in that timeless city for two weeks, surrounded by places he'd only ever dreamed of seeing, had been enough to change him. He'd left with a greater appreciation of the world beyond NU, his hometown, and his family. Beyond football, even. His final night with Liam had cast a further glowing light on the whole experience.

"Zachary."

His name snapped him back to attention. He and Des had developed a million nicknames for each other over their near-decade of friendship. Zachy, QB, 24 were regular options. Des liked to call him Boss Man when he was changing a call on the field and Cap during an inspiring mid-huddle speech. He reserved Cray-Z like he'd used that morning, for when Zach was pushing himself too hard. With all those other options at Des's disposal, it was almost strange to hear his best friend use his given name unironically and in a concerned tone.

"You know we got it this season, right? We're gonna be good. Real good. And all of us," he gestured at the gym, now full of teammates putting in the hard work in the gym, "we got your back, so you don't need to lay yourself out for our sake before we even really get started. Alright?"

Zach let his legs drop to the floor. They were trembling. "Alright," he huffed, realizing how much he'd needed to hear this. Des offered a hand and yanked Zach to his feet. For the morning at least, his workout was over.

—

The exchange of house keys was a major milestone in any relationship. It was a sign of trust and commitment and the first in a series of mammoth steps.

For Zach and Rebecca, though, it had been a practical decision not one steeped in romance. Zach's apartment in Wilson Tower, a modern, high-end, fifteen-story apartment building where many scholarship athletes lived, was closer to campus than her Tri-Delt sorority house on Sheridan Road. When she'd taken an 8 a.m. art class the previous spring that required lots of supplies, it was easier for her to drop them off at his place after class rather than carry them with her all day. He'd given her a key one morning to help make her day easier and never bothered to ask for it back. After a while, she'd started using it for other reasons, and Zach had begun to like having her around, even when he wasn't expecting her.

It was just past eight in the morning by the time he arrived back at his apartment after his workout. He was greeted by Rebecca standing barefoot in his bright, open-concept kitchen. She was wearing a short, floral dress that showed off her shoulders and was singing along to Harry Styles as she pushed eggs around a pan.

Zach and Rebecca had grown up in the same suburban town but went to different elementary and middle schools, so they hadn't met until their freshman year of high school. Rebecca was the type of girl everyone wanted. She took good care of herself, ate well, worked out, and dressed nicely. She was tan after spending the summer as a counselor at an all-girls camp in Idaho. Her head was covered in tight, reddish-brown curls that bounced around her face when her naturally bubbly personality took over. She was a sociology major, the president of her sorority, and sex on legs—even Zach could see that. The irony was that Zach had never had sex with her, and he never would until they got married.

When they first started dating, they'd fooled around like every normal teenage couple, even though Zach had known he would rather have been with a guy. In those early days, they'd experimented enough for Zach to know that making out with a girl wasn't bad. Maybe sleeping with a girl wouldn't be so bad either, when the time came. He was convinced he'd be able to do it, at least, even if it felt like everything was happening through a layer of thick wool, the sensations not nearly enough for him to want more.

One quiet summer afternoon while at a friend's lakeside house for the day, they found a bedroom away from the rest of the guests. They'd been together for over a year, and peer pressure was a bitch. After they kissed for a while, he slipped his fingers into her bikini bottoms, unprepared for the warm wetness he found between her legs. He pressed two fingers where damp hair gave way to silken flesh, moving around and around, and then in. Her reaction had caused a surge of endorphins to rush through him. That was it. They were going to have sex. Strangest of all, Zach had actually felt into it. In that heated moment, he didn't care that he was about to lose his virginity to a girl. The word "bi" had even flashed through his mind the moment before Rebecca had started to cry.

She sat with her back against the headboard, covering her face to hide deep, heaving sobs. Zach was petrified that he'd hurt her somehow.

"I can't," she'd wept. "I want to and I love you, but I can't."

She went on to explain she wanted to stay a virgin until she got married, an imperative of her Catholic faith. There had been something so after-school special about her words like they were coming directly from some formulaic indoctrination. Zach's Judaism, on the other hand, barely even registered in his day-to-day life. It certainly wasn't going to interfere in the bedroom.

"I totally understand if you hate me right now. We can break up if you want to."

But what she didn't realize was that she'd given Zach the perfect cover story. Instead of getting pissed like a normal seventeen-year-old guy might have because he wasn't about to get laid, Zach had played the understanding boyfriend, fully prepared to respect her chaste wishes. She'd fallen even more in love with him in that moment and became hopelessly devoted to the boy who would wait.

As the years passed, Zach was able to hide his lack of any real desire for her behind their virginity pact. He was sustained by the chance encounters with men that he sought out when he could no longer resist. Every time he found himself in a man's bed, he was reminded of how axis-shifting those feelings of desire could be when they were mutual. Wanting his lover as much as his lover wanted him gave Zach a glimpse of what he could have if he were out, and only helped to confirm that, yeah, he was really not straight.

However, each act of self-confirmation was also an act of unfaithfulness to someone he was committed to for the long term. He might not want to have sex with Rebecca, but he did love her. She'd been by his side through everything: tough losses, injuries, disappointing grades, fights with teammates, awful family holidays. She was one of his best friends, much like Des. He could imagine creating a life with her, and it probably wouldn't be a bad one.

His feelings of disloyalty towards her had been especially keen after Italy. The memory of Liam lingered longer than that of any of the guys he'd been with before. But why? What was it about that encounter that made it stand out? Zach assumed it must have had something to do with the European setting, but maybe it was something to do with the risk he'd taken in using his real name. What a thing that had been, actually being himself. The memories of Liam's velvety curls brushing against his naked chest were still so visceral, it felt like it had happened only that morning. The memory of Liam's slim waist encircled with his muscled arms was just as vivid. But strangest of all was the way Zach remembered the sincerity in Liam's eyes after they'd gotten off one last time. Zach had been so desperate to hold onto the emotional and physical high of that night, Zach had even gone so far as to look for Liam on Facebook and Instagram, but with only a first name to go on—and maybe not even his real name—it had been a fool's quest.

Zach dropped his bag, full of sweaty workout clothes, and wrapped his arms around Rebecca's waist. She, too, felt slim in his arms.

"I know you're not supposed to eat the full-fat bacon." She ducked her head away from his greeting kiss. "But turkey bacon is so processed and pretty much tastes awful, so why not eat the real stuff? It won't hurt if you only eat it every once in a while, right?" She slid several slices from a pan onto a plate alongside a hearty portion of scrambled eggs, some whole-grain toast, and cut up melon. She turned around in his arms, presenting his breakfast.

"This looks great, babe. Thank you," he said, in a tone only he recognized as penitent.

"I wanted you to start the semester off with a hearty meal." She handed Zach his plate, apparently blissfully unaware of his inner angst. "It's our senior year, babe." Her hands came up to cradle his face. "Can you believe it?"

He shook his head and kissed her quickly, taking a seat at the kitchen counter as she poured him coffee and chatted cheerfully on.

5

First day. Syllabus day. Professors and students alike were always happy to ease their way back into the semester, turning what was normally a fifty-five-minute lecture into a fifteen-minute cursory review of the basics: come to class, don't plagiarize, use the office hours, and yes, it will be on the exam.

Zach's first class was Statistics 101, which fulfilled a math requirement that he probably should have taken care of as a freshman but had never bothered to put into his schedule. The class was massive—over a hundred and fifty students in the amphitheater-style lecture hall. Zach hung towards the back, trying to keep a low profile.

With Statistics out of the way, his next obligation was a meeting with his new advisor. He grabbed a salad at the student union and hopped on the cross-campus bus, getting off at the main quad where Kresge Hall, the classics building, was located.

The building, constructed upon the founding of Northwestern in the mid-nineteenth century, had felt like home for Zach as much as any stadium or practice field. Here, Zach was allowed to slip into the skin of a young and gifted classics scholar that was as valuable and valid as that of the star athlete. Was it any wonder that Zach manifested the same kind dichotomy in his interests as he did with his private and public personas? Somewhere in the middle, between the two uprights, that was where the real Zach existed.

He'd been feeling a bit anxious about the meeting all morning. His new advisor was a first-year professor who had made all the higher-ups in the classics department positively gleeful when they'd hired him. Fresh out of his Ph.D. program at a school back east, but having grown up in Europe, he'd completed his studies in the States. This gave him the best of old-world authority and youthful perspective. Not even thirty, he was just the type of instructor who could make a dying subject hip again.

Zach checked his phone before slipping it into his back pocket. He was right on time. He knocked, and almost immediately, Eben Barnett, Ph.D., opened the door.

He was tall, almost as tall as Zach, which was a rarity for the nearly six-foot-four quarterback. The professor's blond hair was expertly gelled, his face shaved close. He could have been a Wall Street broker in his cleanly tailored suit of charcoal and sea blues. It looked very modern and very expensive and was a refreshing contrast to the drab tweed and corduroy preferred by the rest of the classics faculty. Zach couldn't help but wonder, though, if this young professor was trying a bit too hard to separate himself from his students and solidify his authority.

"You must be Zachary, Northwestern University Classics Department's very own Achilles. I've heard a lot about you."

He offered Zach his hand, and Zach took it, giving it a firm shake. "I've heard a lot about you as well, Professor Barnett."

"Dr. Barnett, if you would."

Zach nodded, unprepared for the curt response. "Yes, of course. Sorry."

Dr. Barnett gestured towards the chair across from his desk, ready to get down to business. On the desk between them was a manila folder. Zach knew the contents of that folder well. Inside, printed on recycled paper in eleven-point Arial font with one and a half line spacing was the bare bones of his senior honors thesis.

There were few players of Zach's caliber who took the "student" part of "student-athlete" quite as seriously as Zach. It had been a bone of contention between Coach Williams and himself on more than one occasion. Coach sometimes worried that Zach's class load was too ambitious and that it would affect his focus on football.

"How's the schedule looking for this semester?" Coach had asked at one of their first practices back on US soil. He and Zach had been taking a break, watching wide receivers and tight ends practice running routes from the end zone.

"Light load." Zach had squirted some blue Gatorade into his mouth around the face mask on his helmet. "A few required courses left, but mostly I need to work on my thesis."

"You know you're not going to need any of that, right? You're going to have a long, lucrative career doing this." He'd gestured at the playing field.

"Everyone's gotta have a hobby, though, right?"

"Ancient philosophy." Coach had clicked his tongue. "Hell of a hobby. Ever tried golf?"

Zach had smiled, giving him a repentant look. The last thing he'd wanted was for Coach to think Zach wasn't fully focused on the season ahead. "It'll be fine. Promise. I don't have to turn my thesis in until graduation, anyway. Season will be long over by then."

Down field, Des had called out to him, and with an almost instinctual motion, Zach had cocked the ball over his shoulder and thrown a perfect spiral forty yards to midfield. The look he'd given Coach as he'd jogged away to high five Des had been anything but contrite.

Zach scooted forward in his seat as Dr. Barnett held the document out at arm's length. "The Stoics, then."

"That's the plan, yes."

"Not the most original topic for a thesis, but I can see why this era of Roman philosophy, in particular, would appeal to you."

Dr. Barnett's intuitions were spot on. Zach's fascination

with ancient society had started during his freshman year of high school with a mandatory reading of *Oedipus Rex*. It was the oldest thing he'd ever read, and he adored the epic nature of the tale. Zach had been drawn to the inner complexity of the characters who had been created so impossibly long ago. Swiftly, and without looking back, he'd run down the ancient culture rabbit hole, reading every play, treatise, meditation, and history he could get his hands on. All the while, he'd watched every film or TV show set in the era, no matter how dated, campy, or risqué it was.

By sophomore year of high school, he'd signed up for Latin I instead of Spanish III and shifted his focus away from the Greeks to the Romans. Their society seemed to embody—almost encourage—that same duality Zach felt in his life. Philosopher warriors. Emperor poets. A god of wine and blind prophets. He'd been hooked.

Dr. Barnett swiveled in his chair. "Keeping in mind that I've not gotten all the way through, I don't think you're in terrible shape." He accompanied that statement with a tight smile to make sure Zach knew he was trying to be encouraging. "Check out Elaine Pagels's work on the Gnostic gospels. That will get you on the right track for your part about Stoicism's impact on early Christianity."

Zach pulled out his phone and typed Dr. Barnett's suggestion into a memo.

"I'll admit," Dr. Barnett continued, "I was skeptical before I read your work. I didn't know quite what to expect regarding, should I say, the quality of your work."

"I'm pretty of used to the dumb jock stereotype preceding me at this point. It's fine."

"You've surprised me, though. Seems you're a hero both on and off the field." That could have easily sounded like a backhanded compliment, but when Zach looked up, Dr. Barnett's look was kind, not snide. "I take it you did most of your writing over the summer."

"A bit last spring, but mostly this summer, yes."

"That was smart. You've got quite the season ahead, haven't

you? Lots of expectations."

Zach narrowed his eyes, reading between the professor's statements. "You don't follow football, do you, Doctor?"

Dr. Barnett's demeanor shifted as a smile passed his face. "The only football I cared about growing up involved red cards, fouls for flopping, and a goalie on either end of the pitch. But I fell in love with a girl from Wisconsin my first year of college and quickly learned there is only one *true* form of football to obsess over."

Zach laughed softly. "Green Bay Packers fans are ruthless."

"Tell me about it. Her family even questioned my loyalty to her when I got this job because I was making her move to Chicago Bears country." Fondness filled his face as he put Zach's paper back into the folder. "The sport has definitely grown on me, though."

Zach couldn't have been giddier. While he had become a fixture around the classics department with a reputation for being a good student and classmate, most faculty and peer students didn't understand why he did what he did. Football seemed like some frivolous pastime to them. The prospect of one of his professors actually enjoying the game was new and exciting.

"Let me know if you ever want to come to a game. I can get tickets for you and your wife."

"Well, my wife, Kelsey, she's expecting." Dr. Barnett gave Zach another revealing smile. "Not sure she'd be up for sitting on a cold bleacher for hours on end any time soon."

"I can usually get people into the President's Box unless we're playing Michigan or Ohio State. I'd be happy to get you in there." Zach wasn't being a brown nose. He swore he wasn't.

"I'll have to take you up on that, then. We'll talk again soon, Zachary."

Zach was full of warm, unsuspecting smiles as Dr. Barnett showed him out and he walked down the hall to his upper-level seminar on Plato's Dialogues. He took the closest seat available at the oval-shaped conference table and pulled out a fresh notebook. A quick scan around the room revealed familiar faces of fellow classics majors he'd been in class with for years.

The face directly across the table, however, was a new addition, though no less familiar. In fact, that angled face and silky blond curls had haunted Zach's dreams just the night before.

Liam.

How?

Context, as they say, is everything, and Zach's brain reeled, full of epic confusion. He tried to make sense of seeing Liam in a place he had no right to logically exist, but couldn't muster it. For a moment, Zach was sure he must be seeing things. Or having a stroke, maybe. He looked around the room to check whether other people were seeing Liam sitting there too, even going so far as to surreptitiously open Twitter to ensure he hadn't slipped into some alternate reality. The man sitting across from him was, without a doubt, his Roman Liam, not just some cruel doppelgänger put there to taunt him. Zach's heart thudded so hard in his chest that he felt himself pitch forward in his seat, as memories of his night with Liam flooded his thoughts.

Liam had climaxed from Zach's ministrations with little more than a stifled groan. He'd pulled Zach up and probed his mouth, seeking his own taste on Zach's tongue. "Not bad for a rookie."

"Not a rookie, remember?" Zach had stated into Liam's mouth. "Just benched for a bit."

Liam's smile had been impish, almost carefree, with a small wrinkle to his nose and a soft creasing of his brow. Zach had kissed it as if to capture it.

There had been so much kissing after that, what felt like hours of idle kissing. Kisses so deep Zach had felt like he was drowning. Kisses so light he had felt like he might evaporate into stardust. It was the kind of aimless exploration that made time stop. They'd kissed and touched until they'd needed release again. Liam had turned away, pressing his backside into the angle of Zach's hips. His skin had been slicked with sweat from the night's heat, and Zach had bucked into the friction. He'd wrapped his palm around Liam, and together they'd found a steady, long-lasting pace. Liam had felt so alive and responsive in Zach's arms as their bodies mimicked the one act Zach had insisted they avoid. Even so, he'd loved the way Liam had moved closer to him, feeling smaller in Zach's arms the nearer Liam came to his climax.

"I love this, Zachary," Liam had murmured, and Zach had bitten the skin of Liam's shoulder for fear of saying something completely obscene.

Later, Liam had stood in those dangerous gray sweats, watching as Zach put on his shoes. "Do you have Snapchat?"

"Not one that's public." Zach had grinned at him and stood up with a soft grunt. His muscles had gotten a good workout. "I do have IG and Twitter, though. I have over ten thousand followers. Why? You gonna follow me?" He'd given Liam a rogue smile, and Liam had rolled his eyes.

The night was long gone by that point. It was closer to sunrise than sunset. Zach had found a series of messages from Des when he'd finally gotten up to check his phone. Each one had been composed of ever-increasingly drunken misspellings until the last message arrived, letter-perfect, that read "You better not be fucking dead," and was accompanied by a crooked picture of his empty bed at the Airbnb.

"It's too bad you're leaving tomorrow." Liam had refused to make eye contact with Zach and examined his nails instead. "You're kind of fun. You know, for a beefy American jock."

Zach had felt a surge of amused affection, which had arisen entirely too soon and felt out of place in the unfamiliar setting. Still, he'd played along. "You aren't half bad either, for a pretentious European fuck boy."

Liam touched his bare chest gently with the tips of his fingers, simmering with genteel indignation. "Oh. *Oh.* You think I'm a pretentious European? You wound me."

"I like how that's the part you decide to be offended by."

"Well, when the shoe fits..."

He'd grabbed Zach by the front of his shirt and pulled him back into his apartment with a rough kiss. Zach had made the bus to the airport by mere minutes. He'd given Des a look that made it clear it was best not to ask. The whole flight home his skin had still smelled of sweat and the semen of two men. His lips had burned with the memory of Liam's mouth.

And now Liam was sitting across from him, alert and interested as the professor began the class. His jaw-length curls were styled and tucked behind his ears, creating a careful side-part. His pale pink T-shirt, with a wide V-neck and trim European fit, was a bold and uninhibited choice. He had a brand new spiral-bound notebook open in front of him and balanced a pencil, sharpened to an exact point, between his first two fingers.

As the professor handed out the syllabus, making her way around the table, Zach kept his eyes firmly fixed on Liam. He took the offered paper from her without even a cursory thanks. When she reached the opposite side of the table, Liam lifted his gaze Zach's way. He looked right at Zach and then right through him. Not a single muscle on his face twitched with even the vaguest indication of familiarity.

Less than two weeks ago they had shared one of the best nights of Zach's life, but now Liam didn't even recognize him. Or maybe even worse, Liam had forgotten all about him.

6

"*Merda, merda, merda.*"

Sometimes it was immeasurably helpful that Liam knew how to swear in three different languages because, in that current moment, he needed every curse word in his arsenal.

Motherfucker. Here? Zach played football *here?*

He hurried from the classroom, leaving with a brusqueness that was borderline rude to the professor. Of all the schools in this sprawling, over-populated, behemoth of a country—*Madonna santa! Ici?*

"Liam!"

That strapping baritone, interwoven with something melodic and shy, made Liam's spine tingle. He kept his back to the sound, as he walked away from the classroom and Zach's long strides. Liam knew Zach would eventually overtake him unless Liam broke out in a full sprint, which would have only made his panic even more obvious. He pressed his eyes closed before turning crisply on his heel. They were closer together than either expected, and Zach had to pull up at the last minute to avoid crashing right into Liam. Zach's gorgeous blue eyes were disbelieving, just as desperate to understand the situation as Liam was.

"You are Liam, right?"

Liam pulled a bland face, hoping it passed for calm. "Yeah. And?"

"Do you really not—it's me. Zach?" He stepped in closer and dropped his voice. "From Rome?"

Zach looked nervous, much like he had when he'd first arrived at Liam's apartment. And like that night, Liam felt some instinctual need to quell those nerves. As quickly as he could, Liam sought a private place for them to talk. He remembered seeing a study lounge on the far end of the building on his way to class earlier and pausing to wonder who would use that space with its old desktop computers and shitty printers. Lucky for them, the answer was "Absolutely no one," so he nodded his head in the direction of that empty room and Zach quietly followed. There was just enough space for Liam to begin pacing between the banks of computers. Zach closed the door behind them.

"Of course I remember you," Liam shouted. "It's not every night you have a guy in your bed claiming to be some future draft pick for the NF-whatever-the-fuck."

"I thought maybe you'd—I don't know. How is this happening?"

"Hell if I know."

Liam had sought some anonymous encounter that night because he'd assumed it would be just that: anonymous, there for one night only, never to be seen or heard from again. The fact that Zach was American hadn't felt like a big deal. Plenty of American guys came through Rome in the summer. When Liam had realized he was a fellow college student, that hadn't bothered him either. He'd asked Zach where he went to school because those sporty types usually had an immense amount of school pride, right? It had been a bit of flirtation to add to the mood. Liam hadn't actually thought there was even the remotest possibility they would end up at school together, let alone the same bloody class.

"What are you doing in my upper-level classics seminar?"

Liam snapped.

"Um, I'm fulfilling my degree requirements," Zach snapped back. "What are you doing in *my* upper-level classics seminar? You live in Rome."

"No, I was regrouping in Rome. I'd been going to school in Paris before that but—Wait, degree requirements? You're a classics major? Mr. Hotshot-starting-quarterback is a classics major?" Liam's voice came out shriller than he would have liked.

Zach set his hips back against the table, crossing his arms with a sudden smugness. "A classics major focusing in Pax Romana philosophers with a 3.7 GPA, you mean? Yeah. I am. How do you think I recognized that ridiculous *Metamorphoses* quote on your Grindr profile?"

"I figured you Googled it like everyone else usually did."

Zach's face softened at Liam's unintentional reveal. "Why didn't you say anything about coming to school in the States that night?" Zach asked.

Liam leveled him with a look. "I don't remember us doing an awful lot of talking."

"We talked enough. You could have mentioned it."

"I'd only decided to come here a week or so before we met," Liam explained. "I barely knew anything about Northwestern aside from the fact that it has a pretty well-respected music program. Certainly not enough to know it has some big deal football team. And besides, what were the chances?"

"I'm not a betting man, but I definitely wouldn't have taken these odds." Doe-eyed panic lingered on Zach's face even as he shifted to a more conversational tone. "So, the music school, huh? That's cool. I remember you had music on your desk. What do you play?"

"Piano mostly, but I'm a composition major. I added a classics minor 'cause I can, here. My other school didn't offer liberal arts courses." Zach nodded, and Liam realized it was probably his turn to attempt conversation. "A jock with a brain, then. Color me impressed."

Zach gave a bored lift of his shoulder. "It makes for a great human-interest story. I think every bad pun about Greek gods or Roman gladiators has been made about me at least once. The ESPN announcers think they are so fucking clever."

Liam stared at him. "You keep saying these things thinking I know what they mean."

"ESPN." Zach gave him a patient grin. "It's a cable sports network that shows games. You know, on the TV."

"Yeah, alright." Liam's pursed lips morphed into an unbidden smile.

It was impossible not to note how the tension in the room had slipped away. The looks that passed between them carried a certain playfulness once they were forced to accept the inconceivable fact that they were both here in the same city, at the same school, and even in the same class. And into that ease slipped the feelings of attraction and memories of the intimacy they'd found on Liam's mattress by the end of their night together. Liam had sought hidden parts of Zach's body with his fingers. That small, insinuating touch, burned into his memory, had ignited such terrified want in Zach's bright blue eyes that Liam had known that he would have been allowed to feel Zach from the inside if only they'd had more time. One more night. One more hour, even. And now here Zach was, standing before him. It was as baffling as it was thrilling. Liam certainly wouldn't mind if they were able to find that extra time together.

"Look," Zach started, "This is crazy that you're here, and I hope you love your time at Northwestern as much as I have, but it's probably for the best if we don't interact."

Liam was rendered mute.

"I mean, I know we're in class together," Zach continued. "We'll have to interact, discussion grades and everything, but what I mean is, we shouldn't be friendly."

"Why not?" Liam asked after another stunned beat.

"It's nothing personal. In fact, I think you're—" Zach stopped. He pressed his eyes closed and took another steadying breath before speaking again. "It would make things really difficult for me. Like I told you in Rome, no one knows about me. About me and..." He spoke the next word at a careful volume. "Men. In fact, you're the only person on this entire campus who does."

Zach's sexuality was a secret that should have bound them. But instead, Zach was using it to put a wedge between even the possibility of them. Liam didn't think the conversation could get any more ridiculous.

"Do you think I'm going to out you or something?"

"Well, are you? There are plenty of reporters that would pay lots of money for that story." Zach was wound tight.

Liam wondered if Zach's pulse was jumping through the veins in his throat the way he had felt Zach's heartbeat race there before under the lap of his exploring tongue. Liam brushed the visceral memory away with a callous scoff.

"Jesus, give me some credit. I'm not that kind of guy, okay? Why do you think I acted like I had no idea who you were when you walked in, huh? I wasn't about to make a scene. And I'm not going to post something to Snapchat either, like, 'OMG, you'll never guess who I fucked in Rome this summer!'" Liam dropped the Valley Girl voice he'd adopted for something made of carbon steel. "No, wait. Sorry. Didn't fuck."

"Will you keep your voice down?"

Liam glanced around the small room as if trying to find a single human soul who could possibly overhear their conversation. "Are you seriously clinging to the back of the closet so hard that you can't even associate with people who sleep with men? Am I really such a threat to your carefully curated machismo?"

Zach let out a sigh, a sound so heavy it seemed to take on a physical weight. His next words were just as burdened. "I'm very grateful for what you did in there. And that night with you was..." He tossed his head sadly. "But that still doesn't change the fact that when I'm here, the guy that you met that night doesn't exist. Okay?"

There was a desperate, end-of-discussion quality to the way Zach spoke, his handsome frame folded inward on itself. Liam would have almost felt sorry for Zach if his summary rejection hadn't left Liam unexpectedly crestfallen. He reacted to that uncomfortable emotion the best way he knew how.

"You know what? Fine. I don't even want to be at this school.

So, don't worry, champ," Liam delivered the derisive snub like a stab, "this conversation never happened. And neither did Rome."

With a swing of his backpack and a slam of the door, Liam was gone.

—

People at Northwestern were just too damned happy.

Liam spent much of his time trying to identify the root cause of this overwhelming difference between this school in American and what he'd left behind in Paris. Maybe the persistent cheeriness was a result of the sheer size of the university. With a student body of over twenty thousand and eighty different majors, plus a medical school and a law school on offer, Liam's exclusive former music conservatory felt minuscule, boasting less than five hundred students.

Maybe the upbeat mood came from the sprawling campus, home to trees, green spaces, and a lake so big it looked like an ocean. Liam's Parisian metro-scape school housed on one city block could never compare. Maybe it was the fact that most students lived in close quarters, either on campus or in nearby student apartments, as opposed to being dispersed all across the city, living wherever rent was cheapest. There was also a student club for everything—sports, debate, improv, video games, religious affiliations, you name it—so everyone could find their people. There was even a Northwestern Quidditch team. Quidditch. From the Harry Potter books. It was absurd.

Even the transplants from other nations or the opposing coasts seemed to have adopted the chipper Midwestern niceness. Passing exchanges were always met with a "please" and a "thank you." Doors were held open, even if it was an inconvenience. When someone asked, "How are you?" it felt like a genuine inquiry and not just a turn of phrase.

Liam knew this façade of limitless kindness had its limits; human heartache existed everywhere. But it felt like everyone around him had been handed a pair of rose-colored glasses and Liam was the only one who had lost his. Where were the people suffering for their craft? Struggling to find their purpose? Lost in their early-twenties existential angst? Maybe that wasn't the model for life in an American college, where there was support staff for everything from mental health to job placement.

Ultimately, maybe it was just Liam and his European upbringing that made him side-eye his fellow classmates with reserve. Even with dual citizenship in Italy and the United States, his Americanness felt woefully underdeveloped now that he was living in the lower forty-eight. He spoke the same, American accented English, but his syntax and cadence were decidedly steeped in the Romance languages he'd spoken while growing up in Florence and studying in Paris. His whole life had been spent across the pond, save the occasional visit, and he felt more like a tourist walking the campus grounds than a fellow civilian.

Add to all this the impossible reconnection with Zach, the hook-up-turned-classmate that had left him stinging from an unexpected wound, and Liam wished he'd never decided to come here at all.

He missed home, but more so, he missed Paris. He missed the conservatory with its historic legacy. Centuries of the world's best performers and composers had been trained and taught in the very same rooms in which Liam used to sit. He missed the fashionable spirit of the city, the cool laissez-faire, the Métro, the rain on the sidewalks, the night life, his friends, the faculty...

Well, best not to dwell.

The Greek system at Northwestern boggled his mind, too. The fraternities of brothers and sisters had little to do with the ancient societies they claimed to emulate. The massive old homes along Sheridan Road their members inhabited must have belonge to high-class families at one time but were now decorated with garish Greek lettering on the side, their lawns trampled and littered with slews of red cups come Sunday morning.

Even the School of Music had a fraternity, and Liam had been encouraged multiple times to pledge during the first week of classes by fellow well-meaning music students. While he had zero intention of joining, he was more than happy to go to their party on the first Friday of the semester and drink their alcohol.

The frat house, painted red with a glossy black door and the Greek letters Phi Mu Alpha over the front porch, looked dark from the outside. Inside though, endless strands of Christmas lights lined the walls, while black lights and strobe lights placed in corners helped to further set the mood. The music that pumped through the house's speaker system was miles away from the etudes and symphonies his fellow party-goers practiced during the day.

He saw some familiar faces manning a keg, and they greeted him with an overly excited "You made it!" and "Psyched you're here, bro!" and a shot of something cinnamon-flavored. The beer they handed him, in one of those godforsaken red cups, was lukewarm but it was free, and no one had carded him—another thing Liam missed dearly—so who was he to complain?

As he wandered deeper into the house, the music swelled, and he found a place against the wall to view the dance floor. He watched the bodies in motion, lines, and curves, male and female. He hadn't been with anyone since Zach, and this night seemed as good a night as any to try to get the bitter taste of Zach's immediate dismissal out of his mouth.

He moved to the dance floor and let his body react to the bass-heavy beat: all shoulders and hips, smooth and carefree. He tossed his head back to expose the length of his neck.

The people around him were already friends, classmates, bandmates, and lovers—past, present and future. They'd taken classes, performed, and partied together since freshman year. Even though the university was massive, the School of Music was small—only about six hundred students—so he was the unknown entity in their midst. He wasn't sure what rumors were being told, but he could only assume that whispered speculations about why someone would leave Paris Conservatory for Evanston abounded.

A pretty girl started dancing nearby. Slim with long dark hair, she was wearing pale blue skinny jeans and a bright yellow top that showed off her midriff. Liam smiled at her and she smiled back, tucking a bit of hair behind her ear.

Bingo.

Liam danced closer.

"I'm Mackenzie. Flute performance," she introduced herself over the volume of the music. "You're Liam, right? You transferred from Paris?" Liam nodded, aligning his movements with the beat. "Someone said you're from Italy, though."

"*È vero,*" Liam replied, and her face brightened.

In very broken Italian she explained that she had spent the summer in Italy, at the prestigious Spoleto Festival. Liam was beginning to wonder if everyone from Northwestern had been in Italy that past summer.

They ended up on the front porch, their bodies glistening with dance sweat. Their shoulders brushed sloppily as they shared a cigarette, and when Liam kissed her, she yielded, turning into him like she'd been waiting for it.

"Should we get out of here?" He liked the loose way she nodded, her eyes heavy and conspiring.

They fucked twice. Once on Liam's couch—his pants barely pulled below his hips before he had a condom on—and then again in his bed, limbs messy and eyes blurry. He woke up the next morning to a face full of her hair, wild, on the pillow next to him.

In the absence of the usual post-hookup awkwardness, they took the L downtown to the Art Institute of Chicago. Liam was impressed by both the art collection and the company. Mackenzie was smart and inquisitive, and she happily listened to Liam prattle on about the art and artists. She didn't seem bothered by the fact that even though his mother was an award-winning painter and his father a well-respected art historian, Liam had no real authority on the subject.

As they walked through Grant Park, the sun setting behind them, Mackenzie began speaking of a boy back home, confiding in Liam like a potential friend instead of a potential lover.

"We're not together or anything." The breeze caught the scent of her perfume. "But I've had a crush on him for ages. When I got home from the festival this summer, it was the first time he really took notice of me. We had a good time if you know what I mean."

"I can hazard a guess." Liam matched the twinkle in her eye.

"Now I just can't get him out of my head even though I know it's not going to go anywhere."

"Yeah," Liam confirmed without her having asked. "I know how that is, too."

They went to a small house party back on campus that night. There couldn't have been more than fifteen people in attendance. Mackenzie introduced Liam to her upperclassmen and grad student friends. They drank craft beer and smoked a bowl of weak Midwestern weed. Liam played a round of poker, losing on purpose. Later he sat on a worn couch, sinking low into the cushions with Mackenzie's bare feet resting in his lap, and flirted with a first-year grad student cellist. If the furious blush that raced across the guy's round cheeks was anything to go by, he was either totally straight or hadn't considered the possibility that he might not be. The boy introduced himself as Sam because his Taiwanese name was too difficult to pronounce.

"I speak three languages fluently. Five, if you count the dead ones. Try me." Liam was drunk again and showing off. Mackenzie bit her thumb around a smirk. Liam leaned over her legs to watch Sam's lips as he stated his given name. It was several, complex, pitched syllables long, and Liam gave it an honest try before resigning that, polyglot though he was, he was totally out of his depth with Asian languages.

"Sam it is, then," Liam relented and Sam laughed loudly, clapping him on the knee.

Mackenzie kissed Liam when she left early, her fingers hooked into his belt loops. It was short and distracted, nothing like the way they'd kissed the night before.

"See you Monday. I'll show you where that coffee place is," she said, leaving him to his new people.

Liam followed Sam back to his apartment once the party dwindled down and fell asleep on Sam's floor as they listened to the slowest recording of Tchaikovsky's Fifth Symphony Liam had ever heard. The following morning, he woke up right there in front of the speakers with a pillow under his head, a blanket over his legs, and a large glass of water with two painkillers on the coffee table next to him. Liam popped the much-needed pills in his mouth and thought that maybe, with some time, this place would grow on him.

7

The first home game of the season, and Northwestern's second victory, was a game where everything worked for Zach. Every pass felt easy and hit its mark. The defense clicked. Special teams did their job. They developed such a large lead over University of Akron that the second-string quarterback was able to take the last few snaps of the game. Even though Zach hated watching from the sidelines, leaving him in to complete the game hadn't been worth the risk of an errant injury in the final minutes.

Afterward, there were hearty hugs from the coaching staff, and the team sang a rousing, though out of tune, rendition of the school's fight song in the locker room that was live-streamed straight to Facebook. After a few minutes in front of the mic at the post-game press conference, a shower, and a drive in the back of his parents' rental car, Zach found himself seated in a plush leather chair between his mother and girlfriend, poking at the remnants of his steak at one of downtown Chicago's nicest restaurants.

This sort of post-game extravagance had become tradition about midway through Zach's freshman year when it was evident that his parents were not going to be casual participants in his college career. They had come to the first home game and the Big Ten opening game each season, waving their purple and white pom-poms proudly. They'd flown from Seattle down to Florida, Texas, and Georgia for Bowl games. When Zach had been injured during his sophomore year, his dad had even come to campus for a week so he could watch the Michigan State game with Zach as he sat on his couch with his foot elevated.

His parents were pretty great, really, making sure their only child lacked for nothing. Zach's affinity for football was always met with a methodical organization on his parents' part. They sought out the best equipment, personal trainers, and summer-long football camps out of state. His father had pulled strings at his law firm to get behind-the-scenes access to members of the Seattle Seahawks. His parents sought out the best advice from those in the know because if Zach were anything less than exceptional, it would not be because of Zach's failure as an athlete, but theirs as parents.

He'd often wondered how they would react if he told them he was gay. He knew they'd voted for Obama twice, though he was pretty sure that had more to do with his stance on Israel than anything else. He'd always sensed they would be okay with it, really—maybe a little confused or worried, and definitely shocked, but Zach didn't think they'd disown him or anything like that. And maybe that made it worse that he'd kept the truth from them for so long.

He'd presented the lie about his sexuality to them too, living it so convincingly that they who had rocked him as a baby, comforted him as a nervous first-grader, and handled him as a moody teenager, never had cause for doubt. They knew and loved their son as a straight man with a girlfriend he planned to marry. Rebecca was essentially already a part of the family, even though his mother, after one too many gin and tonics, would sometimes comment, "A good Jewish girl, Zachy, that's all I ask. Surely there must be at least one at that school of yours?" To tell them he had been deceiving them all this time would almost be cruel.

Regardless of whatever well-researched and zealous support he'd get from them if he came out, it would do nothing to change the culture of the sport around him. It remained imperative that the façade hold and that the people in his life remain blissfully unaware of Zach's sexuality. Thus, the problem with Liam.

Liam, more than anyone alive, knew with immediacy just how Zach's body reacted to a male lover. It was biological, primordial, almost chemical. But Liam's knowledge expanded past the simple physical acts they'd shared, peering through the emotional windows that were opened that night, too. With their bodies spent and their libidos sated, Liam had threaded his fingers through Zach's hair, mindful and reverent. He'd kissed Zach's temple and murmured words that sounded like praise, though Zach's blood-deprived brain realized several long moments that they were French. Their bodies had fallen into a close embrace on that exposed mattress, and, already half-asleep, Liam had breathed, "Stay."

Wrenching himself from Liam had been like pulling himself away from the most perfect dream. He had been so happy that night. Happy and whole. Wholly Zachary.

This was why he could not have Liam in his life. The temptation to have that side of his identity satisfied again was far too intense, the draw impossibly strong. Being reminded several times a week of what they had experienced together, while their professor lectured about the tenants of justice proposed in Plato's Republic, was difficult enough. Zach had even toyed with the idea of dropping the class, but he needed the credit to graduate. If he could get through this semester, he couldn't imagine any reason he would ever have to see Liam again, a thought that made him sick as much as it filled him with relief.

Back at the steakhouse, Rebecca kissed him on the cheek and Zach flinched, unprepared for her sweetly feminine touch. "I'm going to use the restroom before we go." Rebecca looked at him for a moment before smiling carefully. She placed a hand on his arm. "You okay?"

Zach nodded.

"I'll join you." His mother swayed a bit as she lifted her purse off the back of her chair and followed Rebecca, leaving Zach and his father alone. The meal had been cleared away and his father's platinum AmEx card waited on top of the bill. Zach didn't bother looking at the total, but he was sure it was hefty.

"So." His father settled back in his chair with the remnants of a scotch on the rocks. He smoothed his tie across his belly. Zach shared a similar build to his father, as far as height and width went, but too many hours behind a desk and martini lunches had left his father in less than fighting form. "How have practices been going?"

"Good," Zach answered, uninterested in his dad's banal question. He was starting to feel every one of the tackles his offensive line had let through today and was ready to get home to a heating pad and his bed.

"How's the ankle?"

"My ankle's been fine since the end of sophomore year."

His dad met Zach's petulance with a placating lift of his hands, staking claim to his innocence. "Southern Illinois should be no problem next Saturday, but then you've got a big game the week after that."

"They're all big games this season." Zach adjusted his water goblet so it lined up with the corner of his placemat. "Coach will have us ready for Ohio State though."

"I'm sure he will. What about things with you and Rebecca? How is that going?"

Zach looked up, his brow creasing in the middle. "Good." The word was stretched, inflected up at the end, hinting at Zach's confusion. "But what does she have to do with us playing the Buckeyes in two weeks?"

His father shrugged, a shrewd, narrowed expression on his face. Zach wondered if this was the same look he wore when he was about to destroy a prosecutor's argument at trial. "You two have been together a long time."

"Nearly six years."

"You ever think about what will happen after graduation? Come this time next year you could buy her an awfully big ring."

"Dad!" Zach was not ready for this turn in conversation, and his father's question was completely gauche, besides.

"Well, it's true. The contract you'll get in the draft? You'll make me look like a poor man." His dad appeared to be tickled at the thought, and Zach wished his dad had drunk one fewer of those scotches. "I know Mom goes on about marrying a Jewish girl, but she likes Rebecca, really. And you could do a lot worse."

"I know that," Zach snapped.

"So, have you? Talked with her about popping the question?"

Zach calmed himself, clenching, then stretching his fingers wide under the table. "Right now, I'm just focusing on the season ahead and finishing school."

His dad grinned as Rebecca and his mother returned. "Good answer, son."

After his parents drove them back to campus and Zach said his goodnights outside Rebecca's room at the sorority house, he walked back to his apartment. He stuffed his hands deep into the pockets of his pants and tucked his expensive suit coat ungratefully over his arm, mulling over his dad's tipsy prodding.

Asking Rebecca to marry him was always part of the master plan, he supposed. The question was just a matter of when. Maybe he could do it after her birthday or graduation. She'd love the kind of spectacle they'd create if he asked her at the Draft once his name was selected and cameras were rolling nationwide. Maybe it would just be best to wait until after his rookie season when he'd bought his first house and become a multimillionaire at the age of twenty-five.

They'd have a beautiful wedding; he was sure of it. They could have it at one of the many vineyards in eastern Washington state or maybe right here in Chicago with some rooftop, city affair. They'd have beautiful kids, too. And maybe if he lived with this straight-boy ploy long enough, he'd even trick himself into believing that this life, forever hidden in the closet, would actually make him happy.

8

There was a certain smell that Liam associated with academia. It was a smell that seemed ubiquitous across all subjects and continents. It was found in historic buildings with long-trodden hallways and musty offices piled high with books as old as the subjects written about within them. It was the smell of tattered sheet music stacked on the back of a rounded grand piano that hadn't been touched in decades because the notes contained within the tomes had long since been committed to memory. Sometimes it was the smell of turpentine and cut pine frames ready for the stretch of canvas in light-filled art studios with vaulted ceilings.

Liam grew up in these spaces of learning, and he linked these smells to people in his life. His father was an esteemed Renaissance art scholar whose brain was a magical place of knowledge and insight but whose office, in the back of the Uffizi Gallery in Florence, was in a constant state of disarray. Liam would always remember being young and sitting in his mother's studio, watching her work in her paint-splattered jeans, her wavy blond hair sticking out everywhere while she worked away on her next masterpiece. He'd spent countless quiet hours with his professor at the Conservatory, their heads bowed over one of Liam's compositions. Now, it seemed, Liam was destined to associate these smells with his brother, too.

Liam sat in his brother's his new office, eying the new nameplate with "Dr. Eben Barnett, Ph.D." emblazoned in black against gold.

"So, how are you finding Dr. Ellison's class?" Eben asked. His tone was pleasant enough even though his arms were crossed. He swiveled back and forth in his chair, eyeing Liam from every angle of the arc.

Liam thoughtfully considered the question. If he didn't have to sit across from Zach each class, trying not to fester with resentment while pretending he couldn't remember with exact detail how it felt to have Zach's heels hooked around the back of his thighs, he'd probably think it was fantastic.

"It's alright."

His brother was silent for a moment, letting Liam's mediocre review settle. Then his eyes narrowed. "She's a thrice-published, award-winning author and teacher and a highly sought-after Greek translator."

"Yeah. Like I said, it's alright." Liam glanced up through his lashes as Eben settled his still-crossed arms on the edge of his desk.

"You know, I had actual classics majors emailing me last week, trying to get into that class during the add/drop period."

"I need it for my degree, too," Liam contested.

"I don't even understand why you bothered to add a classics minor. You never seemed very interested in the subject before."

"Dad made me take Latin and Greek, just like you," Liam retorted, hotly. "Might as well put all those *amatas sum, amatus es, amatus ests* to good use somehow."

Six years separated Liam's birth from his brother's. Six years, a miscarriage, and a pregnancy his mother and her doctors called *miracoloso*. The children of older parents, Liam, and his brother were born into an already well-established life. Having fully embraced the lifestyle of their chosen home, the Barnett parents lived a European life, full of travel and sunshine, the arts, politics, a multitude of languages, and late-night dinners al fresco. They were constantly surrounded by brilliant friends and even more brilliant thoughts. So instead of separating from this way of life when they had children, their parents simply let their little boys exist within it.

Liam and his brother had been gifted with a liberal upbringing in a sprawling Florentine apartment off the Via di Mezzo, where there was little talk of bedtime or curfews and no hard and fast rules about cursing. They'd been exposed to the intense German films their mother loved long before either of them should have been and had been offered wine at the dinner table before it was technically legal, even by loose Italian laws.

Liam's parents hadn't freaked out like many might have, when at sixteen, he brought a girl home and quietly took her to his room. Nor had they been bothered when, a few months later, Liam had brought a boy home and done the very same thing. They'd simply asked one morning over breakfast after a different boy had left Liam's room if he knew where to buy condoms at the *farmacia*. When he'd answered with a sassy, *"Ovviamente,"* they'd let the matter slide.

It wasn't reckless or lazy parenting, just progressive. For Eben and Liam's parents, their sons' thoughts and wishes were as valid as any adult's, and this upbringing created a special bond among the four of them that Liam learned was unusual only after he left home. Liam and his brother were especially close.

And then, they weren't close at all.

The distance that developed between Liam and his brother over the years was first forged by a physical barrier an ocean wide. His brother had left for college in America when Liam was only twelve years old. Liam had cried for days. Grown-up and living his own life a continent away, Eben had made little time for Liam's pre-teen saga.

That distance changed into resentment as Liam had continued to be mollified by an easy home life, while Eben had insisted on making his own way. After all the goings-on in Paris during the previous year, Eben's bitterness had codified into a downright dislike of his younger sibling. Liam's parents had stayed by his side, despite their disappointment, throughout the whole ordeal. But Eben, who'd always seen the world in stark black and white, had been unwilling to condone any of Liam's poor life choices.

By this point in his life, Liam was quite used to his older brother looking at him with disappointment, seemingly exhausted by Liam's ingratitude. He gave Liam one such look then. Eben sighed heavily, then tempered his face. "I heard from Mom the other day."

"Yeah, me too. I haven't called her back yet, though."

"That's why she texted me. She's worried."

Liam groaned, slinking lower into his chair. He flung his arms out from his sides in a desperate gesture. "What was I supposed to say?"

"I don't know. 'Everything's fine. Missing you,' probably would have sufficed. You know, polite, normal stuff. She just wants to know you aren't dead and that you haven't—"

"That I haven't what?" Liam cut him off with a chill in his voice that dared his brother to finish his sentence.

It had been their father's idea for Liam, in need of a fresh start, to join his brother at Northwestern University that fall. Liam had met the idea with total petulance and a firm and inebriated, "Hell no!" His brother had, apparently, had a similarly visceral reaction. They shared the same blood, after all.

When they'd both conceded to their father's logic and their mother's weepy guilt, their concessions had come with conditions. Liam insisted that under no circumstances would he share an apartment with his brother. Eben had demanded Liam not take any of his classes, even though they would satisfy requirements for Liam's minor.

Eben had still been surly about his little brother's presence on campus, even as he'd helped Liam move into his apartment on a late August afternoon.

"This job is important to me," Eben had reminded Liam as he'd pulled a cardboard box full of sheet music off the elevator in Liam's apartment building. "It's an amazing start for my career and closer to Kelsey's family. I have to focus this year. I can't be distracted by you and whatever drama you're going to create. I can't be your babysitter."

Liam had done all he could not to rage at his brother's assumptions and jerked the box roughly out of Eben's hands. "Well, that's fine, 'cause I'm not gonna fucking need a babysitter." That had been the last time they'd spoken.

It had been the unanswered voicemail from their mother—the one where her voice had quivered with love for both her sons—that had prompted Liam to swing by his brother's office that morning. He owed it to his parents, whom he'd let down to an immeasurable degree, to make nice with his brother. Maybe he owed it to the little boy who'd once looked up to his older brother with something bordering adoration too.

Liam took a deep breath. "How is Kelsey doing?"

If any topic was safe, it would be his brother's impending fatherhood. "The nausea is better now that she's in the second trimester. We'll find out the sex next month."

"Cool." Liam stood, gathering his things. He had class across campus in a bit, but he would have time to do some composing beforehand if he hurried. He'd woken up with a chord progression in his head, jazz-influenced and brooding, and he was eager to get it down on paper.

Eben's voice delayed him a while longer. He rubbed at the back of his neck. "Kels was wondering if you'd like to come over for dinner this weekend."

"Seriously?"

"Yeah. I mean, she thought it would be nice."

Liam caught his brother's eye. Maybe he, too, was putting in an effort to make things better between them. "Yeah, okay. Just let me know what time."

"Will do." Eben placed his hands in his trouser pockets and offered a small, pleased smile as Liam opened the office door directly onto a waiting Zach. It took Liam a second to process what he was seeing, his head still stuck on the conversation with his brother.

"Hi," Zach said, dumbly. His ridiculously broad shoulders

took up nearly the entire width of the door frame.

"Hello."

Liam shouldn't have been so dazed to see him. He'd been seeing Zach on Monday, Wednesday, and Friday from 10:10-11:05 for the last three weeks, after all. Zach usually rushed into their class, running late and apologizing for it. He would take the chair closest to the door and farthest from Liam, barely comment on anything, and then hurry out the door as soon as class was through. Zach couldn't have been more obvious in his avoidance. This felt like the first time Zach had looked Liam in the eye since the first day of class. Liam had forgotten how intoxicating Zach's undivided attention could be.

Eben crowded in behind Liam to see who was at the door. "Ah, Zach. Congratulations on your win this weekend."

Zach's eyes flitted over Liam's shoulder for a moment. "Thanks, Dr. Barnett."

"How many points did you put up against Southern Illinois?"

"Fifty-six. But they're a Division II school. It should have been more."

"Still, no small feat. Three and oh to start the season, right?" Zach gave him a tight little nod. "No better start than that."

Neither of Zach or Liam had moved from their impasse in the doorway. They hadn't stopped staring either, paralyzed by the face-to-face weirdness, and Eben took notice. "Don't tell me you're star struck, *fratellino*."

"No. We're in the Plato seminar together," Liam answered grumpily.

"Ah, I was talking to Liam about that class. What do you think of Dr. Ellison, Zach?"

"She's fantastic," Zach answered. "One of the best at the whole university, I think."

Eben made a smug noise at the back of his throat as if to say, *Told you so.* Liam didn't bother to hold back his eye roll. "You ready for our meeting, then?"

Liam's eyes snapped back and forth between Zach and his brother, feeling betrayed. Then it clicked: his brother was Zach's advisor. His head rolled back with an internal groan.

With a sheepish look to the floor, Zach stepped out of the way, making room for Liam to pass. Eben's phone rang at the same time, and he pulled it out from his pocket, checking the screen for the caller.

"Can you spare me five minutes, Zach? It's a colleague from overseas I've been needing to reach."

"No problem," Zach replied.

"Five minutes," he repeated, showing the matching number with his hand. That same hand then landed on Liam's shoulder. *"Richiami la mamma, per favore?"*

Liam was unsure if Eben even realized he'd slipped into Italian. That had been their trick as kids: jumping from Italian to English when they were trying to keep a secret from their neighborhood buddies. Whether or not Eben's transition was intentional, it softened Liam's mood.

"Si, si," he replied. *"Oggi.* Today. I promise."

"Thank you," Eben said, as he swiped his thumb across the screen to answer. "Ingo, how are you?" His brother's voice faded as he shut the door behind him, and Liam lifted his backpack over his shoulder, ready to vacate the hallway as quickly as possible.

"Wait."

Liam turned at the insistence in Zach's voice. Zach's brow was furrowed with concentration. "Dr. Barnett is your...He's your brother?"

"Liam Barnett, Eben Barnett. *Il fratellino,* the big bro." Liam gestured between himself and the door with each statement. "Is it so shocking that we could be related?"

Zach stared openly, his jaw slack. "No, I can see the resemblance. It's just...I didn't even know your last name until now."

Liam tutted with faux empathy. "It must be so confusing for you out in the real world where our names aren't stitched to the back of our shirts like you're used to."

Instead of reacting with an equally caustic remark, Zach smiled. The soft curl of his lips was completely disarming, and Liam's cheeks flushed. It was unfair that Liam's rudeness made

Zach amused.

"This is wild." Zach pushed his hair off his face and leaned against the wall next to Eben's office. "Your brother's brilliant. I read his dissertation this summer before I went to Italy. I can't wait to see him published."

"Yeah, well, he also slept with a stuffed lion named Gaetano until he was thirteen because he was afraid of the sound the radiators made in his bedroom."

Zach snorted. "Is he why you're here? I mean, did you follow him here or something?"

"Kind of?" Liam bit at his lower lip for a second. "I needed to leave my old school, so my parents thought it would be a good idea if I wasn't...well, it seemed to make sense at the time."

"Why did you have to leave?" Almost right away, Zach added, "I'm sorry if that's too personal."

Liam was suddenly struck by the utter bullshit of this situation. Zach had zero right to stand there looking so good with his easy hair, his gray hoodie with the NU seal over his left pec, and his shorts showing off those gorgeous legs. He shouldn't have been asking Liam these spot-on questions about his past in a tone that made it sound like he was interested in the answer.

"Well, it is. Personal," Liam snapped. "So why the hell are you asking?"

Zach looked disarmed like the shoe was suddenly on the other foot. It was exactly what Liam had hoped for with his swift turn in mood. The hallway was empty. Behind his office door, Eben's jovial conversation with his foreign colleague continued, muted and undistinguished. Liam checked over his shoulder to ensure no one was coming down the hall. He might be seething mad, but he wasn't a total asshole. He stepped in towards Zach, his voice rash and quiet.

"Just because you know what my cum tastes like, doesn't mean you have to pretend to be nice to me. We aren't friends, Zach. You said you wanted nothing to do with me, so do nothing."

Zach went pale, looking at Liam with another gut-punching stare.

Eben opened his door then, phone loose in his hand, and surveyed the situation. "Everything okay, boys?"

"Fine," Zach replied, but Liam knew Zach wasn't answering Eben's question but his own demand.

9

At first, it had been singing. Singing while playing with blocks. Singing while coloring. Singing at the dinner table. Liam sang little songs he'd learned at his Reggio Emilia preschool and melodies from his parents' nineties indie-rock inspired CD collection, all rendered in his sweet, boy soprano. He joined the boys' choir at the cathedral for the length of a season before his firmly atheist parents became uncomfortable with all the *Pie Jesus* and *Hallelujahs* Liam was forced to perform.

By the age of six, it was the violin at Liam's insistence. But by age seven, he was finished with the fussy posture and slow progress he was making because his parents never made him practice unless he wanted to.

He loved the immediacy of the piano. Two lessons in, he could already play melodies—one-handed and choppy, granted, but melodies, nonetheless. He would sit for hours, his fingers wandering across the keys, creating, exploring—but not necessarily practicing—which would result in stern looks from his teacher at his following lesson.

It wasn't until he was fourteen that Liam realized he could put all these aimless creations down on paper. With little more than two staves, five lines, and note heads etched in pencil, Liam could follow a melody from start to finish, change it, bring it home. Liam could compose his own music.

Getting admitted into the Paris Conservatory had been one of the proudest moments of Liam's life. The legacy of composers who had studied at that school was richer than perhaps any other school in the world, besides the St. Petersburg Conservatory. He often wondered if leaving that lineage, and not by choice, would prove to be one of the biggest regrets of his life.

Even as a composition major at Northwestern, Liam was expected to have a high proficiency in his main instrument. After all, until you're established, who the hell is going to play your compositions, if not you? Between coursework at the School of Music and university-required classes he was sorely behind on, Liam's days were stacked full. Late-night practice sessions were a must, as were nighttime caffeine runs.

"Usual?" Sam asked. Liam nodded and clasped his hands above his head, cracking his back. Sam and Mackenzie got in line. She tucked her arm through Sam's as they waited.

The three of them were a package deal by that point in the semester. Both Mackenzie and Sam had quickly latched their affections onto Liam, but their friendships had jumped circuit and linked Sam and Mackenzie together too. According to Sam, they were like a three-atom molecule with equal bonds. But Sam had been stoned when he said it, so Liam had no idea if the analogy was accurate. Liam didn't do the hard sciences.

He wandered through the student union as the espresso machines hissed and let his mind rest. This break would do him good, as he'd already practiced for over three hours. He stopped in front of the community board with flyers for yoga classes and visiting lectures tacked on with pins. There was a very serious-looking poster that asked, "When is stress ANXIETY?" and, as the music school was just across the street, there were scads of posters advertising upcoming student recitals. In the lower corner was a high-gloss, full-sized poster promoting this season's football schedule. In the center was a giant image of Zach. Liam let out a long sigh. He'd hoped that on a campus of over twenty-thousand students, one guy would be easier to avoid.

The picture showed Zach in his football uniform: tight white pants, purple jersey with the number twenty-four on the front. Under the white-strapped helmet, his blue eyes stuck out even more than usual, thanks to Photoshop. His hand was cocked back over his shoulder, his fingers expertly curled around a ball, ready to throw. Liam's eyes lingered, remembering those fingers, those biceps, the arch of that neck. Zach's body still felt familiar, even after only one night together and one month gone. Liam could still remember the way those parts of Zach felt on his skin, like a ghost who came to visit him in the night.

It was strange to see Zach presented in that role, as Liam had only ever spent time imagining Zach all geared-up in his football uniform as a thought experiment. Possible but not provable. To see it now, the words "NU - All the Way In 2020" printed large above his head, Zach's alternate persona became all the more real. He did exist in that other world, didn't he? This other life wasn't just about a game, either, but a whole complex collegiate sports machine, with a lot of money behind it and Zach at the very core. It wasn't empathy or sympathy that settled over Liam as his eyes remained locked on the glossy image of Zach, just maybe a bit of understanding.

"We should go to a game sometime." Sam came up behind Liam and handed him his half-caff, single-pump, skim hazelnut latte with no foam.

"It's pretty fun, actually." Mackenzie sipped her chai tea. "I was in the marching band freshman year."

"You were what?" Liam's face contorted with disbelief. She may as well have told him she liked to eat inchworms for breakfast.

"Let's go, then," Sam said. "Isn't that what you do at schools like this? Go cheer for the alma mater?" Sam's education, until now, had robbed him of any type of big-time school sports. And much like everything else, Sam was always ready to embrace new experiences with gusto.

Liam looked at them like they'd both grown antlers. He

turned crisply on his heel. "I'm going to practice." He was pretty sure he heard Sam and Mackenzie share a giggle at his expense as he walked away.

Two hours later, Liam reached a point of exhaustion where any further practice was no longer going to be productive. The trio lumbered back to Liam's place and three beers in, Liam was feeling quite content, his legs stretched the full length of his couch. One thing he did enjoy about American universities? Thirsty Thursday.

"My housemate is at a mixer," Mackenzie said as she scrolled through her phone, sending out texts and checking Instagram in hopes of finding something fun to do. Neither she nor Sam seemed eager to stay in for the night.

"Where?" Liam asked.

"At Hillel. I think that guy she likes is there."

"Is that the Jewish frat?"

"No, it's not a fraternity. It's a nationwide community organization that promotes commitment to Jewish life and learning," Sam stated definitively. Liam and Mackenzie shared flummoxed looks, both wondering how their Taiwanese friend could know that. But then Sam turned his phone their direction, a Wikipedia article open on his screen.

"How the hell do you Google stuff so fast?" Liam wondered aloud as Sam contentedly read on in silence.

Liam was always a little weary about anything affiliated with organized religion. In a city dominated by monuments to Catholicism, Liam's parents had drawn their ethics from secular humanists, poets, and philosophers. Liam was brought up to believe that he didn't need religion to dictate what was right and wrong, just his own humanity. Some days he wondered if that mindset hadn't been quite sufficient for him, though.

"I'm up for going there if you two are," Mackenzie said, and Sam agreed with a good-natured smile.

Liam tossed his head back on the couch. His friend's expectant looks were heavy on him. Mackenzie and Sam could, in theory, go without him, but that would only happen if they all weren't so damned co-dependant. "Alright, fine," he relented. "But if anyone tries to recruit me to join something, I'm leaving."

The minute they arrived at the Hillel building, Mackenzie flew off to play wing-woman for her housemate. Sam got beers for both Liam and himself but then disappeared too, leaving Liam in a room full of people he didn't know. Traitors, the both of them.

Much as Liam had suspected, the evening had definitely started off as an info session—pamphlets littered across the food table were proof of that—but now it had dissolved into a regular college party. The partiers had gathered in the main meeting room, past the reception desk and through a set of double doors. The lights were dimmed. Someone had brought in a pair of speakers and a small set of LED disco lights that swirled around the room in a range of rainbow colors. It was thrown together last minute, but now that alcohol was involved, it wasn't all that different from other parties Liam had attended.

After promptly finishing off his beer, Liam got a cup of the dangerous-looking red punch others were drinking. The alcohol was so strong it nearly burned his tongue, despite being masked by gobs of artificial sweetener. He didn't know anyone here besides Sam and Mackenzie and was in no mood for making friends. He took another large gulp and was thinking about leaving when he saw him.

There could be no mistaking Zach. His body was too large, his jaw too square, his eyes too soulful. Zach stood alone across the darkened room, propped up against the wall with his arms crossed. He watched the party around him with a bored expression.

Liam's head began to swim. Christ, what was in that punch? The only thought he seemed capable of forming was *I've had him*. And damn all the subplot, he wanted him again.

Liam realized he'd been staring only when Zach started staring back, not hiding from Liam like he had tried to during class, not averting his gaze towards the floor, stricken, like he had after Liam's epic 'fuck you' the other day. It was bold. Unflinching. The kind of lingering eye contact you couldn't walk away from. Liam swallowed his drink, one final rush of liquid courage, and started his way.

10

A wave of exhilaration passed through Zach as Liam started to walk over. His reptilian brain screamed *Danger! Danger!* while the rest of him watched the ease of Liam's long-legged gait.

Of all the random, incongruous places on campus, of course, Liam would end up here. Fate seemed pretty damned determined to thrust them together. If this were a test, Zach felt like he was failing. If this were a game, then Universe: one, Zach: nil.

"Sugarman." Liam said it like Zach's name was the answer to the most obvious question in the world. He let out an audible huff.

Zach watched as Liam settled his back against the wall, leaving ample room between them. He lifted the hand not holding his drink and tucked it between the small of his back and the wall, his hips jutting forward for a flash of a second. There was something supple and pacifying about that single motion, like a young lion rolling onto his back for the alpha male.

"Kinda like a bad penny, huh?" Liam said over the music.

"Not sure which one of us is the penny in this scenario, but yeah, kinda."

The corner of Liam's mouth curved upwards, and Zach's heart skipped a beat. There was a sluggishness to Liam's movements. His eyes were heavy-lidded, his limbs, slack. That's when Zach realized Liam wasn't being acquiescent or apologetic, he was just drunk—or at least, well on his way to being so.

"Didn't think this was really your type of thing." Zach's voice acquired a disappointed edge.

"No, it's really not." Liam gave his head an emphatic shake. His curls sprung out of place then perfectly back in. "My friend Mackenzie's roommate is here. I don't know. There's some guy she likes evidently." Liam turned his head toward Zach and lifted a suspicious brow. "I didn't think this would be your sort of thing either."

"Seeing as I'm pretty much the most high-profile Jewish guy on campus, the student committee for Hillel is always asking me to make an appearance."

"So, you thought you'd grace the mere mortals around you with your presence tonight?"

"I wouldn't—" He stopped as he realized Liam was just making fun. Their eyes fell away from each other at the same time, furtive smiles crossing each of their faces.

"We leave for a road game tomorrow," Zach said, suddenly aware of how bottom-heavy his voice sounded when he was trying to sound calm. "Coach let us out of practice early. He's been riding us pretty hard all week, so I figured, why not come? Unwind for a bit. The president of Alpha Epsilon Pi was here earlier, too. He wants to make me an honorary brother, I think."

"A frat?"

"Jewish frat."

"Would you join?"

"No," Zach answered. "I mean, being Jewish feels like an afterthought for me. We went to Synagogue growing up a few times a year, the important dates, you know. I got bar mitzvahed, but only because it was something that mattered a lot to my grandparents." Even in Liam's drunken state, he seemed to be listening to Zach's oversharing with interest. It sent the good kind of chill down Zach's spine. "Anyway, if I were going to join a frat, I would want to do it the real way. I mean, you gotta be hazed, right?"

Liam laughed at the ridiculousness of the statement, but

his expression quickly turned steely, as if he'd remembered any sort of friendly behavior wasn't allowed in Zach's presence. Zach couldn't blame Liam for being standoffish. He didn't even blame Liam for the dramatic show the other day outside Dr. Barnett's office, either. How could he, when Zach was the one insisting on all this pretense?

Would it matter if he told Liam how much he hated faking? That when he'd been on a morning run or when they were sitting in class together, he'd imagined all the different realities where the two of them were friends—more than friends. Zach kept finding himself back at this precipice where both he and Liam seemed ready, almost eager, to slip a tentative toe into the pool of friendship. But then one of them would flail back from the icy edge, remembering how much the frozen water had stung them before. It was exhausting, and all Zach wanted was to give in. He didn't want to fight how much he wanted Liam. He wanted to give himself over to their mutual desire and explore Liam's prickly exterior which evaporated from time to time, offering glimpses of gentleness. What he wouldn't give to separate himself again from his faux-heterosexual life here, like he had in Rome, and have another soft night with Liam.

"I need a refill," Liam stated. "You?"

Zach lifted his empty hands. "I can't drink during the season."

"At all?" Liam sounded incredulous. "That sucks."

"Don't worry, I make up for it in the spring and summer. I wasn't exactly sober in Rome if you remember."

Liam swirled what was left of his drink in his cup. He pressed his lips together, releasing them with a pronounced pop. "Can you do other stuff?"

"If I can't drink, I obviously can't do drugs. I'd get kicked off the team in a hot minute, and besides, that shit is terrifying."

"I don't mean drugs." Liam lolled his head to the side, locking his eyes on Zach. Even in the low light, Liam's eyes were honeyed and unmistakable in their insinuation. "I mean, can you fuck?" The sound of his 'f' was crass. The 'k' was positively vulgar. Zach wilted, shivering internally.

"Of course I can."

Liam's eyelids hovered low for a moment. "Then why the hell are we still standing here?"

The room around them went silent and still for Zach. The only sound left was his heart pounding in his ears.

"I thought we weren't going to be friends?"

"We're not," Liam answered with a businesslike tone. "This has nothing to do with being friends. This is just about getting off."

Zach didn't say a word. He couldn't. He wanted to ask Liam what the hell he was thinking of suggesting something like this in a public place. He wanted to grab Liam by the scruff of his neck, catch those curls between his knuckles, and demand Liam make good on his offer. What he did instead was walk away, not even bothering to look over his shoulder because he knew, beyond a shadow of a doubt, that Liam would follow.

—

Anyone seeing them would think nothing of them walking away, but if they could hear the thoughts racing through Zach's mind, they'd be privy to a very different narrative. Sneaking off with Liam was beyond reckless, but maybe that's why it felt so good. A heady mix of nervous anticipation and foolhardy impulsiveness settled in Zach's gut—and lower—creating a feeling, not unlike those he remembered from their first night together. He felt drunk though he hadn't touched a drop of alcohol.

He glanced back at Liam, his narrow fingers trailing along the metal railing of the stairs, his head bowed and displaying a crown of curls. His movements seemed serene and unflustered by the prospect of their rendezvous while Zach's heart pounded out an impatient rhythm.

Upon reaching the second-floor landing, Zach turned and used his hips to depress the crossbar on the fire-safe door. He backed up, opening the way for Liam with a glib smile. Though there was plenty of space for Liam to pass, he crowded in close to Zach, using his whole body to tease him. Liam's eyes went dark, idling on Zach's face. Liam's tongue clicked softly on the roof of his mouth then rolled between his open teeth as if at the ready. When Zach gasped, Liam meandered away with a simpering smirk on his face. Zach was grateful for the door behind him. The hallway was dark, the only source of light a red exit sign at the far end. The classroom they found was even darker. Zach could just make out Liam's shadowy outline as Liam spun, taking it in.

"How romantic," Liam said.

"Getting off, right? Last time I checked, you don't need much romance for that." Zach pulled his belt loose from his buckle for emphasis. At the sound of the metallic clink, Liam snickered.

Using that laugh like sonar, Zach reached into the shadows and connected with Liam's wrist. They staggered and swayed, their feet aligning, their breath audible. Zach pressed their bodies together just long enough for the heat between them to register. Then swiftly, squeezing Liam's hip, Zach spun him around and pushed him backward until Liam's shoulders collided with the wall. Liam let out a surprised exhale.

Zach loomed large over Liam's much slighter frame in what felt like a complete role reversal from their first time together in Rome. Liam clearly liked it, if his already ragged breath was any indicator. Zach bracketed his arms around Liam's face and kissed him roughly, letting the weight of his whole body sink into Liam. He hid nothing of his arousal.

"I knew it." Liam bucked his hips to create room for his hands to get to Zach's fly. They worked together to shift Zach's jeans over on his hips. "I knew you'd be ready for me."

"Shut up."

"Gladly."

In one silken movement, Liam slipped his hand into the front of Zach's pants and kissed his mouth. Liam's touch was hot, almost blistering around Zach. Zach's limbs went weak. He tried his best to concentrate on the zipper of Liam's pants even as blood evacuated his brain, southbound.

What must it be like, Zach wondered, to not only want a partner but to crave him? It must be remarkable to share these impromptu rendezvous, which made Zach burn, with a person who was also his best friend, his emotional outlet. Would Zach ever have that? Or was he cursed to make do with sporadic evenings, stolen hours, and one-offs for the rest of his life?

With the realization that Liam was the only man to have touched Zach twice, he spilled into Liam's hand with a muted cry: high, vulnerable, and unstoppable.

"God, you're pretty when you do that." Liam mouthed Zach's neck below his ear. His grip around Zach relaxed and slowed to a tender pace. He'd done that in Rome, too, eased Zach through the come down.

"You can't even see me," Zach panted, vehemently ignoring how cared for he felt and concentrating instead on returning the favor for Liam.

"No, but I can remember." The words whispered past Zach's ear, turned into a throaty groan. Liam's fingers tightened on Zach's shoulders. Liam shuddered, then went supple against Zach's chest, spent.

"Zach, do you—"

At the sound of fellow party goers laughing out in the hallway, Zach lifted his clean hand to cover Liam's mouth, stopping Liam's question in his mouth. Zach's other hand was still down Liam's pants but he didn't dare move. They both went horribly still. Liam's eyes were wide. The voices vanished as quickly as they had appeared, but it had been too damned close.

"Fuck!" Zach yanked himself away, pulling his pants back up. His heart was beating like he'd just run a hundred-meter sprint at full speed. "Fuck!" He cursed again, meeting the emphatic yell with a snap of his semen-covered hand. "Fuck, fuck, fuck." He paced as he started shaking. Behind him, Liam let out an unruly, grotesque, and inappropriate laugh.

Zach stared in Liam's direction, disbelieving Liam's callous reaction. "What the hell is wrong with you?"

Liam was doubled at the waist, laughing so hard he'd stopped making noise. "I was thinking," he gasped, "we wouldn't exactly have been caught red-handed, would we?" He lifted the hand where Zach's spunk cooled between his fingers. "I'm sorry, I'm sorry," Liam gasped again, but his apology lacked any sincerity.

Zach was such a supreme idiot for entrusting Liam with the encounter. It had been a risk of monumental proportions, and for what? Some piddly hand job? Maybe Zach had been wrong about Liam from the get-go. Perhaps those quiet moments in bed together have been an act. Perhaps the brash, heartless exterior was all there was to Liam, and every moment of sweet flirtation had been the delusion of a desperate, connection-starved man.

"Fuck you," Zach spat.

"Oh, come on," Liam pleaded as if willing Zach to see the amusement in the situation. When it became clear he wouldn't, Liam scoffed with a sorry shake of his head. He wiped his hand on the outside of his boxers, then did up his jeans. "You know, you were a lot less uptight in Rome."

"No one knew who I was in Rome."

"And nobody knows you are in here. Lighten up. *Madonna!*" A very Italian gesture highlighted his Italian curse as he walked past Zach like he was ready to leave. But Zach grabbed for him, securing him around the bicep.

"You really don't get it, do you?" He needed Liam to understand. Even if Liam didn't give two shits, Zach needed Liam to get why it had to be like this. "Anything, even a whisper of something like this, would ruin me. My whole life, everything I've worked for—"

"I know that, okay?" Liam snapped, yanking his arm away.

Zach could make out the look on Liam's face, his eyes having adjusted enough to the darkness. It was not callous or flippant but twisted with something very much like sadness. When Liam spoke again, his voice lacked any brittle edge.

"Look, you're fine. They didn't see us. No way they even knew anyone was in here. And if, by some impossibility of physics, they were able to see through that sliver of a window to that nearly pitch-black corner," he pointed to where Zach had had him pressed against the wall, "and they happened to be using high-tech night-vision goggles, and they were somehow able to recognize it was you, then they probably thought you were hooking up with a girl with a cute haircut."

Zach gaped at him. Liam tossed his head like he had downstairs. "The curls come in handy." Though he didn't quite smile at Liam's quip, his pulse began to return to normal. "There was a bathroom on the right as we came up the stairs. You go in there. Clean yourself up. Go home. I'll wait in here a while, text my friends to tell them that I left ages ago, then leave out the back."

It was like Liam had flicked the switch again, from spiky to mild. It would be so much easier for Zach, his heart, and his urges if Liam would be one or the other: friend or foe.

"Why are you being nice to me?"

"I don't know." Liam plastered on his face a smile so obscenely fake it looked like it hurt. "Last time, though. Promise. You should go."

Liam sank to one of the folding plastic chairs, rubbing at his eyes, and Zach found himself frozen there, watching. Wishing.

"Go!" Liam shouted with an emphatic wave towards the door.

Zach had no choice. Without another word, he left.

11

A fleet of Northwestern University buses idled outside the Horseshoe, the Ohio State University stadium. They'd been there since the game ended, so the whole cabin smelled of gasoline and hot steel as Zach climbed on board. Late night bus rides were a standard part of any road game weekend, but they were so much better after a win, especially one as big as the one they'd had earlier that day.

Everyone in the Big Ten conference loved to hate the Ohio State Buckeyes, and the Northwestern Wildcats were no different. The crowd at OSU's stadium had been ravenous for a win, and Northwestern had been happy to play the spoiler. Zach's defense had an interception on OSU's first possession, and he'd used the resulting short field to score the first points of the game. Even though had OSU fought hard, almost tying things up in the third quarter, the Wildcats had regained control early in the fourth and refused to give it back.

The omens for the rest of the season after this win were tremendous. Zach high-fived buddies and teammates as he made his way toward the back of the bus where Des had saved him a seat.

"You seen it yet?" Des asked before Zach even had the chance to stuff his bag in the overhead bin. "It's a doozy this time, man. I think she's really stepping up her game this season."

Zach groaned as he sank down into the seat next to Des.

"Alright, lay it on me."

Des handed over his phone. The screen glowed bluish-white with Rebecca's Instagram profile. There were about twenty stories chronicling her evening spent watching the game at the Delta Delta Delta sorority house. There were heavily tagged selfies with the usual cadre of sisters gathered to watch, all dressed in various shades of purple and white. In each shot, Rebecca was front and center, an exaggerated smile on her face. There were Boomerang videos of the sisters cheering after Northwestern's first touchdown, a shot of the television itself when the camera had panned to Zach resting on the sidelines between plays. He was sweating and trying to catch his breath, but she'd written "#hubbahubba" and "#mine" across his face in purple letters.

Zach sighed and Des looked on with a droll smile. As Zach's best friend, he'd been putting up with Rebecca for years. Zach kept watching.

She posted this kind of extensive social media content during every game. What she posted rarely had anything to do with the actual sport, even though she knew most of her followers were there to get info on Zach. She was always happy to play up her relationship with the star player and work it to her advantage.

The final story scrolled past, a picture of Rebecca and Zach from last spring's Greek Life Formal. Written over the top in a glowing neon font were the words: "You want your own varsity co-ed? Pledge Tri Delt! 'Cause the best sisters get the best misters."

"Nice plug, huh?" Des teased dryly.

"Well, it is Fall Rush."

Des made an unconvinced noise as the bus pulled away.

When Zach got back to his apartment around 3 a.m., he found Rebecca asleep on his couch, curled on her side. Her knees were tucked into the hem of one of Zach's oversized T-shirts. He crouched down beside her, his quads complaining a bit as he did. If he had wanted to, he could have lifted her up and brought her to his bed. She was light enough for him to carry.

Instead, he tried to wake her. "Rebecca." She didn't react.

He scooted in closer. "Becca."

Her nose crinkled before she opened her eyes. She smiled when she saw Zach. "I tried to stay up."

"It's okay. Let's go to sleep."

She nodded, getting up off the couch with a quick stretch. She was asleep again, on the far edge of his king-sized bed, by the time he'd brushed his teeth. He slid into bed next to her, brushing a lock of hair that had fallen across her face out of the way. Her freckles had started to fade; the summer, once evident on her skin, was slipping away. There was a micro-tinge of regret around his heart.

Who was he to complain about her tireless support? Okay, maybe it was a little much sometimes. None of the girlfriends of the other guys on the team did it. But Zach knew it came from a place of love. He was lucky to have a girlfriend like Rebecca. Being with her should not make him feel trapped or incomplete. Who cared that her bottomless well of peppiness sometimes wore him thin? So what if the curves of her small body, which had sought him out the second he'd gotten into bed, did next to nothing to rouse his libido? She was here—warm, safe, and predictable in a way Liam would never be as a partner.

Suddenly terrorized by the fluid way his subconscious had inserted Liam into bed between him and Rebecca, Zach slid halfway across the sateen sheets in an instant. Where had this idea of dating Liam come from, anyway? It had just been sex, pure and simple. Once for fun and once by mistake. He and Liam were over. Hell, they'd never truly begun.

Carefully, Zach made his way back across the mattress and flipped his pillow to the cool side. He tucked his head against Rebecca's neck and wondered, as he fell asleep if she'd started to wear a new perfume.

—

Liam was the last one to class the following Monday morning, wearing an expression of total ire. Instead of avoiding all eye contact with Zach like he usually did, Liam made sure to meet Zach's gaze, proving how seriously he was taking his pledge to not play nice anymore. Even though the look was full of ice, the intensity was hot as hell, and Zach flushed from it.

Dr. Ellison began her lecture on Plato's *Symposium*, perhaps the most famous of his Socratic dialogues. "We'll be doing presentations in class next Friday on each speech. And since the *Symposium* centers around the various iterations of love," she swooped her voice in and around the word, batting her eyes, and the class, save Zach and Liam, chuckled politely at it. "We will obviously be doing this project in pairs."

She began to partner people off, and it was clear enough by the mid-point that the universe officially hated them both, as she paired Zach up with Liam. She assigned them Aristophanes' speech: the dialogue about romantic love. Of fucking course.

Zach watched as Liam dropped his face into his hand and slumped lower in his seat with an audible groan.

12

L iam had noticed that Zach took notes longhand during the first week of classes when the only way to fully ignore Zach had meant being constantly aware of him. Most other students in their seminar typed straight into their laptops, creating a flurry of ceaseless clicks that sometimes drowned out the professor's voice. He and Zach were the only holdovers that preferred to transfer lecture highlights from voice to pen and paper. Doing so felt reverential to Liam. It was a way to honor an educational lineage from the first places of study in the ancient world through the rise of the Oxbridge tradition and the one-room schoolhouses in New England. Liam liked that the same old-fashioned place inside him lived inside Zach as well.

Working side by side on their Plato project in the testy silence of Zach's apartment, he watched Zach again. Their proximity allowed Liam to observe Zach openly. His bare feet, reddened with healing blisters and calluses, were planted wide in the lush cream carpet covering his living room floor. His elbows rested on spread knees as he leaned over the college-ruled notebook that he had folded back on itself and placed on the coffee table. His blue eyes jumped between the Greek text they were translating and the resulting English words that flowed from the tip of his ink pen with little hesitation. The precision with which Zach's penmanship marched across the page was striking. His script was elegant and perfectly spaced like he'd been properly taught how to write in cursive and then invested time to practice it. This shouldn't have surprised Liam, but it did. Zach continued to be a home for contradictions, a trait that was his most intriguing, and therefore his most frustrating, quality.

Liam set his pencil down to rest in the open spine of his Plato book to hold his place. He had developed a mantra on his walk to Zach's apartment building earlier that evening while kicking at the first round of autumn leaves like some boy sent home after not playing nicely with the neighbors. "I will be contrite. I will be a model classmate. I will basically be the exact opposite of what I was on Wednesday night."

Liam cleared his throat. "I'm sorry."

The pen on Zach's page froze.

They'd managed to avoid any talk of the project for a week—long enough for Zachary to fly off to New Jersey and tally another win. The trouncing at Rutgers University was so monstrous that news of it even managed to find its way onto Liam's Snapchat feed.

The rift between them had taken on a hardened edge since the party at Hillel. It had become brittle in a new and more complicated way. This wasn't just the standard post-hookup weirdness, but active tension. Friction like anger, like hurt.

Liam had sat in that darkened conference room for nearly twenty minutes after Zach left, stewing in the aftermath. His veins had coursed with a disorienting mix of their tandem orgasms, Zach's freak-out, and that disgusting red punch. He was wracked with the nagging insistence that things could be different for them if Zach had never thrown a perfect spiral or if Liam didn't need to walk through the world shrouded in a rigid cloak of regret.

He'd been so nervous to see Zach again that following Monday that he'd delayed his arrival to class with another trip to his brother's office. Their conversation had flowed with something creeping towards familiarity until Eben had looked at his watch and asked, "Don't you have class?" Liam had rushed down the hall, his eyes narrowing into what he hoped was a menacing glare when Zach had looked up at his harried entrance.

At the next class on Wednesday, Liam had been reading a series of messages on Facebook with a soft smile on his face. He preferred other social media platforms, but on this day, in particular, it was an easy way to hear from his old piano teacher in Florence, his aunt, and several friends from Paris that he had been sure he'd never hear from again. He hadn't noticed Zach coming up next to him.

"Give me your phone," Zach had demanded with all the conviction of a first-time mugger.

Liam had looked at him, then glowered at his extended hand. "Why?"

"So I can put my number in and you can text me your address. We have to start working on the project."

"Why my place?" Liam had asked before quickly ascertaining the answer himself. "Oh, right. Can't have anyone like me around your apartment. What would the neighbors say?" He'd gasped, letting his voice become as sibilant as he'd dared.

The room had emptied, so Liam had turned towards him, placing one hand on the table and the other on his hip. He'd canted his pelvis forward just enough and watched Zach's eyes flit down. Zach's body had swayed as if at war with itself about whether to lean in towards Liam or pull back. Liam had so desperately wanted Zach to do something, say something, to acknowledge this complex song and dance they'd found themselves in.

Instead, Zach had spoken, quiet yet cross, "I have to stay at practice late, but I'm free after 8:30."

"Wait, you want to do it tonight?" Liam had faltered.

"The presentation is Friday."

"We can do it Thursday, then."

"We've put this off for over a week. And I don't know about you, but I'd prefer not to fail this class."

Liam had handed his phone over with a growl.

Sitting in Zach's apartment Thursday night with their project still not done, Liam's apology hung in the air. Zach shifted forward on the couch cushion and cleared his throat.

"Doesn't matter. We can still get this done in time for tomorrow." Zach didn't even look away from his books.

"I mean it, Zach. I am sorry."

"I heard you. Let's get this finished, okay?"

"Yeah, sure." Liam turned back to his notes, but only for a moment, compelled to explain. "It's just, yesterday was my birthday. My twenty-first."

Liam had been able to drink legally in his home country since he was sixteen, so the day before hadn't been the massive milestone it was for most American college students. But the minute Mackenzie had gotten word, she had insisted on celebrating.

She'd shown up at his door only an hour before Zach was meant to come over, her hair piled up in a messy bun on top of her head. She'd staggered in, her arms full of junk food and a massive bottle of cheap vodka, beaming up at Liam with the utmost affection.

"Kenz," Liam had groaned, trying to let her down nicely.

She'd immediately forced her way into his kitchen, ignoring his plea and opening cupboards and drawers for supplies. "Sam will be over after he goes to that recital, and I told him to bring people. And more booze, of course. We'll all go out to some bars after that."

"I can't tonight. I told you. I have to do this thing for my Plato class."

"Nope, no work. Not allowed. It's your birthday."

"Yes, and I have one every year right around this time." Mackenzie had not appreciated his wit. "It's really not a big deal."

"Well, it's a big deal to me." She'd dropped her hands, totally crestfallen.

It was only then that Liam realized how frazzled she looked, like she'd been rushing around trying to put something nice together for him. They'd been friends for a little over a month, and no matter how dear they had become in that short amount of time, celebrating something important like a birthday would create memories strong enough to bind them together for life. She'd wanted to give tonight to him so they could be forever friends.

Liam's shoulders had slackened, and he'd pulled her into a hug, kissing the top of her head where it rested against his chest. Her arms had slipped easily around him. He wasn't sure how exactly, but he always seemed to wind up with people in his life he knew he didn't deserve. When he'd released her several long moments later, she'd been smiling again.

After a deep breath, Zach folded his book over and turned to look at Liam. He seemed receptive to this possible excuse. "Your birthday? Why didn't you say anything?"

Liam scrunched his face. "When, exactly, would I have done that? Yesterday morning when you insisted that we had to do our work right away or later that night when I made you run for the hills?"

He and Mackenzie had broken open the vodka right away. They'd drunk strong screwdrivers from pint glasses while cozying up on the couch watching old episodes of *The Office*. All thoughts of Zach's arrival had disappeared quickly, along with any thoughts of Plato or Aristophanes, with Mackenzie snuggled up against him, her ankle hooked around his calf. They hadn't slept together since that first time, but their friendship was a touchy-feely one. People made assumptions, and they would only be half wrong. Liam was sure that if they were ever in the same place, he could easily tilt her face towards his, kiss her, and she'd say yes.

At some point, Liam had spilled a nearly full glass of cranberry and vodka on his shirt. He'd tossed it halfway down the hall in an attempt to get it into the washing machine. He had no memory of why he'd never bothered to put another shirt back on.

By the time Zach rang the buzzer from the lobby, he and Mackenzie had been so screwed up that it had taken them a minute to recognize the sound.

"Is that your doorbell?" Mackenzie had wondered aloud.

"Is it?" Liam had asked with dramatic trepidation. They'd both fallen into a fit of giggles before Mackenzie had clamored towards the door.

"It must be Sam! Come in!" she'd sung into the intercom, before the voice on the other end of the line could ask, "Wait. Who?" with total confusion.

A few minutes later, there had been a knock on the door, and Liam had flung it wide open, expecting Sam and maybe a few other School of Music friends to be on the other side. What he had gotten instead was Zach, looking like the earnest kid next door from some 1950s studio movie, picture-perfect and ready for his close-up. His hair had been slicked back, looking several shades darker from the product he'd used. He'd smelled of testosterone and pine, post-practice clean. Even Liam's addled brain had recognized how dashing Zach had looked standing in his doorway.

Never before had Liam been so aware of their difference in size. The contrast between their physiques wasn't limited to the inches of height that Zach had over him, because Zach was only a few inches taller. Instead, it was the width of Zach, the roundness and prominence of his muscles, that separated them. Zach was the Golden Ratio personified whereas Liam's body was made of straight lines that never met. Somehow though, when they came together, the math worked.

"Zach." Liam had tossed his hair off his brow. "I'd say I'm happy to see you but..." He had given a dismissive flop of his hand. The insolent movement threw him off balance, and he'd had to grab onto the doorway to keep himself upright.

"We're supposed to be working on our project. You texted me, remember? 8:30?"

"Oops," Liam had deadpanned.

Zach had leaned forward, his brow creasing. He'd searched Liam's eyes, which had to have been blown wide-open and red-rimmed by that point. "Jesus, Liam," he'd cursed softly. "What are you on?"

Mackenzie had decided to make her presence known, at that moment, calling from inside his apartment. "Liaaaam!" Her voice had sounded overtly feminine and drunk. "Where did you go? I need you."

Liam had flushed as Zach had scanned him up and down. There had been only one logical assumption for Zach to make, considering Liam's state of undress, his intoxication, and his company. Liam had watched as the conclusion collated on Zach's face. He'd made a soft noise that might have sounded like dismay if Liam hadn't known better.

"I'm gonna go."

"No, don't." Liam had reached for him, both his hands finding the narrowest point of Zach's waist. Liam had stepped closer. The skin above Zach's belt had quivered as he took an uneasy breath. Liam had cocked his head, becoming demure and coy, and looked up at him through his curls. Zach hadn't pulled away. A swoop fell through Liam's stomach.

"Why settle for two when we could make it three, huh?" He'd felt so breathless, reckless, and oddly possessive of both Zach and Mackenzie. "God, she'd love you."

Zach had stumbled away, mortified by Liam's lascivious, and slurred, suggestion. He'd looked over both his shoulders, making sure no one had seen them. "I can't believe you." With one last terrible look that had cut right through Liam's buzz, Zach had walked away.

"Shit, Zach!" he'd called after him, realizing he had crossed a line. More than crossed. He'd obliterated it with a fucking nuclear bomb.

When Sam had shown up a few minutes later, Liam had no longer been in the mood for partying. He'd kicked everyone out of his place well before ten, never even making it to a bar to get carded.

"You were messed up last night." Zach finally lifted his eyes away from their books. He spun the delicate silver length in his curled fingers as if warning Liam that this pause might not last long.

Liam rubbed at his temples. He'd been hungover all day,

feeling hollow-boned and weak, even after eating nothing but junk food. "I know. And I don't want to throw my friend Mackenzie under the bus or anything, but it would have been nice if she'd told me the cupcakes she'd brought were of the, um, edible variety before I ate three of them."

Zach snorted sharply through his nose, smothering a rapidly growing smile by a press of fingers to his lips. "Sorry. Your friend made you pot cupcakes for your birthday?"

"Eh," Liam shrugged. "She's from Colorado." That seemed like a reasonable enough explanation to them both. "Look, I really am sorry if I—" Liam stopped and reset his approach. "No, I really am sorry because I know I was an asshole last night. I didn't mean to blow our project off." He gestured at the coffee table and their work. "And I certainly never meant to put you on the spot or make you feel uncomfortable."

It was about as sincere as Liam got, and he was relieved when Zach took note, replying with equal frankness.

"I think it was what you were offering that surprised me more than anything."

Liam laughed softly. "You were surprised that I wanted to sleep with you again or that I wanted to include a girl?"

Zach blushed at Liam's bluntness. "Both, I guess." He blinked up at Liam, his blue eyes receptive. Liam liked this look on Zach, free from complications. It was a look similar to those he gave in their most intimate moments when it seemed as if nothing else in the world mattered.

Liam liked the sincerity in Zach's eyes that offered forgiveness for everything that had happened the night before. Liam liked the way such a look changed the shape of Zach's cheekbones, rounding them at the corners, making him look less like a chiseled god and more human. Liam liked how he felt good and kind and all those things he'd doubted about himself for far too long when Zach looked at him this way.

Fuck it. Liam just liked Zach, and he couldn't help but hope that Zach felt the same.

13

The irony was, the first guy Zach ever hooked up with was a football player, too.

They'd met the summer after Zach's sophomore year of high school. That June he'd spent three weeks at a camp in Atlanta for rising football players hoping to showcase their skills for college recruiters. Camps like this existed all over the country, but his parents had chosen this one in particular because they'd heard it was the best place for quarterbacks to get visibility.

It had been the summer before Zach had really become himself. He hadn't started dating Rebecca yet. He was missing the twenty pounds of muscle and the inch of height that he tacked on as an upperclassman. He hadn't even been the starter on his team the season before, having played backup to a senior headed to UCLA. He wasn't Zachary Sugarman yet. Not *the* Zachary Sugarman, writ large, whose name was in capital letters on the backs of T-shirts at the campus bookstore. He was a kid from Seattle who'd just turned sixteen, just gotten his driver's license, and just come out to himself.

The other boy's name was Ray Bordeleau. He was blond and a running back. Zach noticed him right away. There was never a spoken moment when they had asked one another, "So you are too, right?" That would have been far too risky. Instead, their mutual attraction had been established with looks that held one heartbeat too long, a press of a knee under the breakfast table that was too firm to be a mistake. Ray asked if Zach wanted to come to his dorm room, a single that Ray had somehow lucked into, to play some Xbox one night. Zach was sure what that meant and was as terrified as he was thrilled.

He had sat on the bed, propped on his elbows, and Ray had been quick to follow, offering another unmissable sign. Zach's mouth had been parched in those panicked moments before Ray's lips had touched his. They'd fumbled at first - too much tongue, then not enough, a clack of teeth. But eventually, they figured it out, and god had Zach liked it.

He'd almost shivered away when Ray had put his hand down the slack waistband of his gym shorts. Zach had whimpered and closed his eyes at the amazement of being intimate with another person for the first time. It had been exhilarating, and a little bit embarrassing, because he hadn't lasted long.

"Do you want me to..." Zach had gestured towards Ray, and he had given Zach a faltering nod. Ray had laid back on the extra-long twin bed, and Zach had toyed with the idea of using his mouth. Instead, he had fit his body behind Ray's, breathing in the sweat on his neck as he'd returned the experiential touch.

They'd ended up playing Xbox eventually, once they'd done everything they'd been bold enough to do and before the counselor knocked on the door to tell them they were violating curfew. They hadn't talked the next day, or the next—not out of any regret but because, at that age, neither of them had the words to encapsulate what had happened.

Sometimes Zach looked back at his skinnier, younger self, and wondered if that version had been the braver one. Or maybe that Zach had just been stupider, not fully aware of all of life's risks.

On the last day of camp, Ray had found Zach before his parents picked him up. He'd slung his duffel bag over his shoulder and punched Zach on the arm. "Thanks, man." He'd been very chummy, totally innocuous as if they'd shared nothing. It had broken Zach's heart a bit.

Zach had followed Ray's ranking in the combine and looked for his name on signing day two years later. Ray ended up at Ole Miss but got injured during his freshman year and quit playing altogether. Zach hadn't bothered to send him a message when he saw the news, unsure if Ray would want to be reminded of what they'd done together that summer. To Zach, though, it had been a landmark in his life.

The quiet moment of absolution between him and Liam on his couch felt just as momentous. For the first time since Rome, he and Liam were on the same page. They now had a clean slate, a fresh place to start from.

"You want something to drink, birthday boy?" Zach pushed himself up off the couch, then turned back towards Liam with a pointed look. "Some water, maybe?"

Liam, whose bout with sincerity had left his cheeks the same soft pink as his lips, tipped his head forward with a small laugh. "Water would be good, even though I'm pretty sure I drank half of Lake Michigan today."

"Hasn't helped though, has it?"

Liam stood and stretched. Something in his shoulder or back popped back into place, and he moaned in satisfaction like an old man. "Nope."

Zach grinned as he watched. "Well, it's the day after your twenty-first birthday." He walked towards the kitchen. "If you aren't horribly hungover then you've done it wrong."

"Oh?" Liam's face brightened. "Do go on, Mr. I-don't-drink-during-the-season. Please tell me you have a spring birthday."

"May. And all I'll say is that I woke up around 4 p.m. the following day in a T-shirt from a bar in St. Louis that claimed I'd won some sort of chicken wing eating contest."

"St. Louis?" Liam cackled. "The hell?"

Zach put his hands up, claiming innocence. "Des swears he has photographic evidence, but he won't show it to me."

"Who's Des?"

"He's my best friend. He's on the team too, wide receiver.

I've known him since we were kids."

Zach collected cups for water and a bowl for some snacks. What good host offered only water, anyway? He pulled out a bag of pita chips and got some hummus and veggies from the fridge. Sometimes he hated his mid-season diet restrictions. Zach filled two tall glasses with ice, then watched Liam move through his apartment as he filled them at the sink.

Liam stopped in front of his CD collection. They were relics, left over from his high school days. When Liam pointed to the play button on Zach's stereo and looked over his shoulder to ask permission, Zach nodded, hoping nothing too terribly embarrassing came out. The jazzy notes of a piano, bass, drums, and a gentle saxophone filled the space. Liam listened for a moment, then nodded, giving it his stamp of approval.

"It would be cool to listen to some of your music sometime," Zach said.

"I don't write anything like this."

"More classical?"

"More French," Liam answered, with a smug grin.

Liam crossed his feet, one over the other in a slow meander, looking at the pictures tacked to the wall like one might at a museum. There were a few framed photos of his family and a bunch of his teammates, but most of the pictures hanging on Zach's walls were of him and Rebecca.

He wondered what Liam saw when he looked at Zach's false life. Did he pity him or find it pathetic? Was it possible Liam was a little jealous? Not of Zach, but of Rebecca?

"That's the girlfriend, huh?" Liam asked as he came to the kitchen to make himself useful. He used his teeth to rip open the bag of chips and poured them into the waiting bowl.

"Rebecca."

"She's pretty."

"Thanks. I guess." It felt strange to talk to Liam about her. Almost like talking about one in front of the other was a form of betrayal to them both. A needling thought began to buzz at the base of his skull. "You and...Mackenzie, was it?" Zach asked.

"Mm-hmm."

Zach cut through a red pepper and added it to the plate. Liam picked it right back up and bit it. "She's your..."

"Friend?" Liam chewed around the word. There was a curious lilt to the end of it as if unsure what other answer he could give.

"Right." Zach laughed uncomfortably at himself. "I only ask 'cause, well, last night. You weren't serious. About, the three of us. I mean, you guys haven't..."

Liam waited. Something about his posture made Zach think he was almost enjoying Zach's discomfort. The innocent tone of Liam's next question confirmed it. "Haven't what?"

"Slept together?"

"Oh, no, we have." Liam brought the rim of his glass to his lips. "The night she and I met. Twice." He drank long, set his glass down, and swallowed. The ice clunked against the side. Liam appeared unphased.

Zach decided to focus his attention on some baby carrots in need of cutting instead of daring to look at Liam's face. He forced the knife through lengthwise, and it landed with an aggressive snap against the cutting board. "So, girls too, then."

"Yep."

"That means you're..." Another carrot, another crack of the knife.

"You can say the word, Zach."

He set the knife down on the counter and forced himself to look. "You're bi."

Liam nodded once. "Correct." Then, with slightly more regard, "Is that weird for you? Considering we've hooked up?"

"No," Zach stated firmly. "I just didn't think people like you really existed."

Liam snorted. "You're a quarterback classics major. I didn't think people like you really existed either, and yet, here we are. It's almost like the start of some joke, isn't it? 'A gay football player and a bisexual pianist walk into a bar...'"

Zach laughed gently, dismissing the fluttering feeling in his stomach as Liam looked up at him, playful and affectionate.

"Anyway," Liam went on, "you're the one with the girlfriend."

He tilted his head towards the wall of pictures. "If anyone here in this room is bisexual, it's you."

Zach considered the pictures of Rebecca, her things that lived in his bathroom and the bottom drawer of his dresser, "just in case," and the way he'd felt nothing when she'd kissed him after dinner earlier that night. "I have a girlfriend, yes. But a girlfriend I really have no interest in taking to bed."

It was Liam's turn to be perplexed. "Really? Like, none at all?"

"I think of it like this," Zach leaned his hip against the counter, crossing his arms. "I really don't like mushrooms."

"Okay." Liam furrowed his brow, trying to follow Zach's unexpected stream of logic.

"I can't stand the texture, don't really like the flavor. Hate them raw. But I'll eat them if I have to. Like, if I'm at someone's house and they've cooked for me, I'm not going to be rude. Or if they're in something flavorful like a stir-fry or on a pizza, they can be kind of okay. And if mushrooms suddenly became the last food substance available to humanity, obviously I wouldn't let myself starve. But if I had my way, I wouldn't eat mushrooms ever again in my whole life."

"And women are mushrooms?"

Zach realized how ridiculous it sounded now that Liam said it out loud. "Yeah. I guess so."

Liam thought for a moment, biting the inside of his lips. "Maybe you just haven't met the right mushroom yet." They both laughed as Liam's tired cliché met Zach's metaphor.

"It's always felt pretty black and white for me," Zach went on, lining the chopped carrots nicely on the plate.

"I definitely lean towards men, too."

"Really? It's not, like, fifty-fifty for you?"

"Some days it is. Some days it feels like one hundred percent one or the other. It depends, I guess. It's a different kind of desire, men and women. I know it sounds like a catch phrase, but it has to do with the individual and not the anatomy they have. I like people who intrigue me. People who aren't always what they seem to be." He played with the ice in his glass, tilting it one way, then the other. "People kinda like you."

There it was. Spoken. Unequivocal. Zach's crush that had been developing since he first saw Liam's profile picture on Grindr, was reciprocated. He didn't quite know what to do with this new information. He should probably respond somehow. He should tell Liam he felt the same way, smile, kiss him... anything. Instead, Zach picked up the food plate and his water and took it back to the couch. His heart was beating way too hard in his chest to form any intelligible response, anyway. Out of the corner of his eye, he saw Liam's full-body eye roll.

They made room for the food amongst their books, but neither seemed too eager to jump right back into their project. Liam popped a baby carrot in his mouth and leaned back into the cushion, one arm resting behind his head. The music continued in the background, the long-form jazz pieces developing and morphing with harmonies and secondary themes. Liam's long legs, heavily bent at the knees, made awkward angles as he fit himself into the space between Zach's couch and coffee table, and yet it worked. Liam was so at ease with himself, his body, his sex life. He existed in the world rather than trying to fit any mold.

"When did you come out?" Zach asked. He'd never had the chance to talk to someone about this before, at least not someone he'd planned on knowing for more than one night.

"I never really did. I started hanging out with guys and hanging out with girls. People figured it out quickly enough."

"And everyone was okay with that?"

"By 'everyone,' you mean my parents?" Liam sat forward, resting his elbows on his thighs, slotting his thin fingers together. "Yeah, well, they just want me to be happy. To not be a fuck-up or whatever." Liam's face dropped, his eyes going dark for a moment. It was a look that reminded Zach of other times he'd asked Liam about his past. "What about you?" Liam asked, morphing back to an easy, conversational tone. He'd clearly had practice making that transformation.

"When did I know, you mean? 'Cause coming out. Well..." Zach made a futile gesture with his hands, and Liam's brow furrowed with concern.

"You haven't come out? Not to anyone? Des?"

Zach shook his head.

"No one in your life knows?"

"You know." It was stating the obvious, and yet it felt like Zach had just admitted to something more. Something of equal weight to Liam's admission of his interest in Zach, which was that Liam alone held a role, unique and special, in Zach's life. He mattered.

The anticipation in the air was palpable, but Liam didn't move to close the distance. If something was going to happen between them, Zach knew he had to be the one to initiate it this time.

Tenderly and slowly, Zach hooked his forefinger under Liam's chin. His thumb settled delicately on the soft skin below Liam's lip where he could feel the faintest trace of stubble. Liam's lips parted, a gasp sliding out as his eyes softened. He looked desperate and so fucking pretty. Zach wet his lips and leaned in.

It felt like a real first kiss, fluttering butterflies and all. Glorious, but innocent too. They were two boys kissing on a couch in the nighttime while music played. They were kissing just to kiss, because kissing felt good, because kissing was fun. Because Zach liked Liam and Liam liked Zach, too.

Zach shifted his hand, cupping the entirety of Liam's jaw, and pulled him in deeper. Liam surged forward, leaning into the kiss then, almost at the same moment, he began to pull back. He gave a small shake of his head before opening his eyes wide. "We, uh, should finish the project, shouldn't we?"

"Yeah, no. Sorry," Zach faltered. He turned himself back towards the coffee table and their books, wondering if maybe he'd gotten things all wrong.

Liam leaned close, nudging him with his shoulder. "And then we should do more of that." His words were slow, dripping with sweetness. In his eyes was the black intensity of desire, the promise that it wouldn't stop at kissing next time.

"I don't know," Zach pondered. He looked down at their

array of books glumly. "This might take all night."

Liam caught on right away. "Yeah," he matched Zach's dire tone. "Yeah, it really might."

They finished the project a few hours later. Then Liam made noises, more exquisite and needier than ever before, as they finished each other off, head to foot, right there on Zach's couch.

Sometime around 3 a.m., they kissed goodnight in Zach's doorway, their fingers the last things to untangle. Only a few hours later, both giddy from lack of sleep, and with this new thing growing between them, they presented their project to their class before Zach boarded a flight for his game in Nebraska.

They got an A, and Zach got another win.

14

Bye weeks were always strange for Zach. Without a game to focus on that weekend, Coach Williams tended to get creative with their practices. He liked to go back to basics but in a way the team didn't expect. For example, the team might walk out to the practice field on Wednesday to find that all the yard lines and hash marks had been removed, leaving a completely blank field of green. They were then expected to run their routes based off timing and rhythm and not any visual cues from the field. Bye weeks also usually included such ridiculousness as taking new pictures to be used for pregame promos, signing T-shirts to be used as prizes at the next home game, or taping interviews.

Zach hated watching interviews of himself, so he almost never tuned in when they aired. However, things had taken an unsettling turn during the one he'd filmed for ESPN earlier in the day. Nothing would have stopped him from watching this one. Settled on his couch, Zach watched as a sportscaster with too much product in his hair posed inane questions to Zach.

"After your win this weekend and Clemson's unexpected loss, Northwestern is at the top of both the Big Ten and the

National rankings. Your name is getting tossed around a lot these days." The camera cut to the man's face as he began ticking things off on his fingers. "First Team All-American, Academic All-American, Heisman Award candidate, number one in the 2021 draft. Aside from all the successes, the team is having this season, what do these individual successes mean to you?"

Zach watched TV-him mull the question over with a bashful shake of his head. "It's a lot, for sure. But I'm lucky to have the full support of my teammates, my coaches, my family, and my friends. I couldn't do any of this without them."

"Seems you've got yourself one special friend, don't you? A real super fan, if her Instagram is anything to go by." By the time the camera cut to him on screen, Zach was looking towards his lap and blushing through the makeup they'd put on him. Real-life Zach let out a slow exhale through his mouth, relieved about how he'd come across on camera. He looked shy and totally smitten at the mention of his girl. It wasn't obvious to anyone watching that at the interviewer's mention of a "special friend," he hadn't thought of Rebecca. He'd thought of Liam.

Zach knew their rapprochement would go unnoticed by anyone but themselves. The new camaraderie that had them sitting next to each other in class instead of opposing sides of the table, chatting amiably before class started, could be explained away by the fact that they'd worked together on a project and had gotten to know each other in the process. Leaving class together also wouldn't arouse any suspicion, even as they subconsciously took a route out of the building that brought them right past Dr. Barnett's office, giving them the chance to toss quick morning greetings through the professor's open door.

There was no way anyone noticed how once outside, Liam detected Zach's distaste for smoke as soon as he lit up his cigarette and only took a puff or two from the filter before snuffing it out with the toe of his elegant boot. It would be impossible for anyone to know that as Zach walked to his next class, he listened to one of Liam's compositions through his ear buds.

Whatever was between them, it was completely secret. Zach

had no doubt of that. It felt private—unknowable and invisible to the rest of the world.

But the camera, as they say, could see everything. Ever since he had given the interview, there had been a burning hole in Zach's stomach, full of panic that the momentary switch from Rebecca to Liam in his mind had been caught on film and broadcast nationwide. He'd walked around all day like he was already wearing the noose that would hang him. He'd been certain that the expression on his face at that moment had been so obvious that it would start the great unraveling of his life.

Thankfully, all his anxiety was for naught. Zach clicked off the TV and threw his head back against the cushion. No harm, no foul. His Friday night could proceed as normal. Except it wasn't normal because he wasn't on a bus or a plane traveling somewhere or over-hydrating with plans to be in bed by 9 p.m.

There was the extra weirdness of being without Rebecca that weekend, too. She was tied up with sorority business. Fall Rush had finished, and that weekend the selected girls would be initiated into the sorority through a secret ceremony that Rebecca didn't even tell Zach about. She would show up at his place Sunday night after not sleeping for two days, flush full of love for her "sisters," bursting about how amazing Tri Delt was.

With nowhere to be, Zach fired off a few texts to Des, Ruiz, and Jackson to see what they were up to. He checked the score of some Friday night games. They were mostly smaller, non-power-conference schools who had no bearing on Northwestern's future, but Zach was a lover of the game and liked to keep up.

He tossed his phone to the side and took a moment to enjoy the silence, letting his long legs stretch out in front of him. His mind went soft and unfocused, releasing the last of the tension he'd been carrying around from the interview. Unsurprisingly, his thoughts drifted towards Liam. Outside of class, they'd texted a few times, keeping it flirty and light. He'd saved Liam's number under the vague contact name of LB, but even so, he deleted the messages as he got them.

With so many differences between them—Europe versus Pacific Northwest, music as opposed to football, out and proud instead of closeted—Zach still saw something familiar when he looked at Liam. It was like their inner selves vibrated on the same frequency, creating not identical, but parallel wavelengths that erased all the static in his life and left him with a sense of calm.

They hadn't been alone since the night after Liam's birthday. Zach turned his head and reached his fingers across the fabric of the couch as if hoping to conjure a hologram of the pornographic scene they had created there on his couch. He could almost see Liam's lithe limbs and his own toned body, twisted and entwined, writhing. Zach felt his libido stir.

Alone and with nothing better to do, he undid the fly of his jeans and scooted his hips towards the edge of the sofa to make room for his palm. He encircled himself, giving a few lazy pulls. It was just enough to ignite the memory, to make the skin of his cheeks flush hot, and to let out a constricted exhale.

He began wondering what Liam was doing at that moment. He was probably out at a party or a bar, now that he was drinking-age legal. Was Liam looking to get with someone? A man or a woman? Maybe Liam was on his own, too, just like Zach.

There was only one way to find out. Zach stilled his hand and grabbed his phone, drafting the text quickly. "What you up to?"

It was casual enough, but even so, he bit at his thumbnail as he waited for the read message receipt to appear. It did so almost instantly.

"Not much. Just got home from a recital."

"How was it?"

"Meh. Trombone."

Another message came through with eye roll and vomit face emojis. Zach smiled, unaware that one could have such violent reactions to trombone playing. Another text appeared on Zach's phone.

"What about you?"

Zach glanced down to where his pants hung open, his hard-on flagging but not gone. "Sitting here." With a tremble of his fingers, he added, "Thinking about you."

Three little bubbles appeared under Zach's last text to indicate that Liam was typing. They hovered for longer than Zach thought he could stand. Finally, Liam replied with complete understanding. "Show me."

Zach dropped his phone to his belly. "Fuck," he whispered. He'd never done anything like this before, and his adrenaline was thrumming. His phone buzzed again with another text from Liam.

"I promise I'll delete it. I just want to see if the same thing happens to you when you think about me as when I think about you."

Liam knew exactly what to say to drive Zach wild.

Zach typed with a daring smile. "Only if you send me one first."

"Easiest deal I ever made. 2 sexs." Zach snorted at Liam's typo even as another message came through amending it. "I mean secs. Lol."

"Sure you did," Zach snickered out loud. He watched his screen, waiting several long seconds until the picture appeared.

It was yellowy, an indication that Liam's camera phone was unable to pick up enough light for full exposure. But Liam the Man was on total display. He was laid back on his bed or his couch like Zach was. Along with a glimpse of his flat belly and nearly hairless navel, the picture captured the rest of Liam's body. He held himself proudly in his hand, his thumb frozen in a sweet touch.

Zach slid the elastic waist of his boxers over his hips and mimicked Liam's positioning. He could barely process what he was about to do when he heard the click of his camera and the descending swoop of a message being sent.

Liam's reply was immediate. "My place. Right now."

Zach had never raced to his Jeep faster.

15

L iam knew it would take about fifteen minutes for Zach to get across campus and find street parking. As soon as Zach's "Leaving now" message came through Liam immediately began cleaning. He started in his bathroom, sliding all his toiletries haphazardly into the drawer by the sink with a clatter. He gathered up the collection of cups on his bedside table that had been accumulating and put them into the dishwasher. He stuffed his dirty laundry into his closet with a mental promise to actually do laundry that weekend. His place wasn't nearly as fancy as Zach's, but it had a killer view. He pulled the curtains wide open, letting the Chicago skyline fill his bedroom window like a perfect background set.

He paused before lighting some incense, something delicate but not too hipster. He wasn't trying to make his bedroom romantic, was he? Sure, his heart was pounding, and he couldn't stop smiling, but that was just because he was about to get some action. Right? He decided he didn't want his place smelling like a musty college hovel, so he clicked the lighter and blew out the tip of the incense before setting the smoldering stick in its holder.

He hurried back into the bathroom to gather some *accoutrements* from the medicine cabinet, putting his acquired supplies out of sight but within arm's reach of the bed. Liam hadn't suggested they indulge in the act that required these items and Zach hadn't offered, but it didn't mean Liam hadn't been thinking of it. He was ready for tonight to be the night.

Zach's hand was still raised in a fist, ready for a second knock when Liam opened the door.

"Hi." Zach was breathless, proving that he'd taken to heart Liam's demand to come over straight away.

Liam didn't want to wait a second longer. He grabbed Zach by the wrist and dragged him inside, spinning them to kick the door closed behind them with his heel. Zach melted, sliding into Liam's frame with a sharp inhale. He fisted Liam's thin T-shirt, scrunching the fabric at the small of his back. When their tongues met, Liam moaned, greedy and happy.

How different this felt from their first encounter. That night Liam had needed to coax Zach gently open, like the slow bloom of a rose which, once unfurled, had been as beautiful as anything Liam had ever experienced. But now, they came to this uncomplicated coupling as equals, offering each other something that didn't need to be sought after anymore. Once requested, it was happily given.

Even though a part of Liam's subconscious wished it were true, the rest of him—mind, body, soul—knew that this wasn't the start of a relationship. They weren't, nor could they ever be, anything that would be defined by a title except "fling" or "dirty little secret." Regardless, whatever this undefinable affair was between them, it was something mutual. Something egalitarian. That was evident in the way they worked Zach's coat off over his shoulders: Liam at the unzipped collar, Zach with the sleeves. It was evident in the smile that Zach flashed as Liam looked down at Zach's naked toes and laughed, "Flip-flops? Seriously? You do know that there was frost last night, right?"

"Easiest on, easiest off," Zach explained before cupping Liam's face and pulling him into another open-mouthed kiss.

Liam couldn't remember the last time being with someone

felt this good, so a quick fumble against a wall would not suffice. Liam wanted Zach horizontal. He wanted skin, every gorgeous inch of it. He wanted to slow the tempo, be fully conscious in the act of doing, sober, and with intent. Anything less would feel unfair at this point.

Liam led them to the bedroom, shirts and socks falling away as they went. The back of Zach's knees collided with the edge of Liam's bed as soon as they entered the room. Liam stepped out of his pants as Zach shimmied out of his and laid back against the pillows. Zach smiled, small and expectant, as Liam crawled between his thighs and settled between his hips.

Zach's broad arms wrapped across the expanse of Liam's back. His hands cupped Liam's shoulders, and he squeezed with an exhaled hum. It took Liam a moment to realize Zach was simply hugging him hello, pure and tender. Liam kissed Zach's neck and hugged him back.

Greetings exchanged, Zach's hands slid low into Liam's briefs, ghosting over the roundness of Liam's ass. Zach carefully drew the waistband of Liam's underwear away from his skin and all the way off. Zach's hips rose, pressing himself, still contained beneath his own boxers, against Liam's naked length. The sensation was muted but warm, and Liam slid into the friction. Zach's hands felt large and insinuating on the backs of Liam's thighs.

So, Liam laid the offer on the table. "I want you inside me."

Instead of meeting the breathy request with a sigh, a groan, or a "Fuck, yes," Zach went still, the weight of his hands lightening up on Liam's body. "You what?"

Liam sat back on his heels. "Enough with the *primi piati*, Zach. We're both ready for the main course now, yes?" He made quick work of Zach's final article of clothing, tossing the light gray boxers in the corner along with the rest of their clothes. So much for having cleaned up the laundry.

"I, um..."

"Don't worry." Liam sunk back into the warmth of Zach's naked body and watched Zach's eyes roll closed. "I have condoms and lube."

Zach pulled away from Liam's next attempted kiss, his neck craning at an odd angle on the pillow. He shook it with a gentle *no*.

"I've never, um..."

Liam leaned on his elbow, his hips still resting in the cradle of Zach's body.

"Seriously?" He felt a surge of giddiness as Zach blushed. "God, I love an unexpected bottom." Liam's whole body fell forward, his head resting on Zach's pillow. He kissed Zach's cheek, a delicate whisper against his stubble. "I'm gonna slick you up so good that you'll be as wet for me as when you're balls deep in Rebecca."

Liam felt unease take over Zach's body the second he said it. It had been too much, too forward, too crass. Mentioning the girlfriend was probably not his smartest move, either. Zach slipped out from under him, and Liam prepped himself to start troubleshooting the situation. Zach turned towards him on the bed: one hand tucked under the pillow, the other toying with the stitching of the hem. He wasn't annoyed or turned off. Zach was bashful. He was back to First Night Zach, unsure, and Liam couldn't understand why. Not when sleeping together felt like such a natural next step for them.

"No, Liam. I've never done that before, either."

"What bottomed or been balls deep in Rebecca?"

It took Zach a minute before he could bring himself to look up at Liam. "Both?"

Liam propped himself up on one of his hips. "What do you mean? You guys have been together for..." He attempted to count on one hand. "How many years?"

"Six."

"And I mean, I know she's a mushroom, but seriously?" A sweet smile flashed on Zach's face at the reference to their conversation at Zach's apartment about their sexuality.

Zach's long lashes fell against his cheeks, and Liam had to resist the urge to brush his thumbs against them. "Rebecca wants to wait for sex until she's married."

Liam snorted down at him and waited for Zach to break the

joke. Then Liam laughed uncomfortably when Zach did no such thing. Then Liam finally fucking got it. "You're a virgin."

Zach turned to bury his face in the pillow and moaned, embarrassed. Liam scooted closer to him, the mattress bouncing below them as he did. He poked at Zach's shoulder once, and then again. "But our first night you said, you *said*, you weren't a virgin."

"It's 'cause I'm not." Zach's eyes went wide. "I've done plenty of stuff with loads of guys."

"Stuff." Liam made air quotes with one hand. "'Hooked up' with, not fucked. Hand jobs, blow jobs, non-penetrative sex, not all the way. Zach, that doesn't count."

Zach's mouth fell open. "That's a very, you know, heteronormative concept of virginity you're adhering to there, Liam." He took on the holier-than-thou air of one desperately trying to defend himself. "And I think you should reconsider that, you know, considering how you have such liberal views on things like gender preference and the fluidity of sexuality—"

"Zach!" Liam cut off his meandering Ted Talk on the construct of virginity by cupping Zach's face in his hands and locking their eyes. Liam wanted to bring the focus back to the core of the subject, that this gorgeous, smart, gifted, funny, kind, passionate man had never felt the joy of joining completely with another human body.

Liam slipped down the bed, aligning his body with Zach's. He let his hands run over his buttery skin. "Haven't you wanted to, though? Wanted someone so badly that you had to know their heat? Become part of them?" Liam's hand drifted lower, past Zach's navel, dancing to where Zach had gone soft. "Or maybe," Liam settled in even closer, his breath against Zach's ear. "Maybe you'd rather know what it's like to be opened up for someone else, totally exposed. To feel another man's heartbeat throbbing in time with yours from the inside. Have you imagined that, Zach? Wanted it so bad you thought you might break?"

Zach simpered and swallowed heavily, color high on his cheeks. "Of course I have."

"Then why not do it? You claim to have had plenty of chances."

Liam pulled his hands away from Zach's most erogenous zones to move idly across the skin of his flank in hopes that Zach would have enough brain power to answer.

"It was only ever one-night stands for me before." A solitary finger trailed the length of Liam's spine. *Before you,* its path seemed to say. "And doing that with someone who I'd just met, and who might figure out after the fact who I was, felt—"

"Too risky?"

"Too big of a deal to do with someone I'd never see again. Call me old-fashioned."

"No, I like it."

Zach caught Liam's hand where it had meandered into the flat space between his pecs. He stilled it, pressing it against his warm skin and looked to their joined hands. "That night with you in Rome was the first time I thought, 'maybe I could?'"

Liam remembered their night together in that dirty Roman flat with stunning clarity. It had been so incredibly late that it was more morning than night, and Liam had pushed the limits of the boundaries Zach had established earlier that evening. Liam had wanted to see how far this handsome American would go.

"I'd wanted that so much."

"I figured. You touched me here." Zach placed Liam's hand on him. He twisted his hips and spread his thighs so he could press the pad of Liam's finger against the place where Liam would enter him. Liam trembled, hardly able to contain how turned on all of this had made him. Zach's honesty, his audacity, the fact they'd both imagined the same thing all those weeks ago, was almost too much to take.

"Shit," Liam hissed. Zach was scorching hot and tight, and Liam felt more wildly turned on just testing the willingness of Zach's body than he would if they were actually having sex.

"I would have made it so good for you, Zach. I will." Liam offered his own vow against Zach's jaw. "I'm not saying tonight, because we shouldn't. But Zach, god, I'll make it so good. I swear." Liam hardly knew what he was saying anymore. He only knew that it was the utter truth.

"I know," Zach's fingers slid into Liam's hair. "I know you will."

As their bodies took over, filling the night with instinctual pleasure that was made all the more beautiful by the promise of what was to come, words gave way to sounds of slipping skin, of lips pressing and then parting. Zach's final directive speared Liam straight through to his core.

"Don't stop."

16

"What do you think of this one?"

A little Sunday afternoon shopping had been Rebecca's idea. Zach had lobbied hard to come to Ikea because if he was spending his one afternoon off all week on retail therapy, the Swedish furniture store was the best option. The kitchen department was slammed with fellow shoppers, its walls lined with overwhelming amounts of cabinetry options and modern dining room sets. Zach craned his head, following the sound of her voice.

Rebecca was perched next to a sleek-looking table, it's top accented by flashes of red at the corners. Looking like some model from a home decor magazine, she stood with her high-heeled booties crossed precisely at her ankles. She tilted her head, awaiting Zach's answer, but he couldn't even remember what the question had been. His mind was a million miles away, replaying, on a near-constant loop, his last encounter with Liam.

"Don't stop."

Zach thought he'd instructed Liam with sufficient conviction, but to be fair, he couldn't completely remember. Everything that happened that night had blurred together into a heady mix of want and honesty. He'd laid the truth of his virginity at Liam's feet, imparting his secret to a man with a proven ability to react in a multitude of callous or understanding ways. Thankfully, Liam hadn't viewed Zach's confession as something to be ashamed of, but as something to explore and nurture. It didn't matter that Zach had never had sex before. It only mattered that he would with Liam.

So maybe those two demanding words had sounded different to Zach's ears. More ecstatic, surer. For Liam, they must have come across as a whimper, an idle aside of someone not totally within their own head instead of a demand from one lover to another. Because as soon as Zach had told Liam not to stop, he had done the exact opposite.

His head had popped up from Zach's chest. The curls at his temple were stuck to his brow and damp with restraint. "For real, Zach, no pressure."

"No, I like it. It feels good. Really good."

For as naked as they'd both been, Liam's smile had been as innocent as a child's gap-toothed grin. He had tossed his body to the far side of the bed and fumbled behind his alarm clock, revealing a bottle of lube. The unopened box of condoms that tumbled into sight had stayed where it fell.

As Liam spent several moments opening the bottle, ripping the seal off with his teeth, twisting the lid back on, and squirting the viscous liquid across his hand, Zach realized how gratifying his relationship with Liam had become. He'd known Rebecca forever. They'd been together through so many of life's milestones. And yet, the bond that was forming with Liam already felt far more complete.

A tightness had grown at the back of his throat, too. A wish for words he couldn't find. A momentary flash of a future that could exist only in his imagination. He'd traced the elegant arch of Liam's cheekbones with his thumbs. Liam had looked up and nipped at Zach's palm.

"Tell me if it's too much." Next thing Zach had known, Liam's finger was cool, inside his body. "Okay?" Liam's hand had remained totally still; his eyes alert. He'd watched Zach's every reaction. "It takes a while to adjust. Just breathe."

Zach had done so, breathing slowly and evenly. He'd tried to resist the conflicting urges to squirm away and never do this again or press even harder into Liam's hand and demand more.

"You ever done this on your own?"

"No." It had been hard for Zach to speak. "Not like this."

After a while, Zach's breath had become like a metronome, and Liam, like a true musician, had kept perfect time with his unrushed movements.

"I want you to practice this, Zach. You know about practice, right? Not a game. Just practice. Next time you're on your own, I want you to try this on yourself, so you get used to this sensation. I mean, I'm not you or anything, but..."

"What do you mean 'not me'?"

Liam had settled lower on his knees, his other hand finally becoming involved in the proceedings. Zach had licked his lips, ever so grateful. "Not all of us look like models and are hung like porn stars."

"Oh, shut up. You're gorgeous."

Liam's quick tongue had fallen into a demure silence. But only for a moment. "Will you do that for me? Will you practice, so that when we finally do sleep together all you'll feel is pleasure?" It had almost been like the words were magic. Zach had only been able to nod, his body ramping up for one of the most intense orgasms of his life.

Zach tried to pull himself out of the Liam-induced daydream as Rebecca's expression grew even more annoyed.

"Sorry. What did you ask?" Zach sputtered, and Rebecca rolled her eyes.

"The table. What do you think of the table?"

"Oh, yeah. It's alright?"

"Alright?"

"I don't know." He gestured towards the legs. "The red is a little weird."

"Hmm. I like it." She moved on with a breezy wave of her hand and a toss of her hair.

It had been a crazy week—another road game, another

hard-fought road win against a Minnesota team that always played with the grace of invading Carthaginians. Another late-night trip home, this time by plane that had been delayed in Minneapolis by a freak October snow squall. Zach had arrived at his apartment to find Rebecca asleep in his bed, wearing another one of his shirts, her phone still glowing in her hand. Zach had made sure not to pry, letting his already exhausted vision blur over the text conversation she'd fallen asleep in the middle of.

Liam's request for Zach to "practice" had been at the forefront of his thoughts all week. But between the game, classes ramping up for midterms, Des insisting on a midweek boy's night out, and Rebecca being oddly clingy, time to put Liam's instructions to the test had been minimal. That morning, though, he'd managed some alone time.

After a text from Rebecca woke up him earlier than he would have liked, asking for his breakfast order for her to bring over after she went to Mass, he decided to reach out to Liam instead. They weren't to the point in their friendship—relationship, tryst, whatever—where daily check-ins were expected, but Zach hadn't talked to him since class on Friday, so he'd fired a short morning greeting. Liam had gotten back to him a few minutes later with coffee mug and croissant emojis, followed with a long line of Z's. With a smile on his face, Zach had deleted the thread and made his way to the shower.

It hadn't taken long for the heat of the shower and the image of Liam still tucked into his bed to kick Zach's sex drive into the 'on' position. Soapy-slick and bent at the waist, he'd caught his weight against the tiles, overwhelmed by the deep-weighted pressure of pleasing himself in this new way.

He wasn't sure why he'd never done this for himself before. Perhaps his small-town roots and pushy parents had left him with a fear of his own anatomy. Or maybe he had assumed he'd never have cause. He was waiting to have sex until he was wearing Rebecca's wedding ring, after all. He had no doubt they'd be one of those cliché couples who was too tired to even manage a quick fumble between the sheets on their wedding night. Only Zach would know the real reason, and it would have nothing to do with exhaustion.

As sensation grew, he'd let his voice grow louder, too. His moans had risen above the sound of the shower. Rebecca could have come home with coffee and pastries any second, but Zach hadn't stopped. Maybe he'd even wanted her to catch him *in flagrante delico*. Maybe that vulnerable moment would be the way it all fell apart, how she finally learned the truth, and he could be free.

"I'm gay, Rebecca," he could have explained. "I want to be with men. I want to be with Liam."

Afterward, he'd had to sit with his back against the shower door for several minutes to catch his breath. Rebecca had shown up later than Zach expected, so much so that he'd been dressed and making a smoothie in the kitchen when she arrived. She'd been wearing a short skirt with patterned purple tights, an outfit more appropriate for a night out than a morning communing with God. But that was her, always ready for the next picture-perfect moment.

Zach rushed to catch up with her as she wandered towards the living room department of the store. She hadn't even noticed that he wasn't beside her and was still talking away, nonplussed. "I mean, obviously, whatever we end up getting will be much higher-end. I thought it would be smart to start talking aesthetics and make sure we agree."

"Why do we need to agree on kitchen tables, exactly?" he asked. He trailed his fingers over the smooth fabric of a faux-leather couch.

"For next year."

Ice settled in his stomach. "Next year?" He tried to deflect, but he knew exactly what she was inferring. "When we move in together, you mean?"

She tucked herself against his side, slipping her arms around his waist as they kept walking. "At the very least, right? I mean, I wouldn't mind if it were even more than that."

"Yeah. Yeah, maybe. If that's what you want."

Rebecca pulled away with an abrupt scoff. "Seriously?

'Maybe?' That's the best you can do when I bring up getting engaged?"

"Well, I'm sorry," Zach snapped. "I didn't expect for us to talk about this for the first time in the middle of an ottoman display." He gestured towards the offending furniture.

"Most couples who've been together for six years and made chastity promises to each other wouldn't even need to talk about it, but I get a 'Maybe?'" Rebecca's voice rose to a shrill tone. She looked somewhere between stricken and shrewish. Either way, it was entirely unattractive. "And here I was thinking maybe you'd..."

"I'd what?" Zach looked at her, his arms lifted from his sides aggressively. He was filled with his own conflicting set of emotions. He felt caught off-guard, full of guilt and his own duplicity. He looked over his shoulder, embarrassed, as their fellow shoppers gave them a wide berth.

"I thought maybe you'd...I don't know." She crossed her arms, giving him a peevish, spoiled pout. "That you'd made plans."

Zach laughed, heartlessly. "You think I already bought you a ring? With whose money, Becca? My dad's? That's classy. I know you're ready to be the wife of an NFL star and to have all the fame you think will come with it for you, but I don't have any of that yet. We haven't even finished school!" His voice had gotten frantic. He didn't even care about the scene they were making anymore. "Who thinks about marriage at twenty-two? Christ!"

And with that single word, he crossed a line. He'd gotten the "Lord's name in vain" speech more times than he cared to recount, and for all the awful things he'd said to her, this one thing, above all the rest, was the most unforgivable. According to Rebecca, using that word was a mortal sin, and she wasn't joking.

As she wordlessly walked away, he rubbed at his eyes with a sigh, knowing he'd made the day a whole lot harder for himself.

17

L iam woke up on Monday morning with Cole Porter stuck in his head. "I love Paris every moment. Every moment of the year..."

Centuries of artists, composers, writers, and thinkers had fallen in love with that city, and Liam had been no different. While Duke Ellington's bluesy saxophone had preferred "April in Paris" and Georges Seurat had depicted the Seine in high summer dot by dot, Liam always liked Paris best in the fall. There was an aching beauty to the gray skies behind the chestnut trees shedding their yellow leaves along the path at the Jardin des Tuileries and the way the cobblestones in Montmartre shone wet with rain. It felt like the city had been returned to its residents, emptied of its summer guests, a bit more worn at the edges but standing prouder than ever. In the two years Liam had lived and studied there, the days between September and the first snowfall had been his favorites. Those were the days when Paris had been the most inspirational to him, when he'd been allowed to fall in love with the place and with himself.

Fall in Chicago wasn't horrible. He appreciated the maple trees with their punches of red and the way the wind came off the lake, whipping and forewarning. Even though he would say he had adjusted to life in Illinois, it wasn't the same as Paris and never would be. But maybe that was okay, too.

In time, maybe Liam would find Paris again, but never as a resident. The bridge to the small music world he had inhabited was burned for him, and he knew he couldn't return to stay. Perhaps he could become one of her many regular visitors, one who would wholly appreciate what he was missing by just passing through.

The Chicago skyline, visible from his bedroom window, looked dull and flat as he sat up in bed to grab his phone. He checked the weather: a perfect forty-two degrees with a high of fifty and a twenty percent chance of drizzle. He liked a few pictures on Instagram, including a post Sam had made at 3:30 in the morning from one of the School of Music practice rooms, showing Brahms's Cello Sonata in F Major on his stand. It was his first semester of grad school, and the guy was stressed with a capital "S." Liam made a mental note to take him something laced with salt and fat when he headed up to school today.

Then, snuggling back into the warmth of his comforter, Liam re-read a text exchange he'd had with Zach the night before.

"Hope you had a better Sunday than me," Zach had written. "Massive fight with Rebecca. FML."

"Nothing a little sexual healing couldn't fix, I'm sure," Liam had replied. "Or some heavy petting in your case."

Zach had replied with an eye roll face followed by a flipped middle finger. Liam had grinned like an idiot as he'd texted back a series of mushrooms. Zach had promptly replied to their well-established inside joke with no less than fifteen middle fingers. His next message had taken on a different, almost sweet tone. "Night, Li. See you in class."

Liam liked the idea of Zach thinking of him at the start and end of his days, but he tried not to read into it too much. After all, Liam had gotten himself in trouble for misreading signs before.

Liam got out of bed with a stretch, turned on the shower, and examined his face in the mirror. He tended to his jawline with an electric razor but skipped over his upper lip. His facial hair was just as blond as the hair on his head and did little more than cast a shadow. But even so, it was a bold look. The peach fuzz 'stache looked somewhere between sleazy Russian porn-star and pathetic high school freshman. Liam let it stand.

After a shower, he applied several pumps of cologne—neck, chest, below the belt. He selected his most elegant trousers, a trim but not overly tight pair. He wrapped himself in the most pretentious, extra-large gray scarf he owned, twisting it around his neck and pairing it with a tweed jacket buttoned once around his narrow waist. If he couldn't be in Paris this time of year, he would walk out into the suburban American morning wearing the fashion of Paris instead.

The seat next to Zach was open, as it usually was those days. It wasn't like either of them had called "save-sies" on a seat next to each other or anything, but their classmates knew that Zach and Liam sat together now. It was just a thing.

He sat straight-backed and controlled, in contrast to the way Zach lolled over the table, his elbows and knees spread wide. The undoing of Liam's scarf filled the air between them with the smell of his cologne.

"Morning." A flicker of surprise passed over Zach's face after his convivial greeting. Liam was sure Zach hadn't expected his stylized appearance or the facial hair, minimal though it was.

"Hello."

"This is..." Zach gestured at his own mouth. "New."

Luckily Dr. Ellison began her lecture right then before Zach had stared at Liam's upper lip long enough for people started to notice or for Liam said something inflammatory like, "I'll let you taste it after if you like."

It had only been the previous Friday when, in a fit of mid-class fantasizing, Liam had toed off his shoe and slipped his socked foot over Zach's. Just as his toes began sneaking under the hem of Zach's jeans, Dr. Ellison had posed a question to Zach about Socrates' concept of the philosopher-king. Liam had suppressed a giggle, realizing his opportune timing meant Zach couldn't flinch or pull away. Zach had to answer her question

ALL THE WAY OUT   119

with total calm even as Liam continued toying with the skin above his ankle. Zach had stumbled through a surprisingly astute response. When he'd turned, shifting his legs out of Liam's reach, the back of his neck had burned a furious red.

After class ended, Zach had all but manhandled Liam into the same unused study room down the hall from their class where they'd talked the first day of class. Zach had closed the door firmly behind them and turned the lock.

"What the hell, dude? You can't fucking do that to me in class."

"Dude?" Liam had retorted with a mocking snort. "Yeah, okay, bruh. Sorry." He'd dropped his bag to the ground and reached for Zach with undignified haste.

"I'm serious, Liam."

The sternness in Zach's voice had been enough for Liam to go from predatory to docile in a second. He'd awkwardly placed his hands on his waist before tucking them under his arms. "I'm sorry," he'd said, grumpy but sincere. "I was over the line. I get it."

"You think?"

"But you liked it, though, I could tell. You were blushing."

"Well, yeah, but there's a time and a place, and in the middle of a lecture is not it."

"I know," Liam had said quickly, more exasperated with himself than anything. "It's just, sometimes I see you and I..." He'd made some animalistic growling sound, grabbing at the air with both hands as he'd closed the gap between them.

"Yeah, me too," Zach had said with rueful regret. "Come here, Barnett."

It had only been a little make-out session—tongues and lips and contentment—but Liam found the memory of it lingering on even into their present class. As Professor Ellison lectured, Liam was the paragon of good behavior. So much so that Zach spun in his chair at one point to give Liam a quizzical look. Liam merely looked back, bland and innocent. Clearly, Zach was expecting— maybe even hoping for—some more mischief.

Class ended with a reminder about the midterm at the end

of the week. Some students groaned or cursed, having forgotten about the upcoming test, but Liam had little sympathy for them. It was in the syllabus, after all. The room became a clamor of backpack zippers and conversation. It felt like a safe enough backdrop for a question that had been on Liam's mind since the night before.

"So, this fight with Rebecca. It was a rough one, huh?"

Zach paused from stuffing his things into his bag. He took one look at Liam and understood his concern. "Oh. No," he stated. "No, it wasn't about that. She has no idea; I'm sure of it."

How Zach could be so certain, Liam didn't know, but he was happy to believe him. "So, what was it about then?"

Zach inhaled through his mouth. "Kitchen tables? I have no idea honestly." They both stood to leave in tandem. "It was one of those fights that starts off about one thing and ends up about something else, you know? Something way bigger."

For some reason, the stability of Zach's relationship with Rebecca seemed important. Zach had been with her practically his entire romantic life, so there must be something redeemable about her. Plus, she gave them a ready cover. Liam was quite sure Zach would want nothing to do with him if there wasn't a beard already in the equation—a beard who Liam knew happily broadcasted details of their relationship on social media with frequency. He'd convinced himself that following Rebecca on Instagram was a totally normal thing to do given his situation.

"Then everything's good now?"

"I was able to talk her down eventually. But just smack me if I ever start talking about the four C's of diamonds, okay?"

Liam spun at the top of the stairwell, his eyes going wide as he held the door open with his back. "Wow. That fight. Big steps then."

Come spring, Liam knew Zach would graduate from college. He would get drafted. He would move to a new city and start what would undoubtedly be a long professional career. He would marry Rebecca, whether that was only a few months from now or in many more chaste years, but one day, barring some strange change in the society where a gay NFL player would suddenly be A-OK, that was what Zach's future held.

Liam had known all this from nearly the moment they met, and it shouldn't have mattered, but it did. It meant that no matter what happened between them, whatever they experienced, they had an expiration date. This wasn't a wake-up call for Liam, just a tempering reminder of what he'd already been thinking that morning. He shouldn't go looking for more than what Zach would ever be able to give. Liam had to accept where he was and what he had. Chicago fall, not Paris. Zach for today, but not for the future.

"Speaking of big steps," Zach said as they exited the classics building into the muted sunlight of the overcast day. "I've been practicing."

Zach's swerve in subject matter brought them back to where they started as a duo: two men who'd met on Grindr because they were horny. It felt like safer ground, and even in the busy walkways of class changeover, Liam put on the charm. He walked backward, a bounce back in his step.

"Have you now?" He watched the way Zach eyed the crowds around them warily and threw him a rope. "You mean you've," he cleared his throat pointedly, "been practicing that method for memorizing irregular verbs I suggested, right?"

Zach blinked at him several times before understanding flashed across his face. "Yeah, exactly. The verbs."

"How many times have you gone through with it?"

"A few."

"A few times isn't going to cut it on the exam."

"Three times." Liam offered an approving but not overly impressed look. "But the last time was, ah, double." Zach rubbed his pointer and middle finger across his brow and Liam wanted to climb all 6'4" of him, right then and there, and devour him.

"So, I was thinking, maybe we could study for midterms together?"

Now it was Liam's turn to be unsure of the doublespeak. He stopped walking, stepped in just a bit closer, and dropped his voice. "Wait, do you mean actually study?"

Zach laughed. "Probably wouldn't hurt to do a bit of both,

right?"

Liam's heart started pounding as he stepped back and took in the guileless look on Zach's face. "Tonight, then?"

Zach's face pinched. "I told Rebecca we'd hang tonight."

"'Course. Um, Tuesday? No, wait. Tuesday doesn't work. I have this masterclass thing that will go late. And I don't want to have to rush."

"Yeah, we'll need lots of time to study." Liam's stomach flipped as heat seeped into Zach's eyes for a moment. "Wednesday I told Coach I'd stay after practice to go through video for Purdue on Saturday."

"I have my orchestration midterm the next morning, anyway. Thursday night, then?"

"Thursday works." Zach's smile was delicate and darling.

Other students, in a hurry to get to their next class, passed around them as they stood in the middle of the walkway, smiling wordlessly at each other. Some gave them bizarre, even grumpy looks, but with Zach's promise for Thursday, Liam couldn't have cared less.

18

Zach realized he had two ways to face what was to come after they solidified their plans to meet at Liam's on Thursday. He could let Thursday become THURSDAY, this great monolithic thing where something life-altering was bound to happen. He could fret for hours about how it would feel. He could worry about whether he'd like it, if Liam would like it, if sleeping with Liam would change him, or them, irrevocably.

His other option was to just let it be what it was: the chance for another night with Liam where they'd end up doing something normal for people their age. Thursday would be Zach's chance to finally share in an act that was both intimate and sexy with someone he wanted and cared about.

He decided on option two and texted Liam Wednesday night. "7 o'clock, right?"

"On the dot."

"Cool."

Liam managed to read right through Zach's false calm with his next text. "It's not that different from what we've already done, you know. Same appendage. Different orifice."

"That's easy for you to say," Zach responded. "It's not your orifice."

Liam sent several laughing-crying emojis. Zach imagined Liam in his bed, grinning and determined to torture him.

"Nothing happens that you don't want to happen, Zach," Liam wrote back. "And I told you I'd make it good."

Bolstered by the whole "consent is sexy" vibe that Liam was promoting and his own desire to finally "do it," Zach arrived at Liam's place Thursday night bearing a backpack with half a semester's worth of notes on Plato and a bag full of Chinese takeout. He kissed Liam quickly on the cheek once the door was shut, exuding a lightness of pure expectation.

They managed to study for a good hour. Their notes and books were scattered across Liam's kitchen table along with discarded chopsticks and soy sauce packets. Watching Liam's beautiful mouth form those ancient Grecian vowels and reading key passages of the work for emphasis, was an extended form of foreplay. Unable to take it anymore, Zach leaned across the table and kissed him, finding Liam's mouth unctuous, almost greasy. He loved the salty tang on his tongue and was ready to let Liam take him right there on top of his Plato notes. Instead, Zach had pulled away, enjoying the blissed-out look on Liam's face as he giggled, "Umm, what was I saying?"

Once their heads were sufficiently stuffed with Plato, Zach helped Liam clean up the kitchen, tidying the empty cartons while Liam washed the dishes. Liam gave Zach every opportunity to bail, but Zach wasn't about to go back now.

He came up behind Liam, who was busy washing a glass with extra attention and pressed his chest to Liam's back. He tucked his chin over Liam's shoulder and wrapped his arms around him to hold him in place. "Hey," he said, swaying back and forth gently. Liam shifted his head sideways, exposing this neck in a way that was entirely biteable, so Zach nibbled it with lip-covered teeth.

Liam spun in his arms. "Come here."

They didn't talk much after that.

Unhurried but eager, they tumbled back onto Liam's bed. Through kisses, buttons and zippers were undone. They shared smiles as socks were pulled off, resulting in awkward angles and jabbing knees. But every time necessity pulled them apart, they crashed back together, hungrier and needier.

Liam didn't ask permission; their intentions were clear all evening long. He grabbed the lube and spread it liberally across his hand and in the cleft of Zach's ass. Zach's solo practicing was nothing compared to Liam's deft fingers. From his back, Zach watched as Liam reached for a condom. Liam was stoic with concentration as he rolled the latex all the way to the root. Steeling himself for what he assumed came next, Zach rolled onto his stomach.

"Wait, where are you going?" Liam broke their verbal silence. He grabbed the underside of Zach's shoulder and convinced him to turn back over. "I want you where I can see you, where I can kiss you," he continued, smiling ruefully as if part of him was sad thinking Zach assumed sex between two men had to be void of any tenderness. "I want you right here. Okay?"

"Okay," Zach agreed.

With that, Liam hooked his elbow under Zach's knee, tucked Zach's body back against itself. Slowly and evenly, he pressed into Zach.

Zach felt a shot of ice up the length of his spine. "Fuck."

"Too much?"

"No. Maybe." He slapped his hand onto Liam's buttock, holding him in place when he tried to pull out. "But no."

"Take as long as you need. I'm good right here." Liam's words were little more than a patient breath. "Though, fair warning, I might not last. You feel ridiculously good."

Liam let out a disciplined breath, his hips shifting with unintentional motion. It was enough to send Zach's head back, a long moan at the back of his throat. He tightened his glute muscles experimentally.

"Fuck." It was Liam's turn to curse. "I definitely won't last if you do that again."

"Well, that would be anticlimactic." Zach did it again anyway.

Liam whimpered through a laugh, his curls brushing against Zach's jaw. "You're such a little shit."

Zach laughed too, finding it strange to be so carefree in that moment of ultimate exposure. After a few more moments his body adjusted, and he rolled his hips once, carefully. Liam's breath stuttered. When Zach did it again, Liam met that motion at its apex with a gentle thrust of his own hips. A rush of pleasure ran through Zach.

What followed was nothing less than what Zach would call amazing sex. Though he had no basis for comparison, Liam was both delicate and powerful. He was completely responsive, always attuned to Zach. They muttered words of encouragement and praise, only stopping occasionally to find each other's mouths, grab a hasty breath through clenched teeth, or catch the happiness rolling off each other in waves.

So much of Zach's life was a façade, false and hidden. He spent so much time wrapped in pads, both figurative and literal, to protect himself from injury and from his own lies. But some people were worth letting his defenses down for. So worthy, in fact, Zach would dismantle every last one of them so he could be completely free. In Liam, Zach miraculously found such a person.

He wrapped his arms around Liam's back, held on tight, and let everything go. They filled Liam's bedroom with sounds and volumes he never dared to before. Tension, hot and tingling, built in every muscle of his body, as he waited for the pending explosion.

"I'm close," Liam panted.

"Me too."

A rhythmic breath later.

"Yeah?"

"Yeah, don't stop."

Those pleading words, again. Only this time, Liam heeded Zach's imperative, not stopping until they collapsed together, both sweaty, breathless, and wearing dopey smiles.

—

Zach woke sometime later to the brush of evening air across his face and the smell of cigarettes. He'd not slept, just rested in a sated daze for some indeterminate amount of time. It had probably only been a handful of minutes but had felt like forever. He rolled from one side to another, noting the heaviness in his limbs. It felt different from the post-game, metabolic exhaustion he was so familiar with. This felt more subtle, juicier. There was a warmth across his shoulders and in his biceps, a slight tremble at the back of his thighs. The distinct ache between his ass cheeks was like a bruise faded enough that you wanted to touch it to see if its tenderness remained.

The Chicago skyline was miles away, but it felt close there on the eighteenth floor, invited into Liam's bedroom along with them. The window was open on its track just wide enough for Liam to exhale the smoke from his cigarette through the crack.

Liam sat next to Zach on the bed, his elbows propped on the bedside sill. He was naked but for a sheet drawn loosely over his propped-up knees. The full expanse of his back was exposed to Zach as he tapped the ashes into a NU coffee mug that Zach imagined still contained the dregs of that morning's brew.

The same lights that cast a sulfur yellow hue into the broken cloud cover outside seemed to make Liam's already pale skin even more ethereal. Iridescent and silver. Alabaster and mother of pearl. Zach had loved that skin from the moment he'd seen Liam's profile picture, black, white, and filtered on his phone. He loved it all the more now that he had worshiped it with his tongue and teeth, felt it bead with sweat and shiver with goosebumps. Zach feathered his fingers across Liam's ribs. He looked back at Zach, having been unaware he was being watched.

"Sorry." Liam exhaled a large puff of smoke. "I haven't had one in weeks, but it just seemed fitting. Considering." He shrugged with a smirk.

Liam reached for the coffee mug to extinguish the cig, but before he could, Zach propped himself on his elbow and covered Liam's hand with his own. He matched Liam's hold on the cigarette between thumb and first finger, slipped it from Liam's grasp, and put it to his lips.

It wasn't the first cigarette Zach had ever had, but it was his first in a very, very long time. The nicotine rush added another layer to his bliss, as did the bemused look on Liam's face.

"Don't tell Coach." He handed the cigarette back. Liam took one last quick drag before jabbing it out in the mug, producing a small hiss.

"I think there's plenty I won't tell your coach."

Zach snickered, then took a deep cleansing breath, sealing the memory of what they'd shared inside himself. Liam's eyes skipped over Zach's body with concern, looking for a wince of pain or any sign of remorse. Zach just smiled and kissed the curve of Liam's shoulder before resting his head there. Liam nuzzled into his hair, the smell of smoke still lingering around them.

"When my parents convinced me to come to school here, they told me it was a school in Chicago. Bunch of liars. But I figured I could exchange one city center for another. The *dix-neuvième* for the Windy City."

Zach shivered at Liam's exquisite French.

"Imagine my dismay when I'd ended up here." He reached forward and slid the window closed with a sealing thud. "In suburbia."

"Oh, come on. Evanston's hardly some sleepy little village. Besides, look at your view! I mean, would you rather be the king up in one of those tall towers, your only view the drab, ramshackle huts of his kingdom? Or the pauper who simply needs to look out his window at the castle on the hill for a glimpse of total splendor?" He pointed towards the John Hancock building with its distinctive shape and matching spires on the top, red airplane lights flashing in and out of sync.

Liam stared at Zach drolly. "You really don't know me at all if you have to ask me that question."

They both laughed as Liam shoved him lightly, but Zach's point had been made. Liam crossed his arms over his knees and rested his chin on the resulting perch. Doing so put several cool inches between them. As always happened when Paris was mentioned, Liam's mood had turned inwardly contemplative, his body language self-protective, and he seemed to need the space.

"Do you still wish you were there?" Zach asked.

"Sometimes." Liam answered quickly enough for Zach to know he was being truthful. Then he looked at Zach, blinked softly. "Not right now, though."

"Look, if you ever want to talk about what happened, I'm here."

"Oh, I've talked plenty." Liam sounded tired. "My parents and shrinks and school administrators and counselors and lawyers."

"Lawyers? Jesus, Liam." Zach knew the time was upon them. They'd just been as intimate as any two people could be, and he refused to speculate any longer. Zach had to know. "Please, just tell me what happened."

With a small shake of his head, Liam cast his eyes upward. "You don't want to know, trust me." He reached for another cigarette and angrily bit the filter between his front teeth.

Zach scooted closer, pressing their bodies together again. "Yes, I do." Liam's lighter clicked but didn't catch. He tried shaking it but to no avail. Zach went on, insistent. "I want to know everything there is to know about you. The good and the bad." Zach cupped the far side of Liam's face, turning it towards his. He waited until Liam met his gaze. "Please. Just tell me."

Zach combed his fingers gently through Liam's curls, a jumbled array on top of his head after their lovemaking. He looked unprepared for this conversation and uneasy, but Zach could see the moment Liam's willpower broke. His face became lax and childlike, and the line of his spine collapsed into a bowed curve. "I'm not a good person, Zach."

"Stop it," Zach scoffed.

"I had an affair with my teacher."

Of all the things Zach thought Liam might say, that had not been one of them. "Seriously?"

"It's not what it sounds like, though, okay?" Liam asserted. "It wasn't physical. At least, not sexual."

"But then—"

"There were looks." He gazed deep into Zach's eyes, his lashes dropping low and flirty for example. It made Zach's stomach flip. "And touches." He caressed Zach's cheek with the back of his hand, then ran it down his neck and over his collarbone. "Things were said that made me think..." He trailed away. Zach settled his hand at the small of Liam's back.

"I don't know what it's like with coaches," Liam said eventually. He rolled the cigarette back and forth in his fingers. "I only played football—sorry, *soccer*—one term as a kid. But a teacher at the conservatory becomes more like a mentor, a master to his protege. It's always one-on-one. You and your professor, alone for hours at a time in their music studio. Honing your art. Giving your soul up to the music. Your entire identity is wrapped up in what you're creating. It's not just some game, you know, where either you win or you don't. It's more nuanced than that."

Zach nodded obligingly, taking no offense to Liam's comparison.

"These teachers, the best of them at least, they learn how to pull at the most secret parts of you, forcing them out onto the page in dots and lines. And once the secrets are out, they pick them apart—judge them, critique them, and berate you and your abilities when they fall short. But then they'll turn around in the same breath and praise you. It leaves you totally confused and emotionally vulnerable. And they are the ones to pick you up and remake you. It's fucked up, right?"

"Yes," Zach agreed. How could he not?

Liam was wildly intense now that the dam had broken. His eyes were a terrifying and heartbreaking mix of unresolved emotions.

"And yet," Liam continued, "there is something completely intoxicating about it, too. Getting that kind of attention from someone so accomplished? So renowned?" He shook his head. "It makes you feel like you're the most important person in the world to them."

Zach made slow circles at the base of Liam's spine with his thumb, ignoring the glint in Liam's eyes.

"He had a reputation." It was the first time Liam had defined the gender of the teacher. It wasn't like it mattered to Zach, but it helped to clarify the picture. "Especially with boys like me: talented, young. Pretty." He gestured at his face, with a cold laugh. "Well, I didn't want to hear any of it. I was sure I was the exception to the rule, that I was different and it was just a matter of time before we..." He trailed away as if it was too awful or too embarrassing to define. "When it turned out I was nothing different, that I was just another in a long line, I didn't handle it well."

"What did you do?" Zach asked gently.

"I reported him. Went straight to the head of the school and the administrative board. Hashtag 'Me Too' was about to explode at the Paris Conservatory."

"Well, good!" Zach said, fiercely protective and sick at the thought of what had happened to Liam. "No way he should have ever treated you like that."

"No, Zach, not good." Liam rubbed at the space between his brows with his fingers. "I should have just kept my fucking mouth shut."

"Why? So he could just treat someone else like that?"

"Because saying something only made it about eight thousand times worse."

"For whom?"

"For everyone." Liam's chest heaved. "Because when I told them that he'd made advances, they made assumptions."

He waited for it to click for Zach. "They thought you had slept together?"

"And I didn't correct them." It was a hollow, pitiful admittance. "I lied about it. Repeatedly. Made shit up. Places and occurrences. Things that I'd only fantasized about, but that we never did." He stopped with a shuddering breath, like this one fact out of all of it had haunted him the most. "I was hurt, you know? Embarrassed. I was pissed off and wanted vindication."

He wiped brusquely at his eyes and shook his head, trying to wipe away all emotion there. He blew out a long puff of air.

"My parents hired lawyers, expensive lawyers. It got harder and harder for the school to keep it out of the press. The other students would barely look at me because I'd had the audacity to complain when everybody knew what he was like. But then they brought my professor in with an army of his own lawyers, and the truth came out. Nothing had happened between us. Not really," he amended when Zach tried to contest. "He told them it was all in my head, that I'd misread his tutelage as something more. So, then there were threats of defamation of character lawsuits, meetings behind closed doors where his lawyers questioned my character. They even brought up my sexuality and my past partners, like that impacted it somehow. My parents were ready to sue them back, but by then, I just didn't want to fight anymore. I was shunned by my classmates. My brother wouldn't even talk to me. I just wanted it all to go away." He swallowed, hard. "*Alors.*" With an elegant twist of his wrists like a magician's assistant revealing the trick, he indicated the apartment around him, the city beyond, his new life. "*Voilà.*"

Zach felt drained by Liam's story but relieved to finally know what had happened. It made his life as a closeted football player seem oddly banal.

"What he did to you was still wrong. You know that, right?" Zach said.

"Yeah, I know. During the meeting where I got expelled, the director of the conservatory told me that if I'd just told the truth from the beginning, they probably would have had grounds to fire him, and I would still be enrolled. But once they realized I'd lied, their hands, legally-speaking, were tied." He rubbed at his stuffy nose and looked at Zach, open-mouthed. "So, now you know how seriously fucked up I am. Probably casts a bit of a shadow over what we just did."

Zach chastened him with a look as a quote slipped into Zach's thoughts, one from Ovid's *Ars Amatoria*. He'd read it in high school as part of his all-consuming obsession with the ancient world. That part, in particular, had resonated with him as he'd battled his own conscience, fighting to justify all the lies he had spread about his own life just for the sake of his game.

"*Militiae species amor est.*"

Liam blinked, his brow furrowing softly. "Did you just quote Ovid at me?"

Zach shrugged. "Seems fitting, considering your proclivity for including Ovid in the weirdest of places."

For the first time in a while, Liam grinned. "Love is a kind of warfare," he translated, thoughtfully. "I don't know. I wanted him. I wanted him to want me. I don't know if I loved him, though. At least, not like you should love someone."

"But he mattered."

Liam nodded. "Even if I didn't matter to him."

Zach kissed him, lingering on his temple, and Liam leaned into the touch. Together, they snuggled down to the mattress, adjusting pillows and pulling the comforter up tight around their faces.

"I haven't told anyone all that before," Liam admitted softly. "No one knows the whole story besides my family. And my lawyer," he added with a dejected snort.

"Not even Mackenzie?"

He shook his head, his eyes already starting to drift closed. "No, she's a part of that music world, you know? It's a small one, and it's not worth the risk of her knowing."

"Well, I'm happy to be your outsider."

Liam perked up just enough to ask, "Can you stay?"

To leave then seemed positively cruel, and yet he had no choice. "You know I can't."

Liam let out a low, unhappy grumble. "Probably for the best. You take up more than half my bed."

Zach pulled Liam closer. "I make up for it, though, cause I'm a total snuggler."

"Why am I not surprised?" Liam mumbled. He tucked his head deeper into his pillow and the crook of Zach's neck.

"I'll stay until you fall asleep, though, okay?"

The duvet rustled as Liam nodded, his breath evening out into a shallow rhythm. The minutes extended as Zach watched Liam sleep, hoping one day, he'd be able to fall asleep next to him and never leave.

19

It was near dawn. Liam's alarm wouldn't go off for hours yet, but when Liam reached for the spot on the bed where Zach had been, it was cold. He blinked open his eyes and looked around his room. All of Zach's things were gone too.

Part of him was disappointed Zach hadn't just accidentally fallen asleep, but that probably would have caused more trouble than it was worth. He rolled back over, ready to steal a few more hours of sleep, when he noticed the obvious way his phone was propped on his bedside table, the blue indicator light flashing, signaling a waiting email or message.

He reached out from under the warm covers and grabbed the device, especially curious when he saw that there was an email from Zach waiting. The subject header was blank, but there was an attachment included.

"For your eyes only. Though I may have kept a copy too. Thank you for everything tonight."

Liam's heart fluttered. He tapped the screen with his thumb to open the attachment and could hardly believe what he saw.

It was a picture of them. Together. In his bed just hours before. One of Zach's broad arms was wrapped around his sleeping body, the other held the phone above them to take the shot. He'd used a flash to capture the look of pure bliss on his face where it was tucked against Liam's curls. Zach's eyes were closed as if breathing him in, a gentle lilt to the corner of his mouth. Liam had never seen anything so tender in his life. He felt safe and adored just by looking at a picture of himself he hadn't even been conscious of when it was taken. He flopped onto his back with a stupid grin, his arms falling wide. Sleep was the last thing on his mind now.

God, he was completely fucked.

When his alarm eventually did go off, it blasted in his face from where his phone was still perched in his hand. He quickly went through his morning routine, making his way to campus and hoping to catch Zach before class.

It worked. Liam saw Zach emerge from between two buildings at the far end of the quad. Decked out in a purple hoodie, he matched the extra Northwestern pennants that flew from streetlamps in celebration of upcoming Homecoming Weekend. Zach's formidable frame towered above the rest of the student body. He walked with an assuredness befitting someone of his notoriety on campus, his physical prowess, his looks, his humility, and his smarts. Zach really was the total package, wasn't he?

Seated on a bench, two cups of Starbucks coffee warming his hands, Liam pulled his tongue across his lower lip as he considered how he was the only human on the entire planet to know Zach the way he now did. He may have only been acquainted with Zach for a few months, but Liam knew exactly what Zach's body was capable of in more fiercely intimate ways than any of those who analyzed his moves on the playing field. He knew the truth of Zach's inner soul and the way his id and superego battled to keep the truth hidden to all—all but Liam.

Now Zach knew Liam better than anyone, too. Revealing that rusty, shameful corner of himself that Liam had sworn to leave behind on a different continent had bound them closer than any amount of sex possibly could.

Walking next to Zach was a fair-skinned black man of a

similarly athletic build, wearing clothes of identical purple. Before they parted ways, they clasped hands and pulled each other into a quick, shoulder-tap hug. It was all very palsy, just lads being lads. Though the entire exchange was laced with the affection of close friends, it was still a very heterosexual jock. Zach played that role with terrifying conviction.

Liam stood up as Zach turned his way. Upon seeing him, Zach jogged a few steps. It was little more than a lazy shuffle to bring himself to Liam more quickly, but it was an adorable display, and Liam's mouth contorted into a grin.

Liam offered up one of the coffees, holding it out at arm's length. "I took a guess."

"Soy, no sugar?"

Liam cocked his head to the side, as he considered the coffee he'd ordered: cream, two sugars for both of them. "Close enough."

Zach took it and swallowed. His eyes went wide at the unexpected taste. "Oh, good God," he coughed.

Liam reached urgently for the cup. "Just chuck it. I can get you another after class."

Zach shook his head, pulling the cup close to his chest with a near covetous growl. "This is mine now."

Liam laughed softly as they began walking together. "Should I be jealous?" Liam tossed his head over his shoulder in the direction of Zach's retreating friend.

"What? Him?" Zach asked with sudden concern in his voice. "No, that's—that's just Des. My best friend? I told you about him, didn't I?"

"Zach, I was only joking." Liam touched his shoulder lightly, his palm skating off Zach's shoulder blade. It was an inconsequential touch for two men who had shared all they had the night before, but it was borderline dangerous for broad daylight, and Liam knew it. They both scanned the quad, looking for someone they might have tipped off. Wordlessly, they moved up the steps and towards the assumed safety of the classics building.

"I take it you made it to practice, then?" Liam held the door open for Zach.

"Barely." He rushed to catch the elevator that had just opened to let some students from an earlier section out. Once they were alone, sealed behind the sliding doors, Zach continued. "Needless to say, I was pretty exhausted this morning, so this will help. Especially with the extra sugar." He lifted his coffee in Liam's direction. "Thank you."

"I should thank you too, I suppose. For the little gift you left this morning."

"You liked it?"

"Um, yes!" Liam retorted, extra lippy.

"Ok, phew. I was a little worried you might think it was creepy or something."

"No, definitely not creepy." Actually, Liam thought, it was the most romantic thing anyone had ever done for him. "And don't worry, it's safely hidden away in a subfolder on my phone with pictures from a trip I took to Croatia with my dad three years ago. Our little secret. Well, ours and the cloud's."

Paris Liam would never have tolerated an entanglement with someone as far in the closet as Zach. He had always been open about his sexuality. Why would he want to be with someone unwilling to be honest about theirs? And yet he got it, in Zach's case. This wasn't about self-loathing, just protecting a dream.

Rome Liam wouldn't have dared stick around when such obvious emotions, while still unspoken, were being felt on both sides. He had been reeling from the imagined romance with his teacher all summer, smarting and bitter, and in no way interested in anything of consequence. But here he was, buying Zach coffee the morning after their first time together.

"How are you feeling, by the way? You know?" He gave Zach's nether regions a pointed look.

Zach shifted on his feet, standing up a little taller, then answered. "Yeah, I'm fine, though my trainer did ask why I wasn't getting quite so deep into my squats this morning."

"He didn't." Liam laughed. "What did you say?"

Zach puffed up his chest with bogus machismo. "Told him I took a really hard pounding last night." Liam's jaw dropped.

"On the practice field, obviously." Zach was smooth as silk as he slid in close to Liam. If the elevator door hadn't announced their arrival with a soft ping right at that moment, the fourth floor of the classics department would have gotten a pretty view of Liam pressed against the wall and Zach's tongue down his throat.

"You." Liam pointed at him, shoving him playfully away as the door opened. "You are the actual worst, you know that? The fucking worst."

They tumbled out into the hall, shoulders brushing, bodies jostling. They didn't bother to cover up their laughter or the sunny looks they tossed each other's way.

"Morning."

"Ciao, Ebbie!"

The glittering joy Liam had felt with Zach easily extended to his brother, who was waiting for the elevator with a rather tall pile of books in his arms balanced in his arms. Liam flung himself at Eben and spun them, almost dance-like, in a boisterous circle. As they came to a stop, Eben clapped a hand on his stack of books, making sure the centrifugal force of their greeting didn't knock them all to the floor.

Recovered, but mildly annoyed, Eben asked, "Don't you two have a midterm now?"

"*Si, si. Andiamo pronto.*" Liam's Italian was rushed and breezy, and Eben regarded him critically. Had it really been so long since his brother had seen him happy that he considered this open display with skepticism?

Luckily, Zach came to his aid before Eben started asking if he was on drugs again or something. "Did you get my email with the ticket link?"

"I did. Thank you. And thanks for getting us into the President's Box. Very fancy. But it looks like my wife won't be able to use her ticket after all."

"Oh?" Liam hated the genuine tinge of disappointment in Zach's voice.

"Kelsey's mother is coming in to do some pre-baby preparations." Eben and Liam shared a wide-eyed look. Liam had had the unfortunate opportunity of meeting Eben's mother-in-law at his wedding. He did not envy his brother his relations. "Let's just say, I am more than happy to have plans Saturday afternoon."

"It'll be great to have you there," Zach said, oblivious to the silent chat held between brothers. "It's always nice knowing you have someone cheering for you in the crowd."

"Don't you usually have about forty-five thousand people doing that?" Eben asked.

"Okay, true. But you know what I mean."

Eben gave Zach a charming smile, and Liam realized the two of them, unbeknownst to him, had developed a very nice relationship as advisor and advisee. It felt like joint stamps of approval.

"So, there's a game tomorrow, then?" Liam chimed in.

A slow, amused smile spread across Zach's face. "It's Homecoming Weekend, Liam. Of course, there's a game."

"Well, I could use the other ticket then, if no one else wants it."

Liam felt the looks of total bewilderment coming at him from either side. While his brother looked at him with utter confusion, Zach's was like heartfelt wonder.

"You want to come to my game?"

"It's about time I fully embrace all aspects of my American university experience, right?"

"The games are long," Eben cautioned. "That'll be four hours sitting next to me. Think you can handle it?"

Liam shrugged. "I can if you can."

His brother's smile was warm and homey. If only their mother could have seen them, then. "I'll pick you up tomorrow morning. Kick-off is at noon, right?" Eben asked Zach as he got on the elevator.

"With the anthem at 11:45."

"We'll be there, and good luck on your midterm, *ragazzi*," he called as the doors slid closed.

"You're just full of surprises this morning, aren't you?" Zach brushed past Liam, heading towards their classroom. He was chipper and light and positively giddy.

"It's just a football game, Zach."

Zach turned, walking backward a few paces as he shook his head. "No, it's not."

—

Just over twenty-four hours later, Liam felt very lucky to have secret lovers in high places. The weather that Saturday was total shit, cold and rainy. Even so, the stadium was full of fans ready to cheer on Northwestern against Purdue University. If it weren't for the temperature-controlled comfort of the President's Box, there was no way Liam would have come. It wouldn't have mattered how infatuated he was with number twenty-four in purple and white or how pleased this made his brother.

Before the game go underway, Eben chatted up the big wigs dressed in suits and drinking complimentary wine on the other side of the suite.

"That's the dean of the business school, and the one in blue is from the Board of Regents," Eben said, retaking his seat with a lofty grin and pulling Liam away from his phone. Mackenzie had been texting him frantically.

"Is the box amazing? Do you love it already? I'm in row 45. It's fucking freezing!" Liam could almost hear her teeth chatter through the written words.

When the marching band took the field for the pregame show, Liam recognized several faces from the School of Music— even in their plumed hats and ridiculous uniforms, which made them look like a cross between soldiers and clowns. They sounded pretty good though, he had to admit.

His brother prepped him with the rules, attempting to draw comparisons to the European-style game they'd both dabbled in unsuccessfully as kids.

"There's Zach," Eben pointed to the far side of the field. Zach was too far away to recognize by his face, but Liam knew it was him simply by the way his body moved as he threw a ball back and forth with a teammate.

Liam tried to stay invested as the teams took the field, but it all seemed nonsensical. "Why is Northwestern kicking it away if they won the coin toss? Why do they keep running into the backs of their own players? They're not going anywhere."

Each question was met by as patient an explanation as Eben could manage, but even so, Liam felt his interest wane when Purdue kicked the ball between the large metal beams that reach skyward like a pair of inverted eighth notes.

"A field goal," Eben explained. "It's worth three points."

"Three's an arbitrary number, isn't it?" Liam retorted, and Eben let out an exasperated sigh.

After a short break in the action, the sides switched, and Northwestern had their first chance to move the ball. Zach took the field, and Liam sat forward slightly, leaning closer to the pane of glass that separated them from the outdoors. Zach cupped his hands, blew on them once for warmth, then crouched in the middle of the line of his teammates. From high above Liam heard him call out, shouting in rapid cadence.

Instead of running the boring up-the-gut plays their opposition had tried, Zach stepped back, light on balanced feet. Before Liam even realized it, the ball was out of Zach's hands, arcing perfectly over the heads of everyone on the field. Its recipient caught it mid-stride, having barely looked over his shoulder to see if the ball was there. The player, the same guy who'd been with Zach the previous morning on the Quad, stumbled once when one of the defenders lunged for his feet. Then he caught his balance and ran the remaining yards into the far end of the field where a giant, white "NORTHWESTERN" was painted on purple grass.

The entire stadium lost its collective mind.

"Touchdown!" Eben threw his hands over his head just like the officials did on the field. He high-fived some random people sitting behind them. "What a play!" He didn't temper his enthusiasm for Liam's sake, but even Liam had to admit, it had been pretty cool.

The rest of the first half went much the same way. The Purdue players trundled down the field with short gains. Sometimes they would kick another field goal, and other times they would kick the ball back to Northwestern if they hadn't gotten far enough down field. Then Northwestern would get the ball back, and Zach would work his magic, managing to get the heaving slabs of men to move with precision and accuracy. They'd score again, the crowd would cheer, and the band would play the fight song.

It was near the end of half time, after the marching band had done their show and during another one of the many TV stoppages where nothing happened besides loud music being blasted through the stadium's sound system, that Liam realized just how glad he was to be here, spending this time on a Saturday with his brother. They'd both said things over the past six months that were designed to cut to the core with a caustic exactness only possible with someone you loved deeply and knew well.

As a child, Liam had been a constant source of joy and entertainment for his parents, with his music making and outgoing demeanor. Eben, ever the rule-follower, was more reserved and studious, always trying to do the right thing. He'd even gone so far as to follow in his father's academic footsteps in his attempt to please them. Liam had seemed a better fit for his parents' bohemian world. Add this to the improbability of Liam's birth, and it was easy for Eben to assume Liam was the "favorite."

He was wrong, of course. If only Eben could have heard the number of times his father went on about his eldest son, the doctoral candidate at Brown University and soon-to-be junior faculty member at Northwestern, while Liam listened on, wallowing in his post-Paris depression. If only Eben knew how elated his mother had been when his brother had announced that he and Kelsey were going to make her a grandmother, while Liam's most serious relationship to date was one he'd created in his mind.

That afternoon, watching football, eating junk food, and drinking beer out of plastic bottles that cost far too much, felt like an arrival point for them. It was the final punctuation on one broken phase of their lives and the start of another.

"Let's take a selfie," Liam suggested, spurred on by his

renewed affection for his brother. "Send it to mom and dad."

"An 'usie,' you mean?"

Liam groaned. "My god, you're so hip with the kids these days, aren't you?"

"Oh, totes."

"Stop. Stop that right now." Eben laughed so hard he almost snorted. Liam couldn't help but laugh, too.

They settled into the frame of Liam's phone screen. Liam suppressed an unexpected wave of emotion when Eben threw his arm around his shoulder, their matching blond hair falling together as Eben tilted his head against Liam's.

He showed Eben the picture for approval before hitting send. "Looks good," Eben said, but the softness of his voice seemed to say, "We're good."

As the game extended into the end of the third quarter, Liam started to wonder why this game needed four quarters. Why not three thirds? Two halves? Time dragged and Liam's thoughts became distracted by all the practicing he needed to get done and the writing projects that needed polishing as they moved into the second half of the semester. He toyed with his phone, seeing another set of messages from Mackenzie. There were three notifications from her already waiting.

"Can't feel my toes anymore. Leaving. Text me tonight. Party at ΦMA." And finally, "YOU ARE GOING!"

He was about to write her back when an unusual motion on the field caught his eye. An opposing player in black and gold was speeding up the field like some kamikaze fighter, breaking his way through the protective line of players around Zach. He crashed, shoulder first, right into Zach's side. Zach's hands, still clenched around the ball, were unavailable to brace his fall, and he landed with a disturbing bounce of his head, his helmet whacking face-first into the ground.

"What the fuck!" Liam shouted, standing. His outcry was met with a tempering look from the gents in the suits. "Sorry," he mouthed at them as he sat back down. It was not the first time Zach had been hit this game, but it was the first time he'd been completely blindsided. "They can't do that, can they?" His eyes were still glued to where Zach lay on the field.

"Unfortunately, yes. It's called a sack. The offensive line didn't do a good job protecting him there."

Almost as quickly as Zach had gone down, he reached up and clasped the forearm of the same player who had supplanted him onto the grass. His opponent pulled him to his feet. Zach looked no worse for wear.

"You two have gotten close, haven't you? You and Zach," Eben asked. Zach sat out one play, his helmet off as trainers examined him.

"No," Liam said, with enough fraternal irritation to tell his brother that they most certainly had. He shrugged, hoping to downplay it. "I mean, I guess we're friends. We study together sometimes."

"When I found out I was going to be advising the starting quarterback for the team, I thought, *che palle,* this is going to be a waste of my time. But he's a good kid. Not what you'd expect."

Liam blushed, certain he had just given it all away.

Even with all the clashing and the grunting, the torn-up sod, and their rain-damp uniforms caked with mud, there was a stunning elegance to the way Zach moved on the field. He was light-footed, powerful, and commanding in his play. Liam felt proud to know him. After watching the game, Liam could finally understand the hype. Zach belonged on a field, playing football for as long as he was physically able. It would be an injustice to the universe, and the talents bestowed on him if he didn't.

As the game clock finally ticked down to zero and the two coaches met in the middle of the field to shake hands, Liam was convinced Zach looked up towards the President's box for several long moments, as if searching for Liam's face behind the glass, and smiled.

20

Carrying a secret as massive as the one Zach had borne for the better part of a decade was often a very lonely mission. His resolve had wavered countless times over the years, certain that if he really was the good and decent man he believed himself to be, there was no way he could keep the charade up even one minute longer.

There were the times he'd slithered back to Rebecca's dorm room during his freshman and sophomore years, the memory of some nameless man still burned into his skin. He'd think about how it was fine to mess around on a girlfriend, but that he couldn't do the same to a wife. Especially one whose marriage vows would mean as much as they would to Rebecca. He'd touch her shoulder, warm under the blankets, and choke on the realization that she, above all others, deserved the truth. He'd lie there in hope that, if she truly loved him the way she swore she did, she would find in her devout heart the ability to hate the sin but love the sinner, and offer him absolution.

There had been quiet moments back west on school breaks, sitting by the winter fire with his father while he read his legal briefs or relaxing on the screened-in porch with his mom, the summer air alive with crickets. During those times, he'd feel insecure in himself but safe in his childhood home, knowing he could start the conversation about his sexuality with a simple, "Mom?"

This web of intricate lies, strung up with precision and laced with guilt, had been his alone to maintain. Until now. Now Liam could help Zach shoulder the load. What Zach had with Liam felt anything but false. Instead, it reflected an alternate, authentic version of himself that existed parallel to the one the rest of the world saw. Liam was the other side of the coin, the world behind the veil that made him more riotously happy than he'd ever been before.

In the weeks following Homecoming, Zach was in complete control of both realities. He was Atlas, bearing up the weight of not just one, but two worlds as they spun forward just the way they should, in perfect balance and harmony.

He stole the easy moments he could with Liam before class, chatting like friends—because they were friends. When necessary, Zach manufactured other opportunities that required a bit more mischief but also garnered a greater reward.

On one such night, Zach snuck into the Music School via the loading dock door, the only one propped open for late night practice sessions after the building was officially closed for the night. He walked down the long hallway of the practice rooms. He'd still felt out of place even with a ball cap pulled low over his eyes and wearing an oversized black fleece that Liam had let him borrow with the crest for *Il Luigi Cherubini Conservatorio di Musica* on his chest. He found Liam in the very last practice room, and through the small porthole window Zach could see the back of his head, his body tilting this way and that over the keys with the arc of each phrase. With a soft knock, Zach entered.

Liam didn't drop a single note. "Almost done." He gestured with his chin toward the chair in the corner. The room barely had enough space for the grand piano. The addition of two grown men into the cramped space left Zach with an up close and intimate view. It was the first time he had seen Liam play and would have happily watched and listened all night. Of course, Zach didn't mind when Liam finished his practice, marking something on the page with a pencil before he locked the door behind him, pulled the blind over the window, and pushed Zach's hips back against the keys.

That Saturday, after NU sailed through their day game against Iowa, Zach went to a Halloween party at the Fiji frat house with Rebecca. Even though he didn't drink, he wore the costume she'd picked out for him—a sailor to her mermaid. It was a night out the likes of which they hadn't had since his return from Rome. She looked happy all evening, and Zach found himself enjoying her company as they danced and didn't talk about the future.

He followed her back to her room after, and when she reached for him for the first time since their fight at IKEA, he didn't hold back. Emboldened by all of his experiences with Liam, he stripped her from her costume, laid her back on her bed, and put his tongue between her thighs, something he'd only done, with hesitance, once or twice before.

She keened, arching her back, as Zach imagined that it was not him during this act but Liam with all his interchangeability. Zach tended to one lover even as he embodied the other. When Zach told Liam the next day what he'd done with her, Liam grabbed Zach by the back of his neck and kissed him deeply, seeking the taste of her, though it had long since washed away.

"Do to me what you did to her," he breathed hard against Zach's ear.

"How? You're a guy."

A hot, red blush rushed up Zach's neck as he realized what Liam was asking. Minutes later, Liam mewled into his pillows, completely undone as Zach's tongue found places he didn't know were meant to be sought.

When Coach pulled Zach into his office and began laying into him after practice the following week, Zach defended himself with a level of exacting firmness that he wouldn't have dared express before.

"You missed practice this morning."

"No, I missed an optional workout that only I am expected to do and have done every day for the past four years."

Coach sat back, properly chastened. "Where were you?" he asked.

Liam hadn't left Zach's apartment until nearly 4 a.m. that morning. They hadn't had sex, hadn't even gotten off. Instead, they'd laid in bed together, face to face, talking, laughing, and exchanging delicate touches and long gazes that went soul-deep.

Zach shrugged. "Sleeping." It wasn't a total lie.

"Look, Sugarman. I know it's been a long season. We've got three more regular-season games left before the Big Ten Championship. We're sitting at number one on every list those analysts put out each week. That means we're going to have at least two more post-season games after that. I, for one, am hoping we go all the way to the championship game, so that means one more."

"I'm hoping for that, too. You know I am."

"That's six more games, Sugarman. Now isn't the time to get complacent. We've got this," he insisted. "But you've gotta stay hungry for it."

"Trust me, I have more riding on us winning the title than anyone. I won't let you down." And just like that, he had Coach back on his side.

That weekend, Northwestern beat the University of Illinois by nearly thirty.

A few days later, Zach walked into Liam's bedroom to see him standing at his massive bedroom windows, watching the first snowfall of the year. It was not cold enough for it to stick, but it made for a beautiful sight. Zach settled in from behind, his arms encircling Liam's hips.

"One of my first thoughts upon seeing this apartment was 'Man, it sure would be fun to fuck someone in those windows.'" Liam snorted. "God, I'm twisted."

"Have you managed to yet?"

"Well, have you had sex in front of this window yet?"

"No."

"Then, no." Liam's shoulders shifted uncomfortably, aware

of what he'd just admitted to with his rapid-fire answering.

Zach saved him the distress by not trying to catch his eye. Instead, he addressed the falling snow. "No one else?"

"Not since that night at Hillel. Not since Mackenzie," Liam admitted. Zach was overwhelmed.

The following morning, Zach sat on the opposite side of Dr. Barnett's desk without a single nervous twitch to give himself away. He listened intently as his professor went through suggested edits in his thesis, all the while knowing just how he'd had Dr. Barnett's brother the night before. Liam's pure white skin had reflected back on the night-black glass like a mirror. His pale limbs had been splayed wide, his fingers slack in Zach's grasp, as Zach had fucked into his body for the first time—only it had felt nothing like fucking and everything like making love.

And perhaps that fact explained why there was no moment of existential crisis when Zach realized a few days later, as he and Liam did homework side-by-side on his couch, that the inexpressible, baffling, staggering emotion that was crowding in his chest had a very simple name: love.

The word locked into place like a gear that had been out of alignment and now shifted back, allowed the wheels to turn. Those three little words gained speed and momentum in his brain.

"Hey." Zach's pulse flew. He caught one of Liam's curls between his thumb and finger. Liam looked up, the stylus for his music writing software clasped between his teeth.

"What?" he said around the bit of metal, not annoyed, just momentarily extracted from the zone. Zach simply shook his head fondly, thinking surely Liam must already know.

Occasionally, he wondered if he was getting sloppy. If, like Oedipus, all this hubris would bring about his downfall. Perhaps someone had noticed the brightness that was constantly surrounding him. He wondered if someone hadn't noticed the way he and Liam came and went from each other's apartments at all hours. He sometimes thought that Rebecca's post-game Instagram activity had gotten more reasonable and she seemed to be putting less pressure on his time than ever before. But it was their senior year, exams were coming, and everyone was busy.

As November forged onward, Zach and Liam took advantage of Dr. Ellison's flu and their canceled class to grab breakfast together at Zach's apartment. They did nothing more scandalous than eat cereal in Zach's kitchen so Zach could pretend they'd woken up together. But it was then, in that innocent moment, that Zach's two expertly detached universes collided.

Rebecca unlocked his front door and let herself in, mid phone conversation. "Yeah, I'll be there in a sec. I just need to drop something at Zach's first—Oh, shit!"

She jumped when she saw them, just as surprised to find Zach in his apartment as she was to see he wasn't alone. She hung up her call without another word, dropping what looked like an overnight bag from one shoulder and her school bag from another.

"I thought you had class," she said, staring at the pair of them.

Before Zach could even catch Liam's eye, hoping to convey the nauseating feeling in his gut and the grim realization that they'd been caught, Liam stepped forward, reaching for Rebecca's hand with a charming smile on his face.

"You must be Rebecca." Zach's palms began to sweat. He had no clue what Liam was about to do. "Zach's told me so much about you. I'm Liam Barnett. I'm in Zach's Plato seminar. Our professor called in sick today which was a good thing because I'd lost one of my books, so I hadn't done the reading. Turns out I'd left it here, but I didn't realize it until I saw Zach this morning before class. Ahh, I'm a mess."

It was a perfect, unscripted cover story, and he sold it like an Oscar winner.

"Oh." Rebecca smiled hesitantly as their handshake held. She laughed to break the tension. "Liam. Yeah, Zach's mentioned you before."

"Has he now?" Liam turned, lifting his eyebrows at Zach. Zach remained frozen with panic.

"Yeah," Rebecca answered. "He said you really helped him

ALL THE WAY OUT   151

study before for his midterm."

Liam turned again, giving Zach a look, soft and layered, but one only he could read. "Oh, I don't know. I think we helped each other out that night."

The butterflies in Zach's stomach became something very different.

"Liam has class straight through until after three." Zach lifted his bowl of Cheerios. "I offered him breakfast."

"You could have made him more than cereal, Zach," She tutted.

"It's better than what I would have had, which probably would have been nothing. But speaking of my crazy schedule, I should get going." Liam grabbed his bag from the floor just as Rebecca stepped into the kitchen and put her arms around Zach's neck. He gave her a distracted kiss. "See you in class Friday, then?"

Zach nodded over Rebecca's shoulder, mouthing a 'thank you.' Liam blew him a silent kiss on his way out the door.

"Has your blood pressure returned to normal yet?" Liam texted him later that night.

"That was too fucking close," Zach replied.

It took nearly ten minutes for Liam to get back to him. "Look we've been hanging out a lot. We can cool things off if you need to. I get it."

"Don't," Zach wrote back. "No way you're getting rid of me that easy, Barnett."

Liam replied simply and immediately. "xoxo."

Zach began to consider ways he could do this into perpetuity—reach some sort of agreement with Liam once he got drafted in the spring and stay together. There had to be a way he could have football, the man he loved, and finally, some fucking happiness. Zach felt untouchable and was ready to ride that attitude all the way through the rest of an undefeated senior season.

That was—until Northwestern lost.

21

They lost. They fucking lost. That reality was somehow incomprehensible.

Zach sat in Michigan's maize and blue locker room, his chest heaving as he tried to catch his breath. A last-minute Wildcat touchdown would have evened the score and sent the game into overtime. Zach had sent one final Hail Mary into the end zone, the ball sailing into a cluster of players, all scrambling to make the catch. Zach didn't even know who came down with it in the end. All he knew was that it hadn't been someone wearing purple.

It was easy to place blame. He could blame Coach for his play-calling in the last two minutes. He could blame Des for that dropped pass early in the first quarter that would have helped set the tone and quiet the crowd. He could blame Ruiz for getting that targeting penalty and getting ejected, which let Michigan extend a drive that NU's defense had all but stopped. He could blame his offensive line who didn't hold tight enough around him, which resulted in a sack and a forced fumble—only his second that season—which a lumbering Michigan linebacker had picked up and run in for the go-ahead touchdown.

Michigan had wanted the win more than Northwestern had. It had been the Wolverines' last home game of another mediocre season. Their fancy, multimillion-dollar coach's neck had been on the line for several seasons now, and he had needed a signature win. They sure had one now. Zach could still hear their marching band playing their fight song, "Hail to the Victors."

This wasn't supposed to happen.

Logic told him that losses like these were a perfect storm of little mistakes. Moments that, on their own, amounted to nothing, but once stacked one on top of the other resulted in disaster. But Zach was the captain, the QB, the leader. He was the one with all the accolades, with his name on all the award ballots and an all but guaranteed career at the next level. Zach wasn't supposed to mess up like this, and he couldn't help but place the blame squarely at his own feet.

This felt like a sign, too. He'd had everything under control: Liam, Rebecca, Coach, school, the team, his parents. This loss was the first chink in his armor. If the team's perfect record couldn't hold, then what would be next to break in Zach's life?

Des punched him on the shoulder pad. "Fuckin' hell, Z." He was already out of his cleats and jersey and wearing a soft T-shirt with the sleeves cut off. It made Zach realize he'd probably been sitting there in stunned silence for longer than he'd thought.

"Look, if we win next weekend against Wisconsin then we have the tiebreaker advantage over Ohio State and we're still in the Big Ten championship game. Then if we win that, we're golden for the national title."

Zach knew all this. There was still a road to a National Championship, but this loss meant it wasn't a straight line anymore. The final four teams that would compete in the College Football Playoffs, with a chance to win the championship, were selected by a committee, not a computer algorithm. Even a single loss, especially a late-season one, could look very ugly to easily-influenced humans. Zach had wanted to leave the committee with zero doubt.

Des clapped his hand at the base of Zach's neck. "This isn't a death sentence, alright?"

Zach appreciated what Des was trying to do. They'd been in that situation countless times before, sitting together in a locker room after a tough loss, trying to bolster each other's spirits. But the sting was still too fresh, the consequences too monumental, and Zach couldn't stand to hear Des's attempted positivity.

Later, Zach somberly answered questions at the post-game press conference because even after a loss, the press wanted a sound bite from him.

"How does a loss like this make you feel, Zach?"

"How do you think?" he replied, and the collection of reporters tittered softly. "You never expect something like this to happen when we're having the kind of season we're having." He spoke into the mic, his voice resigned. "Days like today prove there is a reason why you always play the game. Sometimes the way you have things planned out just isn't the way they end up."

He avoided looking at his phone for the entire four-hour bus ride home, knowing what he'd find: vicious gloating from the haters on Twitter, messages from his parents that would be sympathetic and concerned. There would be Rebecca's Instagram posts, full of melodramatics that would ring false to Zach in his present state.

Instead, he watched the landscape fly past on I-94 as it shifted from Michigan suburbs to forest to flat open land, stretching into a sinking horizon. They crossed into the Central time zone before the highway began to hug the lake, Saturday night traffic slowing their progress.

"Chin up, son." Coach Williams grabbed Zach firmly by the arm as he exited the bus. Something about the tightness of his grip seemed to add 'And pull it together.' "This was a tough one, but it was a fluke. Something to bring our heads back down to earth. I'll see you at practice Monday, and we'll get 'em next week."

Zach replied, "Yes, sir." He never called Coach "sir," but it slipped out at that moment. Was Coach thinking of that missed workout as much as Zach was?

When he got back to his apartment, Rebecca was there. She

was watching the night game between Georgia and Kentucky with all the lights off and the sound turned low. She flung herself around his neck, saying, "Babe, I'm so sorry." It was hard to tell, but it looked like she'd been crying. He knew Rebecca loved supporting him, but he was surprised she'd shed tears over this loss.

"What happened today?" she asked.

"We lost. That's what happened."

"But how? Everything looked a mess."

"Thank you for that precise analysis, Becca. Very helpful. Can you turn that off, please?" Zach pointed at the TV, not caring just how cold he sounded. The last thing he wanted to see was number-two-ranked Georgia easily win their game and all but ensure Northwestern got knocked out of the top four in the rankings.

Even though he'd showered back in Ann Arbor, he went into the bathroom without another word to Rebecca and cranked the water as hot as it would go. He let the water beat against his shoulders, turning his skin red. It felt like an ineffective self-flagellation.

Rebecca had some cooking show on when he joined her back on the couch. She snuggled close and snapped a picture of the two of them right away, toying with her phone for several minutes afterward which could only mean she'd posted it somewhere.

He could have pretended to feel better if it hadn't been for the way Rebecca kept looking at him, watching him like one would watch a person just home from the hospital, certain they were about to fall ill again. It felt like she was waiting for him to break down just so she could be the one to mend him.

And that was when Zach realized it wasn't the *what* or the *how* of the sympathy he'd been offered that still had him so rankled. It was the 'who.'

He didn't want Des's sound logic. He didn't want Coach's paternal platitudes. He didn't want Rebecca's public empathy.

He wanted Liam. Liam with his bored indifference to the sport, his wry sarcasm that had resulted in a series of texts sent directly after the game ended. "The hell even is a Wolverine?" followed by, "Just Googled. Damn, they're ugly little things, aren't they?"

Liam was probably the only person on the whole planet capable of both distancing Zach from what happened that day and snapping him out of his pity.

"I'm going out," Zach said abruptly.

Zach hadn't realized just how dark his apartment had gotten until Rebecca turned the TV off. "Now?"

"Yes, now." He got his sneakers, tying the laces quickly.

"It's nearly midnight. Where are you going to go?"

"I don't know," he lied.

"When will you be back?"

"Jesus, Rebecca, I don't know!"

The minimal light reflected off the pronounced whites of her eyes. That was a double whammy: profanity and a raised voice. He put on his coat as Rebecca crossed her arms sternly.

"I'm not going to wait here all night for you."

"Maybe I don't want you to."

It was, it appeared, possible to distill an entire six-year relationship down to a convergence point where things were being said without being spoken. Zach could feel revelations for both of them happening in real-time.

"Zachary." Her voice was a line in the sand, an ultimatum.

He left without looking back.

The night air was icy and empty. It was exactly what Zach needed. He walked and found a bench on the edge of campus, away from any streetlamps. He took out his phone and pulled up Liam's number. "Can I come see you?" he wrote.

The reply came swiftly, the first welcome words of the day. "Of course. At a bar give me 15."

22

It started much like their first meeting.

Liam opened his door to Zach, broad and handsome, but emitting an aura of unease. Just like he had that first night, Liam gave Zach the once over. Only this time, Liam was not cruising him but seeking hints as to his mental well-being.

Hearing news of Northwestern's loss had been unavoidable. Even Liam's fellow music students, who could be hit or miss on their devotion to the school team, had been talking about it backstage before that evening's concert.

"Wait, seriously? They lost?" he'd asked Mackenzie as she'd clicked off her phone.

"They lost," she'd mimicked. "They? Seriously? Aren't you the one who's all BFFs with the quarterback now?"

"We have one class together. That hardly makes us pals for life."

Mackenzie had been in no mood for his semantics. "Yes, Liam, we lost." She'd said it with something akin to heartbreak. Like this bit of information could seriously ruin the rest of her evening.

"I thought we were good." He'd felt so confused. How could

the team he'd watched just a few weeks before that had moved like a finely tuned Swiss watch not come away with a win?

"We are. We're really good. And Michigan isn't even ranked. That's what makes it so bad."

Zach had told him enough about how the sport worked to know that even one loss could seriously impact the results of the season. Liam couldn't care less about this one game. But about the team's captain? He cared very much.

The loss had weighed heavily in the back of his mind during the first half of their concert. Liam couldn't help but wonder how Zach was coping. He sent him some texts during intermission. They'd been dry and trivial, maybe, but hopefully enough of a sign for Zach to know he was reaching out. Then Liam had waited for a reply. Liam knew Zach had a network of support around him. His teammates, coaches, parents, and a girlfriend would all certainly be ready to step up to offer Zach comfort via insider perspective and real-life experiences. Liam had never felt more like a useless little plaything with no real impact on Zach's life or future.

He'd gotten Zach's text just as he and Mackenzie picked up another round of post-concert drinks. With the University of Georgia on the verge of losing their game too, she had been feeling more hopeful that Northwestern's loss wasn't the end of the world. He'd bent towards her ear to speak over the noise of the bar. "I gotta go."

She'd swallowed back her shot. "Why?"

"I'm going to meet someone."

Mackenzie had stood, her chair raking across the floor, adding to the overall din. She'd stared at him for a moment, the smallest, triumphant smile spreading on her lips. "I knew it." Her drink had sloshed over the rim of her cup as she'd poked him in the chest with a finger. "I fucking knew it."

"Knew what?"

"That you've been seeing someone! Who is it? Do I know them?"

Liam had been ready to toss out another denial, but of course, Mackenzie could see the truth. After all, they had started walking down that path towards romance themselves, even if only for the length of one night. It was no wonder she could read the signs. But then another group of friends arrived, and Mackenzie got distracted, so Liam was able to sneak out without any more cross-examination from her.

Liam's final assessment of Zach's status was that he just looked tired. It wasn't an exhausted kind of tired though, more a fed-up kind of tired. It seemed like the only thing keeping Zach's bones upright was mental fortitude. Everything about him, from the slope of his shoulders to the arc of his brow said, 'Can we please not talk about it?' So they didn't.

Liam opened the door wide and welcomed Zach in with a sweep of his arm. He took Zach's coat, tossing it unceremoniously on the couch, and then took Zach's hand. His fingers were icy cold.

"Were you out with Mackenzie?" Zach asked as he allowed Liam to lead him to the bedroom.

"And some other classmates."

"Now I feel bad."

"Don't. It was just two-for-one well drinks at Davie's. You've just saved me from a massive hangover tomorrow."

"Glad I could be of service."

"Take your shirt off." Liam pointed at his bed. "Lay down."

"Liam." Zach shook his head sadly, his lashes dropping to glance against his cheeks. "That's not what I came here for."

"No? Shame." Zach looked regretful momentarily until Liam cupped his face, his thumbs finding the bones of Zach's eye sockets. He resisted brushing against those long, dark lashes. "I know that," he whispered, and Zach sighed. "Just trust me, okay?"

Liam went into the bathroom and retrieved a small vial from the back of the medicine cabinet. By the time he came back out, Zach was shirtless, his body wrapped around one of Liam's pillows. He had kicked his shoes off, and they lay in a pile at the foot of Liam's bed. Liam had half a mind to just let Zach be, certain he would be asleep in minutes if he wasn't already. Then one of Zach's eyes popped open, giving Liam a puzzled look.

"Roll over." Liam crawled onto the bed as Zach obeyed. Liam swung one leg over Zach's hips to straddle him. He popped open the vial he gotten in the bathroom and spread its pungent contents on his hand. Zach moaned as the heels of Liam's palms found the deep muscles of Zach's back.

"This okay?" Liam's thumbs swirled through the slippery liquid and pressed again.

"You're way better than the team PT."

"Thanks, I think."

The silence that filled the air felt sacrosanct, a safe space, so Liam let it stretch on. It felt like a silence that only Zach should fill if he needed or wanted to.

Liam continued to work, pressing deep around Zach's shoulders and the muscles that paralleled his spine. Liam lightened up as he reached the skin on Zach's left side. The bruise Zach had gotten from the terrible sack Liam had witnessed in person had faded from Zach's skin. Liam's memory of Zach falling helplessly to the turf had not.

"What is this stuff?" Zach mumbled against the pillow.

"Part lotion, part balm, part tincture. *Una piccola magia.*" Liam laughed at Zach's noise of utter confusion. "So, my parents live in this big old apartment building in Florence, right? If they hadn't bought it in the eighties when the neighborhood was still a little *cosi cosi*, there's no way they could have afforded it. We have the whole top floor. Arched hallways, a fresco ceiling in the living room. You can just make out the top of Il Duomo from my parents' bedroom."

"God. Sounds beautiful."

"It is," Liam agreed. "The kind of beauty you only appreciate once you've moved away from it." Liam recoated his hands before wrapping his fingers around the back of Zach's neck. He pressed the soft space behind Zach's ears, not worrying when a bit of the liquid got into the hair at the base of Zach's skull.

"There was this old man, Signore Fares, who was in charge of the property. Fixed broken light bulbs in the hallways, picked up your mail when you were out of town, let you in when you got locked out, that kind of stuff. He had this amazing garden on the roof. Citrus trees and herbs. How he managed to get anything to grow up there in the direct sun, I have no idea. Eben and I were the only kids in the building for a long time, and we liked to play up there. We'd pretend we were explorers searching for El Dorado or fighting storm troopers in the forests on Endor. I don't know. Stupid boy stuff." They both laughed softly at Liam's childhood ways.

"Anyway, he liked to keep an eye on us. Felt responsible for us, I think. Like whenever one of us fell off our bikes or got into a scuffle with another neighborhood kid, he was always there, ready to take us home to get patched up. Or if it wasn't too bad, he'd lather us up with this stuff, give us a *limonata,* and send us back on our way."

"And did he lure you away into some dark, locked basement with promises of candy?"

Liam shoved Zach lightly in the back. "You've watched too many crime dramas. It wasn't like that at all. He was sweet. I think he was just lonely. He makes this stuff from herbs from his garden. Claims it helps cuts and bruises heal faster. I think it just makes everything feel better."

"Well, I'm certainly feeling better." Zach's eyes were closed and his lips were relaxed into a curved smile. He seemed at ease for the first time since he'd arrived.

Liam flopped down next to Zach on the bed and rubbed the remaining product into his own skin. He pressed the tips of his fingers against his nostrils and inhaled. It smelled like comfort. Zach tucked himself against Liam's side, and they laid there for a while.

Liam's mother had mentioned the possibility of the whole family coming home for a visit next summer. Eben's baby would be a few months old by then. Summer would be the perfect time to introduce the newest member of the Barnett family to his adopted Italian roots.

In a different life, Liam would suggest that Zach come with him. But Zach would never be able to go home with Liam. They'd never stroll through the tourist-filled streets of Florence at sunset before ducking down a side street and into a cafe only the locals knew. Liam would never see Zach's quiet childhood neighborhood only a few minutes from the frigid blues of the Puget Sound—a place Zach spoke of with such fondness.

There were certain parts of each other's lives that were destined to remain stories. Liam supposed, in the end, that's all they would be to each other. Something that happened once, and was thereafter destined to remain hidden like some forgotten myth.

"Today was the first time I questioned whether I really want to play football professionally. It scared the fuck out of me." Zach spoke in a whisper, and Liam lifted his head to catch Zach's eyes.

"Just because you lost?"

Zach nodded. "I know it's just one game, and the loss today wasn't all down to me, and I know the season isn't over. I mean, last I checked the score, Georgia was down against an unranked team too, so we're probably fine. Rationally I know all that, but what if..." The air from Zach's sigh passed over Liam's neck. "What if they're all wrong about me? What if I'm not as good as they think I am?"

"Then you've been pulling the wool over of a lot of experts' eyes for a long time."

Zach huffed softly, the noise not quite a laugh. "Sometimes I feel like a total fraud. Like, if they only really knew the real me... and I don't even mean about this." He squeezed Liam all the tighter. "At least not this time."

Liam savored their closeness before he replied. "I get that way sometimes, too. You're playing a concert and you miss a note or come in wrong, and you just feel like you've ruined this experience that was meant to be perfect—for the audience, the other players, the composer, even if he's been dead for two hundred and fifty years. And you just can't help but think, 'Why bother? I'm clearly terrible.'"

"Yeah, exactly." Zach propped himself up on his elbow, suddenly animated now that Liam understood. "When it all goes right, it's the best thing in the world. But when it goes wrong? It's awful. Do I really want to put myself through this kind of doubt for the rest of my life?"

Football for Zach, much like music for Liam, was not only his future, it was his whole identity. The center of his universe. It was why he woke up in the mornings and why he'd concocted this complicated life he lived. Zach losing football would be akin to losing himself.

Liam caught his fingers in the thatch of hair at the front of Zach's head and grabbed hold, rocking Zach's head back and forth playfully. "Like you'd be happy doing anything else."

Zach smiled, more deeply this time, and settled back against Liam. He could tell Zach's mood had shifted just by the way he dropped his arm around Liam's waist. Zach yawned, his mouth wide, as he started to say, "I don't know, I did always want to learn the saxophone."

"No," Liam half moaned, half laughed. "All the beautiful orchestral instruments in the world and you pick that? Rachmaninoff tried to make the saxophone happen. Prokofiev tried. Ravel tried. It didn't stick for a reason."

"So what?" Zach laughed gently. "I like jazz."

"We should go to a show sometime at one of the jazz clubs in the city."

"Yeah, I'd like that. Once the season's over."

Liam's fingers began a gentle painting of Zach's skin. Zach interrupted the quiet a few moments later.

"Hey, would it be cool if I just stayed here tonight?"

"You are joking, right? I've been trying to get you to have a sleepover at my house since Rome."

Zach lifted himself up again to look at Liam. He wore an expression of such sincerity, such openness, such warmth that Liam was certain he knew the exact words that would come out of Zach's mouth next. Liam flushed as he realized he would say them back. What Zach said instead felt even more transformative.

"I'm so fucking glad I met you."

Liam pulled him down for a kiss, his eyes closing against the warm tears that filled his eyes. Their kiss was long but chaste, one that would lead to comforting sleep and little more. Still, it left stars behind Liam's eyes and a warm happiness in his chest. A little bit of magic, indeed.

—

The only other time Liam had celebrated Thanksgiving in America was the year his grandmother died. He hadn't known his father's mother well. He'd been left with only vague memories of his time with her. He remembered his parents taking him to their home in Maryland as a toddler, pushing him in a stroller to the base of the Washington Monument, and to an aquarium with sharks in the walls. When she'd visited Florence one summer, she had already been old, and his parents had made a massive fuss about her well-being the entire time.

She'd passed in mid-November, so it had made sense for his parents to tack an extra week onto their trip for the funeral to give his father more time to grieve with relatives he'd drifted away from when he had moved to Europe. It also gave Liam and Eben their first real taste of the American tradition.

At six, Liam had a basic grasp on what the holiday celebrated. Without the time off from school like one would have in the States, his parents usually hosted a get-together on some random Saturday in November with other American friends living in Florence. Whole turkeys were nearly impossible to come by in Italy. Even if his parents did manage to track one down, the bird usually wouldn't fit in their European-sized ovens, so the Thanksgiving feasts Liam had been accustomed to always had a decidedly Tuscan flare.

Sleeping on an air mattress in the basement of a distant cousin's home, with attitude spiraling out of his long, skinny limbs, Liam had been ready to show off the prowess of his *scuola elementare* year-one brain. He had picked the holiday apart. "Why did the pilgrims need the Indians to help them? Why couldn't they have grown food on their own? And what did the native people get out of the deal? Why is there a parade, and who is that flying dog?" He had refused to eat the gelatinous cranberries or the limp green beans, but he'd loved the pumpkin pie.

His first Thanksgiving in Chicago would thankfully lack the unfamiliar relatives. Instead it felt like the natural crest to the semester. The break from classes matched the serenity he and Zach had found as well. It had been ten weeks since Rome, almost two months since that night at Hillel, and a month since they had slept together for the first time. Liam and Zach had found a balancing point. Their relationship—and Liam used that word without hesitation—was no longer about frenetic hookups. Instead, it was about drawn-out moments of intimacy, both physical and emotional. There was no fear in Zach's eyes anymore nor willful equivocation in Liam's. The days since Zach's loss at Michigan had felt effortless even as everything remained behind closed doors. Enduring, if only the world were different.

By Tuesday night of Thanksgiving week, the campus was mostly empty as students departed in preparation for the holiday. Liam slept in late on Wednesday and spent the morning drinking coffee with pumpkin spice creamer while he perused food blogs. He stayed in his pajamas as he worked on a composition that was due when the semester ended the following week: *Impractical Pairing for flute and cello,* by Liam Barnett. Dedicated to Mackenzie and Sam. It was a bit gimmicky—a shift from his usual work—but it felt nice to write something lighthearted for a change.

With Rebecca flying home that afternoon, Zach's parents arriving first thing Thanksgiving morning, and the massive, must-win, final home game of Zach's college career against Wisconsin on Saturday night, Liam had made no claims to Zach's time. He knew Zach would see him when he was able. Liam certainly didn't expect Zach to bang on his door Wednesday afternoon and storm through like a steam train.

Zach grabbed Liam immediately and kissed him so hard he nearly fell over. Zach pulled off with a massive smack of his lips and an ebullient smile. He was so breathless he could barely get the words out. "She's been fucking the point guard."

"Who's been fucking the what now?"

"Rebecca," Zach said. "She's been sleeping with Seth Nuñez,

the starting point guard on the basketball team, for the past two months."

Liam was stunned silent as Zach started to pace across the apartment floor. He spoke so quickly and with hand gestures so broad, Liam couldn't help but wonder if Zach was having some sort of manic episode.

"I mean, I could tell she was getting distant, but I just thought she was still holding a grudge about the whole engagement ring thing. How did I not see this? No, I know exactly how I didn't see this." He gestured at Liam. "But she's actually been sleeping with him. Like actual sex. So much for waiting until she's married!" He tossed his head back and laughed. "He even lives in my building, like two stories up from me. I see him in the laundry room all the time. He's pretty cute, but, god, this explains so much! All the times she'd be wearing something weird or show up at my apartment at some weird time. She'd obviously been with him. I can't believe this. Can you believe this?"

This was not the normal reaction of a guy who'd just found out his girlfriend of six years had been cheating on him. But then again, Zach's relationship with Rebecca had always functioned under rather exceptional parameters, even if she had been totally unaware of them.

"When did she tell you?" Liam asked, finally able to get a word in edgewise.

"Just now before she left for her flight. She said she, and I quote, 'couldn't keep living a double life.' She said that. To me." He pointed at his own chest. "Me!" He laughed hysterically again, spinning as he rubbed both his palms across his face.

Zach had just been given a free pass. He was exonerated from what otherwise would have made him look like the worst kind of user. Liam had only met Rebecca once, and his affair with Zach had been Zach's main source of infidelity, but something about his overt schadenfreude sat unpleasantly with Liam.

"You're not upset about this at all? I thought you two had 'plans,' in the big sense of the word. I thought you cared about her?"

"I do."

"So then, six years." Liam snapped his fingers. "Poof."

A bit of wind fell from Zach's sails. "Look, I was never going to be enough for her, just like she was never going to be enough for me. I can't fault her for going out and finding what she needed, especially when I've done that to her more times than I can count. This is better for everyone, including you. Can't you see that? Plus, I think she really likes this guy." He grabbed Liam by both shoulders, attempting to return things back to his more celebratory mood. "Let's go out. Someplace nice in the city."

"Was Rebecca upset?"

Zach sighed heavily. "You're harshing my high here, Liam. You know that, right?"

"It's just, she thinks she's ruined your relationship because she was the unfaithful one."

Zach moved into Liam's orbit. He linked his fingers between Liam's. "Look, I'll text her in the morning, okay?"

"And say what, exactly? 'It's chill, babe, I've been fucking someone else too. And by the way, it's a guy.'" Liam snorted at his own ludicrous suggestion.

"How about I tell her whatever you think is best, hmm? Something about understanding and being thankful for our time together and wishing her joy and wanting to still be friends? It would all be true." Zach turned the charm back on. "Just, please. I want to buy you a drink. Spend some time alone with you. It's almost like you don't want me to take you out on a date."

That word changed things slightly. "A date, huh? You do realize it's the night before Thanksgiving."

"Yes." Zach placed his hands on Liam's hips, then over the flannel pajama bottoms to where the thin fabric covered his ass. He pulled their bodies together. An inviting pressure began to build. "And I've read that the night before Thanksgiving is one of the biggest drinking nights of the year. Ever heard of Drinksgiving?"

"No," Liam snickered. "God, Americans really have stupid names for everything, don't they?"

Zach plastered a wicked smirk on his face. It became all the more dangerous when his tongue slid out to wet his lips.

"You can't even drink during the season," Liam said, firmly removing Zach's hands from his body. "That's a rule, isn't it?" He wandered over to his kitchen counter, pretending to tidy up, but Zach was close behind.

"Oh, Liam. Haven't you noticed I've been breaking my rules for you all along?"

23

The bar on the ninety-sixth floor of the John Hancock Building had a piano in the corner. A youngish looking man plunked away easy renditions of jazz standards and old-time favorites, graciously accepting tips in a rounded glass bowl. After much cajoling—and his third cocktail—Liam summoned the gumption to ask the pianist if he might have a turn on the keys. Happy for an extra break, the musician obliged.

Liam played something short and simple, one of his own compositions that he had written the previous year in Paris before everything had turned to shit. He looked over at Zach, who watched with a proud smile on his face, the single IPA he'd been nursing all night still at his elbow. Zach was the only one who clapped when he finished, but Liam found that was all that mattered.

"Bravo, maestro," Zach said as Liam retook his seat. He grasped Liam briefly by the shoulder.

The evening had been filled with these kinds of touches. Small gestures, that in effusive Italy, where no greeting or farewell went without a kiss or two on either cheek, would be totally *de rigueur*, but here in twenty-first-century middle

America felt totally brazen.

An older gent had recognized Zach when they'd first come in. Wearing a Cubs baseball cap, the man had given Zach a motivating fist pump and a "Go Cats," as they'd ordered their first round of drinks at the bar. Other than that, he and Liam had been left on their own. Perhaps people thought they were old friends or cousins, reunited for the impending holiday. Better yet, maybe people simply weren't looking their way at all.

To Liam, though, they looked very much like two men on a date. Zach had gone home while Liam showered and had returned wearing a blazer with a fancy pale blue polo underneath. Liam had dressed in a crisp, white, collared shirt paired with textured gray trousers. They made for a stunning pair: dark and strong, blond and lean, young, and lost in each other.

The city looked stunning, too, stretched out below them. The Chicago skyline had been like a backdrop to Liam's semester, always there in his bedroom window. Rain, sun, good night, terrible morning, it felt like his skyline now, and Chicago felt like his city. What a difference a few months could make. He couldn't help but look Zach's way with that thought and found Zach's eyes already on him.

"You look so beautiful right now." Zach looked spellbound and in love. Liam felt himself wilt. It was the first time Zach used that particular word. Not sexy, not hot. Beautiful. If this really had been the first date, Zach would definitely be getting a second.

"I wish I could kiss you. Fuck, sorry." Zach immediately blushed. "I'm such a lightweight now." He lifted his drink and finished it.

"Don't be sorry. I wish that too."

"Even if it weren't me, though. Two men? Here? It couldn't happen."

Liam scanned the bar. It had been gradually emptying as the hour grew later. As subtly as possible, he turned his knees towards Zach. Behind the barricade of their long legs, Liam caught the pads of Zach's fingers with his and curled them back into his palm. It was such a simple thing, just holding hands.

They'd never done this before though, not in public, certainly. It made Liam's heart gush and Zach gasp.

"World hasn't ended yet." Liam smiled softly.

Zach squeezed back. His eyes flitted anxiously over Liam's shoulder before he finally let go. "The world shouldn't care about how two people feel, but plenty of people still do, huh?" Liam nodded in commiseration. "You've never been, you know, harassed or anything, have you?"

"No," Liam said, lifting his drink. It was more ice than gin by then. "The music world is a pretty universally safe space. And I'm not saying Europe isn't without its bigots, but it tends to be more progressive on the whole. The times I've been with a guy, I've been lucky."

Zach's face turned serious as he looked out the window into the night. Liam wondered whether the cavalier way he'd embraced the end of his relationship with Rebecca might be catching up with him. Perhaps he'd finally remembered exactly what was at stake.

"So, you'll probably start dating another girl, then, won't you?" Liam asked. It wasn't a critique, just a genuine question.

"Rebecca and I did just break up, like," he checked his wrist for a non-existent watch, "five hours ago. I should probably wait a little longer before I move on."

"I don't know," Liam mused. "They always say the best way to get over a girl is to get under..."

"You?" Zach's lips shaped around the vowel, and for as cute as he looked, Liam gave him his best annoyed face. Zach was avoiding the question and he knew it. He propped his chin in his hand and exhaled. "Rebecca certainly did make things easier for me for a long time," he eventually admitted. "She provided all the smoke and mirrors without me really having to try. And the fact she didn't want to sleep with me—God, it was perfect. Seems cruel to put someone else in that position again."

"You could always tell her, whoever this next girl is. Explain to her why her boyfriend or husband isn't exactly up to his marital duties." Liam meant that to be a teasing dig, but for Zach, it seemed to be a moment of realization. His expression turned sad.

"But what a miserable life for her. For both of us."

"You really never can come out, can you?" Liam asked, with total empathy.

"After I've stopped playing, maybe, though I doubt the sport would be thrilled to have a gay coach any more than a gay player. And I'd like to do that after my playing career is over." Zach lifted his face towards Liam, a sudden bout of worry across his face. "That doesn't change things for you, does it?"

Way more than he ever thought it would, Liam realized. For Zach's sake, however, he merely shook his head. "Take me home, Zach," he whispered, leaning in closer than necessary. "Make me yours for as long as you're able."

24

Maybe it was because they knew they'd have all night and most of the morning. Maybe it was because for the first time in his whole life Zach wasn't cheating on someone. Maybe it was the minute alcohol flowing in his veins. Whatever the reason, their lovemaking reached new levels that night. Zach felt closer to Liam than ever before, but it was still not nearly enough. As Liam used fingers, lips, and the full stretch of his own body to prime Zach, he wondered what it would be like to have Liam, skin to skin, unprotected, without the antiseptic delay of latex. Zach knew he was clean. He trusted Liam to be so, too; he was too savvy not to always be safe with his lovers. It would be as easy as stilling Liam's hand with a soft, "Don't bother," Zach thought.

But as Liam reached for protection, a repentant smile on his face and whispered, "Safety first, right?" Zach realized this was a conversation for a different night.

Even with the condom between them, Zach felt their bodies fuse together, which was nothing less than exactly what they deserved. Zach's ribs were Liam's ribs. His lungs, Liam's. Two hearts, one body. One soul.

Liam was already awake, drinking coffee at the small raised counter in the kitchen by the time Zach pulled himself out of bed the next morning. They'd slept through the Macy's Thanksgiving Day Parade, and now the NFL pregame show was turned on for Zach's sake, but muted for Liam's. Zach danced his fingers over the bumps of Liam's spine, just visible through the thin fabric of his silky robe. Liam lifted his face to be kissed, so Zach obliged.

"What time are your parents expecting you?" Liam asked.

"Too soon." With another quick kiss to Liam's cheek, he went to the sink, rinsing out a mug when he couldn't find a clean one. Liam clicked off his phone and set it down before crossing his arms on the counter.

"You going to tell them about Rebecca?"

"Guess I should, huh?"

"How do you think they'll take it?"

"They'll be surprised, for sure." Zach poured himself some coffee from Liam's fancy Italian pot. "My mom will be elated, though she'll try to hide it."

Liam gave him a surprised look. "Really?"

"She was never Rebecca's biggest fan. Always wanted me to find 'a nice Jewish girl.'" Liam smirked at his air quotes. "I wish you could come with me."

"And you'd introduce me as what, exactly?"

"My study partner?" Liam snorted through his nose. Zach's suggestion could never fly. "What about you? When you going to your brother's?"

"In a bit," Liam said. "All of his in-laws are going to be there—all of them—including his mother-in-law who is a neurotic monster and his sister-in-law who is always plying me with drinks involving peach schnapps. I think she has a crush on me." Liam groaned, throwing his head on top of his arms dramatically. "Now I do wish I could go with you."

Zach reached across the counter and tussled Liam's hair.

With their coffees in hand, they made their way to the couch. Zach turned the TV volume up just enough to hear it but not enough to annoy Liam, who happily opened his laptop, crossing his feet on the coffee table. Zach's attention was drawn momentarily to those naked toes, and that's when he saw a neatly folded piece of paper nearby with Liam's name listed on the front in bold font. Zach picked it up and turned to Liam.

"What's this?" He didn't mean the program itself; he could read the concert title, venue, date, and time well enough. "Why didn't you tell me about your performance?"

"It's not like you would have come."

"Of course, I would." Zach opened the bi-fold paper and scanned the titles, taking a small thrill from seeing Liam's name listed as the composer not once, but twice. "You know I love listening to your stuff, and I hardly ever get to hear it live."

"That wouldn't have been conspicuous at all. Zachary Sugarman at a School of Music concert?" Liam snorted. He shut his laptop and pushed himself up off the couch with a hand to Zach's thigh. "Refill?"

"People know we're friends, Liam." Zach ignored his question.

"Yes, but friends don't come to end-of-semester composition studio recitals—not unless they're playing in it, too." He blew some steam across his refreshed mug before joining Zach back on the couch. "I can hide in a stadium, Zach. You can't hide in a concert hall."

Zach fingered the corner of the paper. He thought of Liam's bout of questioning last night about duping another girl into dating him, marrying him, perpetuating this dishonest life. He thought about how close he had felt to Liam the night before, and all he was being forced to miss by not being Liam's partner.

"What if I don't want to hide anymore?"

Liam looked at him like he'd gone mad. "Don't be stupid." Liam shoved his hand in Zach's face, almost like he was smashing Zach with an imaginary pumpkin pie. Liam had completely missed the serious tone of Zach's voice. Or if he hadn't, he was choosing to ignore it.

"Besides," Liam twisted, grabbing his phone off the side table before settling back on the corner of the couch, his feet tucked up so his knees nearly reached his chin, "then we wouldn't be able to use the super sneaky emoji text code I've come up with to get us through today."

Zach was forced to abandon his life-altering musings as Liam crawled into his lap, a puckish smile on his lip. Zach's phone buzzed in his pocket. *Seriously?* he asked with a single look. *Seriously,* Liam replied with a look of his own.

Liam had sent him several heart eyes followed by a rain cloud. "Okay, so that's for when I'm remembering the blow job you gave me in the shower last week."

Zach's head fell back against the couch cushions as he laughed indelicately. Next, Liam sent a sleeping face. "Well, I think I know that one means."

"Bored," they intoned at the same time.

Liam typed again and they waited that fraction of a second for the data to rocket into outer space before zooming back onto Zach's phone. It was an eggplant followed by squirting water. Zach laughed again. Liam was just too much sometimes.

"What exactly are you planning on getting up to at your brother's house today, anyway?"

"I don't know," Liam stated innocently. "Turkeys take a long time to cook."

One final text came through. A long series of eye roll emojis.

"Let me guess. When that sister-in-law gets handsy?"

"No. This is for when I'm annoyed you aren't close by to service my needs."

Zach looked up at him. "In other words, it's how you'll tell me that you miss me."

Liam pouted thoughtfully, tossing his phone away and circling Zach's neck with his arms. "It's not so much that I miss you. It's more I just hate everyone who gets to be with you when I'm not."

It was quintessential Liam: revealing a depth of affection, if only you knew how to read between the lines. Luckily, Zach considered himself fluent. He flipped Liam onto the couch with ease, settling gently between his hips.

"For the record," he said. "I hate everyone that's around you when I'm not too."

Liam smiled into their kiss as they made Thanksgiving

memories together.

—

The second Saturday after Thanksgiving, Zach was riding high. The lowest low he'd felt after the Michigan loss was nothing compared to the euphoria he felt after winning the Big Ten Championship game.

"This is just the first championship, boys." Coach was giddy, his hair sopping wet from the post-game celebrations.

They hadn't been allowed champagne to spray all over the locker rooms like professional teams did—half the team was still underage, after all—but the team managers had instead snuck in a small armory of water guns. The effect had been the same. Zach's jersey was positively soaked through from the friendly, ecstatic fire, right down to his pads.

"We got one more championship to go," Coach was saying. "We took care of Wisconsin on our home turf to finish the season and got that regular season title. Then we came here to Indianapolis and got that Big Ten Playoff title. And next? Next, we're going to go to Pasadena." There was a small surge of affirmative cheers after each statement. "We're going to get those Rose Bowl rings."

"I already got my finger picked out for it and everything, Coach!" Des yelled from where he stood at the back of the room. Ruiz was next to him, streaming the whole locker room bedlam to his Instagram.

"It's going to look real pretty on you, Des," Coach agreed.

The communal enthusiasm was growing, a compounding ripple just waiting to burst as Coach stalked across the front of the room. Zach loved the way Coach Williams could rile everyone up without resorting to shouting. He had enough power in his words, like some great orator of old.

"Then we're going to bring it back, right here, to Indy. This is our field, now. We own it." Zach cheered the statement using his best captain's voice. "One month, boys," Coach stated, holding up a single finger. "If we keep working hard for one more month, I promise you—I promise—we will be National Champions."

The locker room erupted into a shower of cheers. Zach's voice was raw by the end. He was certain he'd never sung the fight song louder or with more affection.

The bus ride home had a similar party atmosphere as Zach eventually settled in the back of the bus with Des. There was music playing from phone speakers, loud laughter, broad smiles, and high-fives from players and staff alike. It was a remarkable moment, made all the better because Zach was sharing it with his best friend. Zach gave Des a high five and a fist bump, confident that Des was feeling equally sentimental, even if he didn't say it.

There was a single text from Rebecca, somber, and conciliatory. "So happy for you, Zach. Call me over winter break if you want. It would be good to talk."

They hadn't gone so far as to announce their breakup publicly on any social media platform, but considering she'd spent most of Thanksgiving break tweeting sad breakup song lyrics and about the Maui Invitational Basketball Tournament, Zach figured people would catch on soon enough.

Liam's one message had been sent only moments after the game ended, which meant he'd been watching. "Sparta falls! Fuck yes."

Against habit and his better judgment, Zach left Liam's text on his phone rather than deleting it because at some point between Thanksgiving break and that moment on the bus, racing past the steel mills outside Gary, Indiana, Zach had come to a decision. Much like that morning all those years ago when he'd faced himself in his bathroom mirror and identified himself as gay, Zach felt no panic at this realization, just the calm that came with knowing something with utmost certainty.

By the time they arrived back on campus, it was nearly midnight, and the temperature had dropped considerably. Most of Zach's teammates, exhausted and cold, left quickly, but Zach found himself lingering. He played the part of the team captain, making sure everyone had all their gear, and the senior, savoring every last nuance of his final season.

"Sugarman." Coach Williams approached from behind where

Zach was staring up at the giant Northwestern sign illuminated above the stadium's main entrance. "You did it," he said, pulling Zach into a hug. They'd hugged plenty after the game, but this one felt different. Less coach to player, more father to son.

The first time Zach had come to Evanston was for a recruitment trip. His junior season had just ended with a defeat, losing the State Championship by just one point. He'd already done well at the combine in Atlanta the summer before, so between that and his near-victory at the state level, he'd picked up plenty of interest from schools across the country. Most people assumed he'd stay out west and go to Oregon, Stanford, or University of Sothern California. Northwestern hadn't really been on his radar.

Nevertheless, he'd flown out to Illinois for that January weekend along with Des. They'd been allowed to skip eighth period to make their flight and were chauffeured to the airport in a black Escalade. Their seventeen-year-old selves could hardly get over their coolness.

He'd loved the Northwestern campus, the lake, the proximity to Chicago, and the offer of a full ride. Plus, the chance to start as a first-year freshman wasn't bad either. He'd also loved that he'd be able to do all of this with his best friend.

But most of all, he'd loved Coach Williams. Zach loved the steady way he commanded respect from the players, treating them as individuals, and with unexpected kindness. He loved the way Coach spent several hours going over the video of his losing championship game with Zach, explaining why he would have made a different call for particular plays and how he would have coached Zach to move differently or selected a different receiver to complete the play. He'd been patient and nurturing, a true teacher of the game.

Coach had suggested a book for Zach to read that weekend. "I would give you a copy myself if the NCAA wouldn't crack down on me for recruitment violations," Coach had said with a wry smile. The book was called *The Inner Game of Tennis,* and Zach downloaded it to his phone the second he left campus. In it, the author suggested ways to silence the "inner critic," as he called it, the voice inside one's head that could derail an athlete during competition. This was the voice that was judging instead of concentrating. It was the voice that latched onto past mistakes instead of letting go and adjusting in the present.

Zach had read it on the flight home, touched to the core that Coach Williams could already sense the self-doubt that plagued Zach. He'd arrived home knowing he wanted to be a Northwestern Wildcat.

Zach pulled back from Coach's hug. "Two more games, right?"

"You bet." Coach appeared pleased that his locker room words had gotten through. "But it's okay to celebrate this one, too. No matter what happens in your future, no one can ever take this from you, Zach. Don't ever forget that. I know I won't."

The moon was bright white overhead. The frigid wind and the sincerity of the moment created a tightness in Zach's chest. "Do you think it would be alright if I spent some time here? On my own?" Zach asked. "It's just kinda hit me I'm never going to play here again."

Coach clasped his upper arm. "As far as I'm concerned you can stay all night. Stay until next season, even. Sure would make my job easier."

Zach laughed, the brief exhale instantly creating a white puff of air in front of him. "I'm not so sure about that."

Coach picked up his bag, his keys already in hand. His BMW was parked nearby. "I'm gonna miss you, Zach. And not just on the field."

As Coach started to walk away, Zach asked offhandedly, "I never thanked you for Rome, did I? I mean, not properly, at least. I know you could have taken the team anywhere, but you went there. For me." Coach was getting emotional, his thoughtful face becoming more wistful. It had been a long season for him, too. "That trip changed my life in ways I'm still discovering," Zach said.

"Now you're just making me cry, Sugarman, and it's too damn cold to cry." Coach turned back one last time, saluting Zach with two fingers before unlocking his car, turning the key in the ignition, and driving away.

Zach waited until he could no longer see the taillights of Coach's car before getting his phone out. He bit his gloves, pulling them off to type as quickly as possible with both thumbs. "Meet me at the stadium."

Liam didn't leave him waiting long. "I see. You win one championship and suddenly you're making demands." He followed up, saying "Why?"

"Just get your ass over here."

"Little more specific locale, please? Stadium isn't exactly small."

"You'll know." Zach shivered as he sent the final text. He wasn't sure his goosebumps had anything to do with the temperature. He sent one last text, just in case. "Wear a hat though cause it's fucking freezing."

25

"**H**oly shit." Liam's voice sounded impossibly small as he emerged from one of the tunnels and onto the field.

He'd taken an Uber from his place. The driver had given him an odd look when he'd asked to be taken to the stadium.

"You know the game was hours ago and in a different state, right?"

Liam had simply flounced back in his seat and let Zach know that he was on his way.

The lights at the south gate were on, so that's where he asked the driver to drop him off. Miraculously, the wrought iron fencing was unlocked. Beyond the gate was a ground-level tunnel out to the field, its lights on while the others around it remained dark. Zach was lighting Liam's way to him, a fluorescent trail of rose petals.

Spaces as large as Ryan Field compel the gaze upwards, so Liam craned his neck, trying to take it all in. He felt like he'd just stepped out onto the world's biggest concert stage, and at the very center of it, with his hands clasped gently behind his back and a knit cap pulled low over his forehead, was Zach, attentively awaiting Liam's approach.

Liam came to stop with his toes just over the mid-field line. He wasn't sure what was happening or why Zach had asked him to come to the field. Whatever it was, though, Zach seemed happy about it. He pulled Liam by the wrist into a massive hug before kissing him soundly on the lips. Zach's nose was as rosy-cold as his cheeks; his face was molded out of pure happiness.

"What do you say?" Zach asked, lightly. "You up for a game?"

"Um. No." Liam spun out of Zach's grasp and caught Zach's lighthearted look. Zach had known what Liam's response would be; he hadn't even brought a ball.

The grass was brittle under Liam's boots, icy and trimmed to precision. Without the stadium lights on, the rows upon rows of purple bleachers that stretched up on either side of him looked nearly black. Even so, Liam could make out the huge Northwestern "N" imprinted in white on the back of the seats. The scope of this space had been totally skewed the times he'd watched a game in person or on TV. The field seemed far smaller when viewed from a distance or on a screen. But there at eye level, gaining even a single yard of the hundred that stretched from end zone to end zone felt like an impossible feat. The immensity only further highlighted Zach's talents.

"It must be deafening during a game," Liam said. Zach caught Liam by his elbow and playfully pulled him back against his chest. Liam relaxed into Zach's frame, tapping into that basal stillness that flowed through his limbs whenever he was with Zach.

"Even if they're booing, they're making noise for you. Who knows, maybe one day you'll perform for a stadium crowd."

"I'm not the Rolling Stones. Or Beyoncé."

Zach shrugged with a non-committal noise. "Hey, you never know. It's the biggest rush in the entire world—the crowd, the band, the cameras—but then needing to shut all that out and just focus on the game. It's addicting. There's only one other thing in the world that's ever felt as good," Zach whispered that last bit, nuzzling his face into the warmest part of Liam's neck. Liam shivered at the touch even as he snickered at Zach's cheesy line. "Hey, come on. Don't," Zach complained with laughter in his voice. "I'm trying to create a moment here." He spun Liam so they were face-to-face.

"I came back to school for my senior year to win a championship. And Liam, I'm so close. So close." His eyelids fell softly closed, almost like it pained him to imagine the cruelty of faltering now.

Liam rubbed his mitted hands over Zach's arms in support. Six months ago, he would not have even known what Zach was talking about, let alone cared in the slightest. But now he did. He wanted nothing short of everything for Zach.

"All that I've accomplished this season," he motioned at the stadium, "I've done while giving in to the one thing I thought would hold me back. I've found the one thing I thought I could never have." He cast a pointed but gentle glance down to Liam. "If I win these next two playoff games like I know I can, no one can tell me that I can't be who I really am anymore." He took a quick inhale of frigid air. "Which is why I'm going to do it." He gave a final determined nod. "I'm going to come out."

Liam took a few steps back from Zach. Every single, below-freezing degree of the night air flooded his veins. "But, you said from the very beginning that you never could. You can't, Zach."

"I can because I already have. Don't you see?" Zach closed the space Liam had created with a single step. "I can be both, Liam. Football player and gay. This past semester has shown me that. I've won games this season, I've led my team, all the while sleeping with a man. Falling in love with him." All urgency slipped from Zach's face, replaced with tender simplicity. His breath swirled visibly around them. "I love you, Liam. And I want to hold your hand on the way to class. I want you to meet my parents and not have to hide how much you mean to me. For once in my fucking life, I just want to be honest, and the truth is that I want to be your boyfriend. God, who knows?" Zach's head tipped forward so their hat-covered foreheads touched. "In a few years, maybe we'll be even more than that."

"More?" Liam pulled back. He swallowed slowly as he scanned Zach's eyes, dark and pretty. "You want to..."

Zach was smiling. He seemed bewilderingly at ease with

the idea he was promoting. "Haven't you ever thought about it? 'Cause I know I have. What our life might look like if you and me—"

"Yes," Liam answered too quickly. He felt like he'd just answered Zach's proposal, and, for a second, Liam found himself believing in some perfect utopia where Zach lost nothing and they gained everything. But just as quickly Liam regrouped, slamming them both back down to the frozen earth.

"Okay, so say you do this. Say you come out." He began pacing while Zach listened intently. The first glimmer of concern spread across Zach's brow. "Maybe Ellen invites you onto her show and the Human Rights Campaign names you their Person of the Year. What about the other half of this country?" Liam asked. "What about the vocal, vicious other half that thinks two men together are a sin or an abomination? Doesn't that same half make up a large portion of the fans who fill professional stadiums every Sunday afternoon?"

Zach opened his mouth, most likely to protest Liam's blanket political stereotyping but Liam cut him off with a halting hand. "What if you aren't drafted at all? Or you are, but some bigoted opposing coach tells his players to target you with the intent to hurt you, or worse? What if your career is over before it even starts?"

"Then it would be worth it 'cause I'd have you."

"But then, what if in a few years you decide you don't even want to be with me anymore?"

"Not possible." The edge in Zach's voice gave Liam pause. He turned to look where Zach stood, defiant and determined, unmovable by any amount of reason. Zach meant what he was saying and was acting ridiculous and daring enough with his whole future that he might actually do it. Zach would throw this all away—for Liam.

With the moonlight cascading across Zach's wide shoulders, Liam had never been prouder knowing any man in his whole life. He felt lucky to call Zach his friend and his lover.

An image flashed through his memory, one he hoped he'd carry with him for the rest of his life. In his mind's eye, he saw that first glimpse of Zach in his doorway in Rome. He'd been tanned and hesitant, yet willing to seek out a total stranger for even a taste of happiness. That man and the one who stood before Liam in the frigid dark were so clearly one and the same. Perhaps Liam had fallen in love with Zach right then, on that first night. And maybe one day, Zach would find a way to forgive him for it.

Liam contorted the sob bubbling in his chest into a vicious laugh instead. Zach flinched at the sound.

"You've known me for all of what? Four months?" Liam asked with a whip-quick shift in tone. Zach nodded. "And now you're talking about marriage? We met on Grindr, for fuck's sake, because we were accidentally in the same city at the same time and we were both horny. And yeah, things got intense, but we thought we'd never see each other again."

"So?"

"So," Liam cocked his head as if pitying him, "no one meets the love of his life on Grindr."

"I did."

Liam clenched his jaw. Why was Zach making this so impossibly difficult for him? Liam upped the attack. "You only think that because I'm your first," Liam said with a detached wave of his hand. "Go fuck a few more guys and then get back to me."

"Don't say that." Zach grabbed Liam, then said it again. "Please don't say that, Liam."

The way Zach's voice cracked over his name was enough to break Liam's heart. Zach's fingers curled around Liam's elbow, desperate and pleading and so painfully familiar.

"You know what I think this is?" Liam dove back in. He finally worked up the courage to meet Zach's eyes, throwing him a narrowed, accusatory look. "I think this is about Rebecca. I think you're actually pretty broken up about your picture-perfect wife leaving you for some other hot shot on campus, so you just imprinted that same fantasy onto the next warmest body."

"Fuck you." Zach's hand finally fell away. He stepped back

from Liam with a stuttering breath.

"Well, you did do that, didn't you? Pretty decently too, for a virgin." Liam quite literally felt sick from the vitriol he was spewing. All he wanted was to escape this scene and be allowed to hate himself in peace. But Zach wouldn't let him.

"Don't do this," Zach pleaded softly. Tears fell freely from his eyes. "I know you, Liam. And I know you love me too. Please, just tell me you love me. Just say it, cause then none of this other stuff matters—

"This was always going to end, Zach!" Liam interrupted with a shout. His voice, loud and final, echoed in the stadium. He needed a moment to catch his breath. Each shallow inhale was full of ice and anguish. "So, consider it finished."

Liam couldn't stop the tears that broke through his hate-filled veneer, not when realization finally passed across Zach's face and it looked so very much like defeat. Liam stepped in close, brushing Zach's jaw with the backside of his hand. The fibers of his glove caught in Zach's stubble, almost like even they did not want Liam to let go. He hoped the slight tremble in his fingers did not belie the cruel touch he meant it to be.

"At least we'll always have Rome, right?" He offered one final, ruthless salvo. With a toss of his head to shake off the tears, Liam turned. He stuffed his hands into his pockets and walked back the way he came, ignoring the way Zach's voice was carried off by the wind, desperately calling his name.

26

The entire team had assembled in the atrium of the student
union to watch the Championship selection show. The space
was decorated for the broadcast with massive purple banners
hanging from the ceiling, rippling occasionally when the
heating system kicked on. The cheerleaders and members of the
marching band formed a ring around the second-floor balcony.
It was a massive moment, not just for Zach as an individual
player or the team as a whole, but for the entire University.
It was a chance for NU to be in the national spotlight, so the
university had put its best foot forward.

Zach sat front and center along with the other seniors and
Coach Williams. The rows behind him were filled with the rest
of the team, staff, and trainers, all in their matching purple
tracksuits. The Athletic Director and members of his office, the
operations managers from the stadium, and other fancy people
in suits that Zach didn't recognize sat in the back. His parents,
who had driven up that morning from the game in Indianapolis
the day before, were somewhere in the crowd too.

The ESPN camera crew had its bright lights shining from
behind a bank of television monitors so the team could watch

the broadcast in real-time. Outside, there were trucks ready to livestream their reactions and splice them into the same broadcast.

"We begin with the number one overall seed, earning an automatic berth to the Rose Bowl in Pasadena, CA on New Year's Eve. After winning the Big Ten regular season title outright and also beating Michigan State yesterday to secure a Big Ten playoff victory..."

The room erupted into waves of sound even before the sportscaster's announcement was complete. Zach jumped to his feet. He clapped his hands. He cheered. He smiled. He high-fived Des and pulled him into a strong hug. He accepted a hearty handshake from Coach Williams.

He felt nothing.

Somehow, Zach had managed to walk off that frozen field the night before and found his way back to his apartment. He'd woken up that morning on top of his blankets with his shoes still on. His brain—his heart—was still there on the field, shivering as he watched Liam walk away.

What Zach felt wasn't grief, at least not yet. This was shock. A numbing mix of nausea, anxiety, and crippling distress all twisted together, writhing in his stomach. Liam's words didn't feel real yet. Zach was unable to process the way Liam had not only torn his colossal decision down, but then ripped every beautiful thing they'd created together into jagged little pieces. It was nearly impossible to bear, especially after Zach had offered him so much.

The broadcast ended almost as quickly as it began, and the resulting scene overwhelmed Zach. Everyone seemed to be looking to their captain in the noise of the celebratory crowd. News crews wanted a sound bite from him and an All-American smile. But Zach just couldn't be who they wanted him to be. His thoughts and heart lagged pitifully behind.

Needing to get away before people started to notice the anxiety raging in his veins, he worked his way towards the back of the room, excusing himself from eager teammates and coaches with what he hoped were polite smiles. He brushed past his dad as he reached out to clasp Zach's arm, spinning away almost like he would from a defensive player on the field. His dad let out a disgruntled huff.

"I just need a minute," Zach explained. He pressed a quick kiss to his mom's cheek but escaped before she could even offer her congratulations.

Once out of the atrium, Zach made a break for it, pushing his way through a set of fire doors and down a long hallway. He found some privacy in an empty meeting room. A motion sensor light clicked on as the door closed behind him, filling the space with compact fluorescent light. All the air in the room felt caught too high in Zach's chest. He couldn't get enough down into his lungs to get a proper breath.

The logical part of his brain identified that he was having a panic attack, but reason did nothing to help him as his heart continued to race. He dropped to a chair, his elbows propped so he could wedge the heels of his hands against his eyes. He pushed so hard he saw stars. His breaths shallowed and began to multiply. Inhales and exhales tumbled over each other, until they dissolved into erratic sobs. Zach couldn't remember the last time he'd cried this hard.

There was nothing false about what he and Liam shared. It was all openness and expression—ironic considering that theirs was a completely secret affair. But Zach had performed the whole fake relationship act long enough to be able to tell the difference. He knew emotional connections like the one he felt with Liam did not exist in isolation. Feelings as deep as Zach's could not be felt unilaterally or in a vacuum. There was no way he could have fallen so deeply if Liam hadn't been there next to him, falling at the exact same rate.

He knew Liam loved him. Zach had known for weeks now. Zach could see that truth in the curve of Liam's lips at the top of the John Hancock building, and he could feel it while lying in bed together on Thanksgiving night. The truth of Liam's love had been there the night before when Liam had admitted to imagining a future together. The truth was even there in his purposeful cruelty, as he said anything he could think of to get

Zach to hate him. It was there in his departing tears and in the way he'd reached out for Zach one last time like he'd been desperate to preserve a memory.

"Knock, knock." Des rapped his knuckles against the meeting room door in time with his words. He peeked his head around the door frame. Zach couldn't be sure if it was the sight of his best friend or the emotional catharsis of his crying fit, but he was finally able to fill his lungs with a satisfying breath. The universe began to feel centered back along the plumb line.

"Yo, Cap," Des's voice was soft with concern at the state of Zach. There was no use trying to hide his wet, red eyes now that Des had already seen him. Des pulled up a chair next to Zach and put a comforting hand on his back. "Hey, man. I know this is a lot, but these are happy tears, right?"

Zach laughed around a sob and sniffed. "Obviously not."

Des seemed lost for a moment because this should have been a life- and career-defining moment of elation. "This is about Rebecca, isn't it? That two-timing bitch."

"Do not call her that," Zach demanded so emphatically it set Des back a bit. "This has nothing to do with her. And to be honest, I'm happy she's moved on."

"Okay." Des's voice was still filled with hesitant confusion. "Then what's going on, man?"

Zach thought of the day he and Des met. Everyone at their middle school had seemed hesitant about the new kid with the gentle, Haitian French accent and the different colored skin. Zach had noticed the way Des watched a pick-up game of flag football after school, desperate to play, and had asked Des to join his team.

After that had come years of sleepovers playing Xbox until 3 a.m., travel league, awkward school dances, and JV football. They were inseparable through summer institutes, injuries, Homecoming Court, hoping Des's parents didn't come home during parties in his basement, and fights with teammates. There had been the State Championship games lost and won, Prom, after-Prom parties, and moving halfway across the country together. If Zach couldn't tell Des the truth, how was he supposed to tell the rest of the world?

Zach clasped his hands together. He pressed them to the table so they didn't tremble. "I'm going to tell you something that might make you hate me."

"Shut up."

"No, I'm serious, Des." Zach turned to face him as he felt tears start again.

"Yeah, and so am I. You're my brother. You know that," Des said, just like Zach had known he would. He reached for Zach's shoulder, companionable and strong. "There is nothing you could say that's gonna change that."

"Nothing but this."

"You're freaking me out, man."

"I'm gay."

It was like ripping off a Band-Aid, but instead of the sharp sting dissipating in a flash, the burn intensified as Des scooted his chair back away from Zach.

"What did you say?" he asked with hushed confusion.

"I'm gay." Zach hadn't said those exact words out loud since that long-ago morning in front of his bathroom mirror. Repeating them twice, in the course of a minute, felt immense. "Not only that, but I've been sleeping with a guy all semester behind everyone's back."

"You can't be."

"I am."

An expression spread across Des's face that Zach interpreted as abhorrence. His worst nightmare of rejection had come true, first by Liam, and now by Des. Maybe Liam had been right. Maybe he really couldn't do this, regardless of all he had achieved. Maybe the closet was the only place he'd ever be safe, respected, or loved.

"I knew it. I knew you'd hate me."

Des put up a halting hand in Zach's direction. "Will you just give me a fucking second before you start putting words in my mouth? This is just really is not what I was expecting you to say, like, at all." After a long moment of silence and a tempering exhale Des asked, "How long have you known?"

Zach lilted his head sadly, emoting a touch of desperation in the answer he gave. "I've always known."

"So Rebecca?"

"For a long time, she was the person I thought I would be with for the rest of my life. Truly. I had myself convinced that being with her was going to make me happy. If not happy, at least okay. But at the end of the day, she was just a beard. A cover. I mean, she's my friend, and I care about her. But I was never really in love with her."

Des acknowledged the answer with a soft nod, then sat with it for a long while an unreadable series of thoughts passed across his face. Then he turned towards Zach and punched him square in his non-throwing shoulder.

"Fucking—Ow!" Zach cupped his arm tenderly. "The hell, Des?"

"How long have we been friends, man? What have we been through, you and me? Fucking everything." He enunciated each syllable of the last word. "And you wait this long to tell me? Seriously?"

Des wasn't confused or disgusted. He was pissed. And not because Zach was gay but because he hadn't told him sooner.

"Huh?" Zach asked, unable to come up with anything more intelligent.

"You like dudes." Des shrugged. "So what? I'm almost relieved. 'Cause let me tell you, I was beginning to wonder if you had a screw loose or something. Rebecca's sweet and all but she can be a little much."

Zach let out a stunned laugh. "I was sure you'd lose it."

"For real? You know what I get up to between the sheets. Some of that shit ain't fit for prime time." He smirked, giving Zach a look that was both boastful and scandalized by his own conquests. "So why am I going to judge you for what you want to do in the bedroom? You think it matters to me where you like to put it?"

Zach felt himself blush. "Well, it was usually where *he* liked to put it."

"Okay." Des slapped his hand on Zach's knee, holding it there with a firm grip to stop Zach from revealing any more. "That's a lot of detailed information about a part of your anatomy that I'd prefer not to think about, but if it gets your rocks off, no shame." Des turned serious, the touch on Zach's leg becoming a gentle squeeze. "Thank you for telling me. It means a lot."

The tears on Zach's face felt like warm relief. He couldn't believe his luck at having the greatest best friend ever.

"Have you told anyone else?"

Zach shook his head meekly.

"Good, 'cause if you'd come out to someone else before me, we would've had words."

"I'm sure all the guys I've been with figured it out." Des's eyes went wide at Zach's use of the plural. "Sorry. TMI."

"No, it's not; it's just new. But I'm just glad you were out there getting some action. Shit, thinking about you and that virginity pact for all these years was starting to make me depressed."

It was more acceptance than Zach had ever dreamed he'd get. Unable to put into words just how grateful he was, he collapsed onto Des's shoulder, eliciting a chuckle and a brief one-armed hug from his friend.

"So, what's his name, this guy you've been seeing?" Des continued as he helped Zach sit upright.

"Liam." The name felt like a brutal echo.

"Show me a pic, then."

Zach pulled out his phone. The only picture he ever took of Liam from the night they first made love felt too private to share, even with Des. Instead, he pulled up Liam's Instagram and handed Des his phone.

"Dr. Barnett, my advisor, Liam's his younger brother. But Liam and I met in Rome that last night when I went out on my own."

"You know, I thought you'd hooked up with someone that night. I just didn't want to say anything 'cause of Becca." Des smiled as he scanned through Liam's pictures like he was genuinely happy for Zach. It was a baffling sight. "He's cute. Right?" he added as if to check his ability to judge male attractiveness.

"He is. Very. But it doesn't matter anymore." Des handed him back his phone with a questioning look. "Yesterday after we got back from the game, I told him I loved him and that I wanted to come out for him," Zach inhaled a sad, resigned breath. "And he freaked out and ended everything."

"For real?" Zach nodded, pocketing his phone. "Shit, I guess men are assholes even if they're dating another guy."

"Guess so," Zach said.

"What did he say when you told him what you wanted to do?"

"Gave me a laundry list of all the reasons I shouldn't."

"Well, I don't know this kid but he's not wrong. It's one thing telling me, but coming out publicly would be taking a crazy, monster risk with your career, Z."

"I know that," Zach defended himself. "But he was worth it. We were. I've never felt like this before, Des. Not by a thousand miles." His voice caught and he bit at his lips. He was exhausted by the emotional roller-coaster of the last twenty-four hours and was having a hard time containing his vulnerability. "I'm just so sick of pretending."

"So then maybe this coming out process shouldn't be about him at all." Des rested his cheek on a propped-up fist, turning thoughtful. "It's like getting clean so your girl won't leave you. Or trying to wear some cool clothes just 'cause you think it will make people like you. If your only motivation is someone else, you're going to fail or look stupid trying. So, if you really want to be honest about who you are, then do it for yourself, Zach." Des tapped him in the middle of his chest with his pointer finger. "No one else."

Just then, Ruiz stuck his head in the room. "Hey, sorry guys—that blonde reporter from ESPN wants to interview you guys together." Then, sensing something important had just transpired there, he asked, "Everything okay?"

Catching Zach's eye, Des tilted his head toward their teammate and friend, encouraging Zach to tell Ruiz, too. Zach shook his head, curt and definite. He wasn't ready for that, yet.

"It's just been a lot the past couple days," Zach offered a

vague truth.

"What we've been working towards for four years." Ruiz stepped into the room to share a quick fist bump with both of them.

"Tell her we'll be there in five minutes," Des answered, keeping his eyes on Zach and his smile warm.

Zach was still completely broken-hearted and unsure how to move forward without the first person he'd ever loved. He had a playoff game to win in a month against a team that could destroy them if they didn't play their very best. He still had the terrifying process of opening himself up for the world to criticize, if he ever ended up having the guts to do it. But at least now he knew he still had his best friend.

27

L iam didn't cry again. Instead, he drank.

He bought cigarettes without filters and smoked them in front of his bedroom window, flung wide open to the December cold. He stood there until his teeth started chattering and goosebumps formed on his naked chest, and he finally understood why Chicago was called the Windy City.

He listened to too much Billie Eilish and refused to return Mackenzie's calls. When she finally came banging on his door after several days, he claimed innocence.

"I've been camped out in the basement practice rooms. You know there's no signal down there." He could tell Mackenzie didn't buy it for one second, but she let up on him regardless.

When it came time for their Plato final, Liam watched Zach enter the room and begged silently for him to glance Liam's way. Instead, Zach kept his blinders on, cruelly ignoring Liam. He tried, but Liam couldn't concentrate on the essay exam laid out before him. He wrote some incoherent drivel, knowing his grade would suffer from a lack of focus but didn't care. All he wanted was one second of accidental eye contact with Zach, one smile—as small or broken as it might be. When neither of those things happened during their exam period, Liam waited in the hall after, determined to catch Zach on his own.

"Zach." The name felt oil-slick in his mouth, like some forbidden thing that no longer belonged to him. Zach stopped, lifting his eyes towards the ceiling before turning his head just enough to let Liam know he was listening. "I just wanted to wish you good luck this weekend—at the award presentation in New York."

For a minute Zach's face brightened. "I didn't think you'd remember about that."

"Of course I would."

The Heisman Trophy, perhaps the most prestigious award in all of college sports, was awarded to the most outstanding player of the year. Liam knew it would be awarded the Saturday after exams ended at a special ceremony in Times Square. Zach had been a favorite all season long. An ache filled Liam's chest as he realized that Zach had assumed Liam would forget that fact, even though Zach had told him on more than one occasion how much he'd love to win.

Liam's wish for good luck felt like a possible olive branch. He dared to push himself off the wall and take a step towards Zach. That incremental encroachment was enough for the look on Zach's face to shutter closed. He moved on, brushing Liam off with a negligent, "Right. Thanks," like he would any fan who was desperate to be close to the celebrity they admired. Liam watched Zach round the corner to the elevator feeling nothing but desolation.

When Zach was named the Heisman winner a few days later, it was plastered on all of Northwestern's social media accounts. Liam couldn't have avoided the news, even if he'd wanted to. Hunkered down in his bed with a dark beanie pulled low over his ears, Liam watched a shaved-down version of the hour-long ceremony that had been uploaded to YouTube. On the small screen of his phone, Liam watched as Zach waited nervously in the front row with the other nominees. Then, after his name was announced, he watched Zach get up to hug his parents, his coach, and a man Liam assumed was his newly acquired agent. Zach joined all the past winners up on the stage, holding the giant bronze statue of an old-timey footballer mid-play up over this shoulder for pictures. He delivered a short but sincere speech, offering his thanks to all of those who had supported him along the way. Liam found himself wondering if his name would have been included on that list if he'd let things go differently that night on the field.

Liam thought he'd known heartbreak in Paris. But he realized all too quickly that that experience hadn't been heartbreak at all but rather some far less mortal wound. A damaged ego, maybe. The infatuation that had amounted to nothing and turned him petty. It was nothing like the bone-weary, unrelenting sadness Liam continued to experience even as he flew to the Alps of southern Germany for a Christmas ski trip with his parents.

The weather was wet and cold. Even the delicious smells emanating from the holiday stalls of the *Weihnachtsmarkt* set up in the small town's *hauptplatz* couldn't put him in a festive mood. His mom and dad's renewed kindness didn't help either, as Liam couldn't begin to explain to them why he was so miserable. He couldn't tell them who Zach was or what he'd lost when they'd broken up. Liam's heart hurt in ways they could never know. He grieved, in broody solitude, a relationship that had changed him, moved him, and then evaporated into nothingness.

Liam scrolled through Instagram, seeking out tagged pictures of Zach back home for his truncated winter break. Most of the pictures showed Zach propped up next to pretty blond girls he must have known in high school. His smile had looked sleazy, possibly drunk, and so very vacant for a man who was sitting on top of the world. The images left Liam feeling vile, too, though he wouldn't allow himself to go so far as to say he was jealous.

Liam returned to Chicago just after Christmas. His apartment felt obscenely cluttered after a week in the world of German minimalism, so Liam purged. He binned clothes he no longer wore and donated books he didn't care to re-read, hoping it would help scrub Zach from his life. None of these material things had anything to do with Zach, so in the end, all of Liam's effort was for naught.

Their entanglement hadn't come with any of the sentimental trappings of a normal relationship—movie stubs, pictures on his phone, tags on social media, or pieces of clothing accidentally left behind. They had been exacting in how clean they had left each other's lives, leaving no trail of crumbs for the outside world to follow. If only they had been more careful with how deeply they'd meshed their hearts together.

Liam didn't even have a text conversation to scroll back through while awake at night, feeling alone and sentimental. All he had to remember Zach by was the one picture Zach had taken as he'd held a sleeping Liam close. Liam refused to part with that picture, no matter what kind of closure he might find by getting rid of it.

Eventually, he crawled out of his torpor to make New Year's Eve plans with Mackenzie and Sam. After several bottles of bubbly and a joint of Mackenzie's choicest kind, she insisted on watching "the game"—the semi-finals of the Championship series. Northwestern played South Carolina, and Liam's agitation at having to watch Zach was sky-high.

"Why has everyone become so obsessed with football?"

"Because it's the playoffs!" Mackenzie exclaimed. She held the TV remote in one hand and a pink plastic champagne flute, full to spilling, in the other. "It's a big deal for our school."

"Well, it's not a big deal to me." Liam leered down at her over the back of the couch.

"It's a big deal to your friend Zach," Mackenzie parroted back.

With a pout, Liam flopped on the couch next to Sam, who in all likelihood had already fallen asleep behind his glittery 2021 glasses.

"He's not my friend anymore," Liam muttered.

As the game clock on the screen ticked down to zero and the night edged towards midnight, Liam felt his insides crumble. Northwestern won because of course, they did. This victory was exactly why he'd gone and broken both their hearts. He felt justified now, knowing Zach could live this perfect storyline to completion where there was no room for a male partner. Liam had broken things off so his Zach Sugarman could continue being *the* Zachary Sugarman.

When Mackenzie woke Sam and insisted they go to the roof to watch the fireworks that were going to be set off from a barge just off the coast of Lake Michigan, Liam feigned sickness.

"Too much champagne. Buy the good stuff next time, will you?" he slurred before putting on his coat. The minute he was out of her apartment, he opened his Grindr app for the first time since Rome. It was easy enough for Liam to find some nameless man to help him ring in the new year.

The guy was as drunk and miserable as Liam was. "You know what they say about the person you're with when midnight strikes, right?"

The hook-up's romantic insinuations made Liam sick. He kicked the guy out of his apartment before 2021 was even two hours old and emptied the contents of his stomach into the toilet before he passed out in his bed.

Hungover and bitchy, Liam went to a New Year's Day party at his brother's place. It was a grown-up affair with top-shelf wine and little canapés, crudités, entremets, and other forms of pretentious French finger food. Many of his brother's colleagues from school were there, including Dr. Ellison, who insisted Liam call her Jeanette now that he was no longer in her class. Liam humored her request with a sweet smile and a handshake, all the while thinking, "No chance in hell."

"What's wrong with you?" Eben asked as he dumped a stack of plates onto the kitchen counter after the party was over. The boys had been left to tidy up so Kelsey could catch a nap, a necessity again now that she had entered her third trimester. Liam extracted his hands from the warm water. Soap suds clung to his forearms as he moved the plates into the sink.

"I drank too much last night."

Eben stood with one hip cocked to the side, his arms crossed. He already had the "cross dad" stare down pat for future use. "Well, I don't doubt that. But then what has this month-long temper tantrum been about?"

"What month-long tantrum?"

"Come on, Liam. You've been pissy since before exams, and mom said you moped around the entire time you were in Garmish." A thought flickered across his brother's face. "Has something come up again from Paris? You know he's not supposed to contact you."

"No! What? No." Liam peevishly grabbed a kitchen towel to dry his hands. If being a good brother-in-law to Kelsey meant talking to Eben about what had been going on, then screw being helpful. Eben wasn't going to let him run away from this conversation, though. All it took was one dubious lift of his brother's eyebrow, and Liam felt like he was pinned against the counter.

Liam folded his arms across his chest, as his brother continued to wait. They used to be the type of siblings who talked about personal things when they were smaller, and so were their troubles. Liam exhaled hotly.

"Look, the world is never going to change, right?" he began. "I mean, it's always going to be filled with small-minded little assholes. So why even try and fight that? Why make some big statement about who you are and what you feel? Why try to make a stand when you know it's not going to change a damn thing? Making some grand gesture by coming out to the whole world is pointless when you know society won't accept it, and," he continued emphatically, "if you do come out you're going to lose this massive, professional sports career that you've been training for your whole life." Liam stopped, realizing he'd wandered into specifics.

Eben listened in stillness. Then, with infuriating kindness, he asked, "Is this what Zach offered to do for you?"

Liam's silence gave Eben every answer he needed. He made a chipper noise at the back of his throat, his body suddenly a rush of movement. Eben collected a half-empty bottle of wine, slipped two wine glasses between his fingers, and began to pour. "Much more age-appropriate this time. Well done."

"Oh, shut up." Liam flushed. His brother offered him a full

glass, even though the thought of more alcohol made his head pound. "How did you know?" Liam excepted the wine but didn't drink.

"My life might be more about picking out colors for the nursery and hypnobirthing, but it's not like I've forgotten what it looks like to be in love with someone. Or what my little brother looks like when he's ridiculously happy." Liam cleared his throat trying not to get emotional. "Zach must really love you," Eben stated, "if he's willing to do that."

"He does. He really does. Or at least, he did." Eben pressed his lips together, astutely noticing Liam's corrected tense. "He would have lost everything if he'd come out, though. God, can't you see the shitstorm now? Because I can. And I just couldn't let him do that. Not for me. Not for anything." Liam's voice rode the fine edge between holding things together and breaking down completely. "Why would he even suggest it?"

"Why did you do what you did in Paris?"

Liam balked, unsure why Eben brought that up when it had nothing to do with Zach. "Because I was an idiot?"

"No, because you felt something," Eben insisted. "Something big and important. And when you feel things that are big and important, you want to do things that are big and important. Not always the right things, necessarily, but big things nonetheless. What Zach offered to do for you was no different."

Liam was left speechless. He'd never heard his brother talk about Paris with any sort of empathy, any understanding of what Liam had experienced. It broke the last of Liam's restraint.

"I'm such a piece of shit, Eben," Liam lamented. "He was standing there, telling me these things—these beautiful things— things I want and that I feel too." Liam curled his palm helplessly over his heart. "And all I could think was—I can't go through this again."

His brother shook his head, not quite following. "What do you mean?"

"Say he does it," Liam began to lay out the hypothetical outcome. "Say Zach comes out and he loses any chance at a professional career. You know every news outlet on the planet is going to come after 'the guy who turned him gay.'"

Liam spoke with heinous honesty. Yes, Liam had wanted to protect Zach's future with every fiber of his being, but he'd needed to protect himself too.

"What happened in Paris was a small scandal in an insular classical music community that most of the world doesn't pay attention to or care about. But this? This would make headlines. I couldn't drag Mom and Dad, or you and Kelsey, back into my stupid drama. I couldn't be the bad guy again, Eb. Have someone I cared about resent me. Fuck up someone else's life. Especially not Zach's. Not when he means so much."

Liam had been speaking so constantly and with such vigor that he'd failed to notice the tears rolling down his face until his final words caught in his throat. Eben stepped forward, setting down his wine glass and folding Liam into his arms. It had been ages since Liam felt this kind of brotherly love, and he leaned into it.

"I'm sure you would be the bad guy to some. As you said, the world is an imperfect place." Eben began running comforting circles across Liam's back. "But to countless others, you would an inspiration. The second half of a love story that gave them the strength to finally be honest with themselves and those around them. You've already been that person for Zach. Can't you see that? I get that it's a risk, but maybe it's a worthy one. And maybe one you take together."

If it were at all possible, Liam missed Zach more at that moment than he had in the previous three weeks combined. "I pushed him away, Eben," he rasped. "Hard."

Eben grinned, his hands still on Liam's shoulders. "Then pull him back."

How exactly Liam was supposed to put his brother's advice into action remained a mystery over the next week. It seemed a Herculean task of impossible measure after everything he'd said and done to Zach. Nothing had changed, either. The sports world Zach inhabited was still terrifyingly homophobic and they were two men, in love. Any attempt at a public relationship would make Zach's future complicated, at best. Liam supposed the only real change in the equation was his eagerness to support Zach's decision to come out. Even if it fixed nothing between them, he owed Zach that moral support.

The football team went back to Indianapolis for final practices leading up to the Championship Game mid-week. There was a massive send-off from the stadium that students and fans had been encouraged to attend. Eben sent Liam a link to the Twitter post about it, adding, "Something big and important, perhaps?" But Liam didn't want any public confessions—or to have his brother meddle in his love life, for that matter—so he gave it a pass.

Countless times a day, Liam considered going old school and just calling Zach. Maybe he'd be lucky and get Zach's voice mail, so he could just leave a message begging for forgiveness. "I know I'm a total dick, but can you just call me?" he'd say. "We can get a drink after the Championship or go see that jazz show." That felt hardly enough to make up for what he'd done, so he never bothered.

The following Monday was the first day of classes after the break. It also happened to be Championship Game day. Liam tried distracting himself by keeping busy in the music building. He met with his composition professor to talk about his senior project and plans for graduation the following school year. He left half inspired, half overwhelmed, and still with his mind on Zach.

He emerged into a winter dark and a seemingly deserted campus. All of Evanston's eyes were turned to television screens and computer monitors that night, ready for the College Football Playoff National Championship game between Northwestern and the University of Georgia. There were massive watch parties all over town at bars, the student union, and even at the stadium itself for those people crazy enough to bear sitting outside in the January air to watch the game on the jumbotron. But Chicago was a football town, and people would brave just about any degree of cold for the sake of football when there was enough beer involved.

Liam knew Mackenzie was having a small get-together,

and part of him was tempted to go. He pulled out his phone to check the score before picking a destination. Northwestern was leading by a two-score margin with less than five minutes to go in the third quarter. Relief filled him. He still wanted Zach to win. Of course, he did. As he slipped his phone back into the outer pocket of his shoulder bag, he realized maybe all he was destined to be was another devoted fan cheering Zach on to greatness in his own private way. Liam's lips twitched into a rueful smile, and he began the familiar route back to his apartment.

Snow began to fall as he walked, the flakes fat and especially white as they danced in the light of the streetlamps. His phone rang, and he pulled it back out of his bag. It was Eben.

Liam rolled his eyes, answering the question he assumed he'd be met with. "Yes, Eben, I know we're winning. But no, I'm not watching."

"Liam." The tone of his voice was enough for Liam's heart rate to skyrocket. "You should get to a TV as quickly as you can. It's Zach. He's been hit, two guys at once. He's not moving."

28

He ran to Mackenzie's place, not because it was closest but because it felt safest.

"You made it." Mackenzie opened the door, trepidation already in her voice.

The familiar figures from school who had collected to watch the game all sat forward on the edge of their respective seats, a stunned silence in the room. Liam stood directly in front of the television, not caring that he was blocking Sam's view. His lungs were on fire from the ragged breaths of frigid air he'd sucked in as he'd raced across campus. If he hadn't been shivering, he'd be dripping with sweat.

The announcers spoke in concerned tones, as on the screen, in slow motion and from every possible camera angle, the replay showed Zach fall to the field again and again and again. This hit wasn't like the sack Liam had seen that day at the stadium. It was far more violent. On Mackenzie's small TV, Liam watched a Georgia defensive player break around the outside edge of the offensive line and come at Zach low. The defenseman's shoulder aligned precisely with Zach's knee. Liam could imagine the snap of sinew, the crunch of cartilage and bone a collision like that would inflict. That hit was nothing compared to the next one, inflicted by a massive lineman who, as Zach tried to evade the first hit, struck from around Zach's waist, the crown of his helmet colliding upwards with the underside of Zach's jaw. His head snapped back and forth with terrifying speed, even in slow motion.

In the resulting crumble of bodies, Zach's limbs created completely unnatural angles. He landed on the field, limp and unconscious. The instinctual part of his brain—naturally selected through the millennia for self-preservation—that should have reached out to break his fall, was shut off. Zach was completely helpless as he fell.

Between horrible replays of the tackles, the broadcast cut to live images. A sky camera flew over an army of coaches and EMTs in a circle around Zach on the field. There were shots of horrified members of the marching band, fans wearing both colors with their hands over their mouths in shock, and UGA players forming prayer circles on the sidelines.

The feed jumped to a close-up of a Northwestern player. His helmet was off. The tears on his face mixed with his sweat. It took Liam a moment to recognize him as Des, the boy from the day on the Quad and Zach's best friend. The commentators lingered on his image, gently considering how hard this must be for Des, having known Zach for so long.

Liam wanted to scream at those two microphone-wielding dickheads on the screen. What about what he was feeling? At least Des was there with Zach, breathing the same air. Liam was a million miles away, unable to do anything. He was too terrified to cry, though he choked on the immeasurably large sob that filled his chest.

The game broadcast cut to a commercial for some slick new car, and Liam blinked for what felt like the first time since he'd arrived.

"It's him, isn't it?" Mackenzie's hand came to rest gently between his shoulder blades. "The guy who you've been seeing."

Liam nodded meekly.

"Oh, Liam." She wrapped her arms around his waist from

behind, tucking her head against his neck when words failed her.

They watched as Zach was loaded into an ambulance. For a fraction of a second, he came into aerial view. There weren't any IVs or oxygen masks, just mountains of braces and straps attaching his prone body securely to the gurney.

"That can only be a good thing, right?" Sam asked, having come to stand with Liam too. He must have heard Mackenzie's question or intuited the situation from her reaction. Liam didn't care by that point who knew that he and Zach had been an item. The secrecy of his love for Zach didn't matter anymore, only the existence of it.

They showed the hit one final time, and Liam was struck by how frail Zach's body looked. Liam thought of all the times he'd lain next to Zach, how Zach's body had always been so strong in comparison to his own. Every one of Zach's muscles was primed for maximum power even when in the act of submitting. Zach had felt indestructible, supple, keen, and always so beautiful. Now that same beautiful body was broken and hurting. Liam's arms ached, missing the feel of Zach's solid heaviness in them. He pulled Mackenzie closer.

The ambulance lights turned on, twirling red and white. Everyone in the stadium rose to their feet, blessing Zach's journey with a chorus of hopeful cheers. Then grotesquely, another person took Zach's position as quarterback, and the teams began playing the game again.

"Kenz, I need to borrow your car." Liam was amazed by how level his voice sounded.

She looked from the screen to Liam, then immediately started gathering her keys and coat. She paused once to ask Sam to lock up when he left. Their heads tilted sweetly towards each other, and Sam's eyes fell closed as he kissed her. Liam let out a shattered breath at the tender moment between his two best friends. What a self-pitying douche he'd been for not seeing what was happening right under his nose these past few weeks. All semester, probably.

"I'll drive," she said as she pulled a knit hat over her hair.

"And you're going to tell me everything."

It took until they'd reached Lafayette, Indiana, or about two hours if the clock on Mackenzie's dashboard was to be trusted, for Liam to finish telling the whole tale. Rome. Plato. Hillel. The Symposium. The football game. The John Hancock Building. The Stadium. As he relayed the story, their time together felt so much longer than the four-plus months it had been. Perhaps it was the intensity of what they'd shared that gave their relationship such gravity and not merely its duration.

"I'm sorry I couldn't tell you." Liam had kept himself together through the recounting of their relationship, his thoughts focused solely on getting to Indianapolis and Zach's side.

"I probably wouldn't have believed you if you had."

The snow was still falling—not enough to make the roads dangerous, but enough that Mackenzie kept her windshield wipers on. The narrow stems of plastic dragged back and forth across the glass with a rubbery squeak.

"What are you going to do when we get there?" she asked.

Liam stared out the driver's side window, his thumb caught between his teeth. "I don't know. Something big and important, I hope."

The phone mounted to Mackenzie's dashboard buzzed, announcing a Google alert. They could both read the final score as it popped up on the screen, but it didn't feel official until Liam read it out loud. A minute atom of hope flared to life in his heart.

"We won."

—

It was well after midnight by the time he and Mackenzie arrived at the hospital. He'd scoured Twitter along the way for clues about which hospital Zach would be taken to for treatment. Liam's deductive guesswork had panned out.

Indiana University Medical Center was swarming with news crews and hardcore NU fans waiting for an in-person update on their star player's status. Meanwhile, hospital security was busy keeping the ambulance lanes open and people under control. Mackenzie cranked the wheel, turning her car under the well-lit awning in front of the emergency department. She put the car in park but left the engine running.

Liam gave the crowd a tepid look. "I can wait for you to park, you know."

"No, I'll drop you. Who knows what the parking situation is going to be. It'll be faster this way."

"You're sure? I should walk with you. It's late." He felt gallant offering, but the truth was, he didn't particularly want to walk into that waiting room full of Zach's teammates on his own, either.

"There are cops everywhere." Mackenzie gestured out the window. "I'll be fine. Text me when you know where you'll be, and I'll come find you." She said it like you'd ask a friend to call you after class so you could meet up for lunch. Her calmness and focus had been a magical balm for Liam through the whole anxiety-ridden night. Without a thought for how long the drive might take, where she might sleep that night, the weather conditions, or the classes she would miss in the morning, Mackenzie had jumped into her car with Liam. She hadn't asked why or questioned his motivation. She'd just done it. Because Liam had asked. Because Liam was her friend. He seriously was the luckiest asshole on the planet.

Just as he suspected, Liam felt completely out of his depth as he walked through the sliding glass doors of the emergency department waiting room. The large, modern space, befit a hospital this size. It was overrun by Zach's teammates and coaches, many of whom were wearing matching 2021 National Championship ball caps. Their broad, athletic bodies were sprawled in banks of chairs, their legs extended long and wide. Liam feared he might evaporate into nothingness if he attempted to walk among them.

In the corner, away from the hulking young men, was an older couple, nicely dressed and sitting with the head coach. Liam swallowed. He knew instantly they were Zach's parents. The similarities between Zach and his mother were shocking. Her elegant cheekbones and soft, dark brown waves were so very much like his. Even from this distance, though, Liam could see that Zach got his eyes from his father. His blue eyes, identical to Zach's, were terrified.

Eleanor and Freddie. Their names came to Liam out of a murky memory from a night that had lasted until morning not so long ago, when he and Zach had filled the waning evening hours with unflinching gazes. The looks they'd shared had reflected their shared inspiration and cautious wonder at just how deep their feelings were beginning to run. They'd told each other old stories, so no part of them, not even their pasts, would be unknown to the other. Liam wanted more nights like those.

He had made the grand gesture. He'd driven nearly three hours so he could be here when Zach woke up. But what next? Should he go to Zach's parents and introduce himself as his study partner just like they'd joked about on Thanksgiving morning? Should he just ask a random player and hope they didn't body slam him to the ground, asking who the skinny kid was? Should he try to snag one of the nurses even though they looked frazzled by the crowded room and added scrutiny of the high-profile patient?

"Holy shit. It's you."

A mystified voice came from behind, and Liam turned. It was Des, and he was staring at Liam, a coffee frozen halfway to his mouth. He lowered the cup and pointed. "You're him. You're Liam."

"Yeah. You're Des, right?" Liam offered his hand, slipping into formal introductions. "Liam Barnett. Zach told you about me?"

"Yeah." There was a snarky edge to his answer. "He told me everything."

That couldn't possibly be true. Liam stuffed his hands back into his pockets. "Everything?"

"Yeah, man. Everything." Des repeated with emphasis.

Liam couldn't believe it. Zach had come out to his best friend. "When?" he asked, now breathless.

"The day after you—" Des stopped. He leaned in slightly closer, highly aware of how delicate the subject matter was. "He told me the day we got into the playoffs. The morning after our first game in Indy. He told me you split up, too."

"It's complicated."

Des seemed as displeased by Liam's explanation as he did by the taste of the hospital coffee as he finally took a sip. "Were you at the game tonight?"

"No, I, uh, I drove here. Well, my friend drove here. She's parking her car now."

"You drove here from Evanston? Just now?"

Liam nodded. "When I saw what happened to Zach I just got in the car." Liam looked aimlessly around the waiting room. It was filled with people who had known Zach ages longer than Liam had, people who hadn't walk away from Zach when he'd offered them his very soul. Liam sighed heavily. "Look, I didn't think this whole thing through terribly well."

As if sensing Liam's discomfort, Des guided him over to a chair, taking the seat next to him.

"What have they told you?" Liam inquired.

"Hardly anything. They've been coming in and telling Zach's folks and Coach Williams stuff, mostly. All we really know is he woke up in the ambulance—which is good, but that means he was out for at least fifteen minutes."

"Which, I assume, isn't?"

Des shook his head. "It could go either way. Evidently, he was disoriented when he woke up. Didn't know where he was or what had happened, but not, like, out of it. I mean, he knew his name, the year, stuff like that. They had to sedate him after a while."

"Why?"

"Just to keep him calm while they did the scans. 'Glorified sleeping pills,' Coach said."

"Has anyone been in to see him?"

Des shook his head, again, somberly. He and Des couldn't have been more different, yet there they were, joined together because of Zach. In this sea of unfamiliar humanity, Liam was grateful to have at least one person there who knew Zach's whole truth and how Liam fit into it.

He texted Mackenzie, but she was already on her way to the ER from the garage. She came in the sliding doors only a few minutes later, and Liam called her over with a wave.

"Hi." Des offered her his hand. "I'm Des."

"I know who you are." She gave him a star-struck smile.

Just then, a doctor came through the doors that separated the waiting room from the triage center. She made a beeline to Zach's parents and Coach Williams and sat opposite them.

The room fell silent. Liam leaned forward, Mackenzie's arm linked in his for support. He tried to catch what the doctor was conveying but was unable to hear anything, nor was he able to infer anything from the stoic nods of the coach and the pained looks of Zach's parents. In the end, the doctor ushered the three grown-ups into the back.

"Coach?" Des called across the room just before Coach Williams slipped out of view. When Coach turned at the sound of his name, Des stood, lifting his arms in a desperate, questioning gesture.

"All we know for now is that his ACL is ruptured." There was a generally muted reaction to this news from Zach's teammates, groans and muttered curses. "His patella is fractured too, but we were pretty much expecting that. They're still waiting to get CT results back to know what damage the second hit caused. Keep sending him love and strength, boys, however, you find that most meaningful."

A few offered up a "Thanks, Coach," with an air of utmost respect before Coach turned and followed where Zach's parents had gone.

Liam turned to Des, hoping to gauge how he should take this news. Des sat back with his head resting against the wall. His eyes moved in their sockets as he did the calculations in his head. "ACL. That's four months." He spoke out loud but like Liam wasn't there. "Six if your surgeon has a bad day or if your PT sucks, which his won't. They'll get the best for Z. The kneecap thing though, that might be another...six weeks on top of all that? Depends on where the fracture is, I suppose. The head thing though. If it's only a concussion, he'll get cleared eventually."

"How are you so calm about this?"

Des turned his head Liam's way with a shrug. "We've all been here before—dealing with injuries, waiting on news about whether we're ever going to play again. I mean, most of the time it's not this serious, but it's a risk we take every time we step on the field." He pointed towards the double doors. "That could have just as easily been me in there tonight. Could have been any of us. Tonight, it was Zach."

"This fucking game," Liam whispered. It was similar to the reaction he'd had when he'd watched it live. Being able to appreciate the excellence of Zach's play hadn't changed the violence he saw in the sport. He pushed both his hands through his hair, pulling hard at the roots just to feel something other than concern. His hands dropped to his lap with an explosive exhale. "Why couldn't Zach have played, I don't know, ping-pong or something?"

Des snorted once, then twice. Mackenzie soon followed. And before Liam knew it, Des was shaking with laughter. "Can you imagine?" he asked around a giggle. "Zach? Playing ping-pong? That little paddle?"

That's when Liam lost it too. It felt so wrong to be laughing this way when Zach's prognosis remained unclear. He could tell they were getting plenty of odd looks. But his stress had to find a way out somehow, and a laughing fit certainly seemed like one of the healthier options.

"Shit." Des wiped at the tears in the creases of his eyes. He let out a long, pitched sighed. "I'll get you guys some coffee. It's going to be a long night." He slapped Liam on the back as he rose, using enough force to nearly launch Liam out of his seat. Des grinned down at him. It felt like Des had just put Liam through some sort of initiation and was pleased with the results. But once Des was a few steps away, he stopped and sobered his expression. "Look, I know we don't know shit right now about how he's going to be, and I don't want to speak for him or anything, but I think 24 is gonna be happy you're here."

Liam nodded, grateful for Des's vote of confidence. "Wait."

Liam was suddenly confused. "Twenty-four?"

"That's his jersey number, you doofus," Mackenzie teased. "Some kind of boyfriend you are." Her face went white, thinking she'd inadvertently outed Zach to his best friend. She gave Des a mortified look, but he flashed her a radiant smile.

"I like her."

"Congratulations, by the way," Liam said. He nodded up towards the hat that sat cockeyed on Des's head. Des reached up and adjusted it as if still getting used to the fit and meaning behind it.

"Thanks." Des's eyes became glossy. "We won this one for Zach."

29

Information came in slowly throughout the night. With Zach's knee injury diagnosed, it became the least of the doctors' worries. Their focus turned to his lapse of consciousness and any potential, long-lasting brain injuries.

His brain scan came back clean, which meant there had been no bleeding, but his intracranial pressure was increased, which indicated swelling. "It's a concussion," one of the assistant coaches announced sometime around 3 a.m., and that word didn't seem so scary to Liam. It was just as Des had speculated. "But it's a bad one," he clarified, and the dread in the pit of Liam's stomach settled back in.

Liam, too over-caffeinated to sleep, felt like he was suspended in a time lock. Days could have passed outside, and he'd have no concept of it, sitting in the brightly lit waiting room. He alternated between pacing listlessly through the endless hallways and watching the same miserable CNN headlines on the wall-mounted televisions over and over again from different chairs. Mackenzie fell asleep eventually, her legs and arms in an uncomfortable-looking twist against the hard plastic. Liam tucked his coat under her head to pillow it as best he could.

Sometime well past 4 a.m., Coach Williams came out and told the teammates who had stayed—which was most of them—that Zach had been moved to the main ward for observation. His sedatives were being tapered off, and they wouldn't know anything more about the severity of his concussion until he woke up.

"Time to get some sleep, boys." His voice sounded ripped to shreds with exhaustion and worry. He looked down at his toes, trying to stop himself from getting choked up. "I'm proud of the men you've shown yourselves to be tonight—on the field, but more so right here." He pointed to the floor as his voice cracked. "We truly are the Northwestern Football family, and I love you all."

His drained but poignant speech took Liam by surprise. Weren't coaches all supposed to be screaming, red-faced ass-kickers? This coach seemed like a tender-hearted gentleman, which would explain why Zach always spoke of him with such reverence and affection. The players loaded themselves onto the team buses that showed up a few minutes later, but Des didn't move a muscle, his hands clenched to the armrests like he was glued there. He wasn't leaving until he saw Zach, and neither was Liam.

Mackenzie woke around the time that chain restaurants out in the real world would be opening for business. She offered to go get them actual food and actual coffee. Liam hated the thought of asking her to do even one more thing for his sake, but then he reasoned maybe she was going stir crazy sitting vigil for a man she'd never even met. He gave her a twenty and a long hug and watched her walk out the door into the faint morning light.

Des jumped up to talk to Zach's parents when they walked through the waiting room a short while later. Liam could only watch from a distance as Des played the best-friend-since-middle-school card for the latest update.

"Come on," Des said after Zach's parents left. His eyes were flared with determination.

"What?" Liam's voice cracked. "What's going on?"

"They told me his room number." Des didn't need to say anything more.

They wound their way through the hospital's long hallways, in and out of elevators, past hospital staff that paid them no mind. When they arrived on the ward, Des walked straight up to the nurses' station, turned on that megawatt smile, and tipped his National Championship cap like it was some damn badge. Liam was sure dawn-o'clock wasn't within the hospital's visiting hours, and he was prepared to be kicked out. But Des's sweet-talking worked. His toothy smile faded the instant he turned from the nurse's station. His jaw was set and determined as he pulled Liam down the hall by the cuff of his coat and into Zach's darkened room, completely unmolested.

There was no time for Liam to mentally prepare himself for the sight of Zach in a hospital bed before he saw him lying in one. Zach's left leg was wrapped in a massive brace that ran from his hip to his ankle and was propped up by a mountain of pillows. There was another brace around his neck that seemed to tilt his head back against the elevated bed at an awkward angle. There was an IV attached to his right hand, a nasal cannula resting on his cheeks and over his ears. He was pale and motionless aside from the gentle rise and fall of his chest.

Liam's eyes stung at the sight of him. He'd missed him so much and instinct took over. He reached for Zach's hand, finding it dry and warm where it was nestled in an array of starchy white sheets. Liam bent down to press his lips against the soft patch of skin at his jaw. He whispered, "*Tesoro, mi cosi dispiace tanto*," against the flop of Zach's hair, still matted with the musky-sweet smell of sweat from his helmet.

Liam didn't think how Des might react to seeing his previously-assumed-one-hundred-percent-heterosexual best friend being fretted over by his previously-secret-one-hundred-percent-male lover. Liam extracted himself from Zach's side as Des stepped into his slight line.

"Sorry."

"Don't. It's fine." Des reached out for Zach too, wrapping his fingers around the inside of his calf. It was a purely platonic gesture but carried a sweetness that was impossible for Liam to ignore.

There was only one chair in the room, pulled close to Liam's side of the bed. He wondered if it was Zach's mother, his father, or his coach who last sat there watching Zach's face intently for any signs of wakefulness. Des gestured for Liam to take the seat.

"You can stay, too," Liam offered, but Des just shook his head.

"Redheaded nurse said they're just letting him rest, so they won't be in unless something changes before the morning shift shows up at eight. You should have a couple of hours." *Use them wisely,* his voice seemed to say.

"Will you let Mackenzie know where I am?"

"Sure." Des's voice curled. "I can keep an eye on her."

"She's got a boyfriend. Just, you know, FYI." Liam said. Even only knowing Des for a few hours, Liam was sure neither Sam nor Mackenzie stood a chance if Des was allowed to turn on the charm. "It's new for them, but yeah. Off-limits."

Des wiped at the guilty-as-charged smirk on his lips with the pad of his forefinger. His eyes narrowed into wry slits and locked on Liam. "Noted."

Before Des left, he lifted the Championship hat off his head and placed it next to Zach's head on his pillow. With a single nod, an apparent punctuation mark to his own internal discussion, Des left, and Liam was alone with Zach for the first time in weeks.

The hospital room was high above this unfamiliar city. The sun broke along avenues and boulevards, shining between buildings that Liam didn't know, that he hadn't studied night after night, day after day. He had a sudden wish for home, for Chicago. The sound of Zach's sleeping breath was beautifully familiar, though, as was the shape of him at rest. Even in Zach's current state, being in his orbit again was enough to bring Liam peace. He wished he could crawl into the small space beside Zach in the bed and just be close again. Instead, he picked up Zach's hand, knowing it would have to suffice until Zach was awake and Liam said what he needed to say.

He sank to the chair, keeping hold of Zach's hand. The thick cushions were a welcome change from the seats in the waiting room. There was even a blanket draped over one of the armrests, and Liam pulled it around his shoulders. All the frenetic static that had been buzzing in Liam's ears since his brother had first called him less than twelve hours earlier faded to silence. The background sadness that he'd carried with him since he had turned his back and walked away from Zach that night on the field lifted from his muscles. He felt light and freed. There was no way to know how Zach would react when he woke up and saw Liam here. But at that moment, Liam was exactly where he needed to be and where he hoped he was allowed to stay.

—

Liam hadn't even realized he'd fallen asleep, when a thick, almost clumsy, caress of fingers in hair, woke him.

He couldn't have been asleep long because no one had disturbed him with their morning rounds. It had been long enough, though, for Liam to feel completely revitalized, especially when he stood to see Zach looking back at him. His bright blue eyes swam wide in their sockets, unable to focus on anything for long. Each blink was slow, seeming to require great effort. In those moments where Zach could keep his eyes open, they were filled with a mix of confusion and distress. Surely someone at the nurses' station must have noticed the change in Zach's heart rate, beeping in a steady rhythm on his monitor, yet no one came to disturb them.

"Hey," Liam said, tenderly. "How are you?" Zach pulled at the collar Velcroed around his neck as if trying to understand its function. "No, no, no. Don't. Leave it." Liam gently moved Zach's hands away, their fingers brushing as he did. The bewilderment in Zach's eyes grew more distinct with their contact.

"Am I hallucinating?" Zach slurred. His breath was uneven and shallow.

"No," Liam answered with a fleeting smile. "It's me. Do you know where you are?"

Zach's eyes closed, and he swallowed audibly as he thought.

Then with droll intonation, "I'm not in Kansas."

Liam's next smile held longer. "No, definitely not in Kansas, Dorothy. You're in Indi—"

"—anapolis," they finished together.

"Yeah," Zach continued, "The game." His brow furrowed. "Who won?"

Liam picked up the hat Des had left behind and held it up over Zach's face so it came into his line of sight. The corners of Zach's lips pulled up, and he lifted both hands to grab onto it. There was such simple, childlike joy on his face as he examined it. His thumb trembling over the stitching that read, "Northwestern University NCAA Football Champions 2021."

Zach's hands dropped back to his chest, the hat falling from his fingers. The weight of it must have been too much for him to support any longer. Liam made a quick grab for it before it tumbled to the ground. Zach didn't seem too bothered by his show of clumsiness.

"Sons of bitches won without me."

"I think they won because of you. Congratulations, Zach."

Zach closed his eyes again, a guileless smile on his lips.

"Do you remember anything about the game?"

Zach nodded the best he could with the brace still on. "Second half, I think. I was trying to go long for Des, but the offensive line broke. Their left tackle, the guy with the Thor hair, I saw him coming at me." He reached for his knee, attempting to confirm his incomplete memory.

"It's your ACL." Liam tried to break the news as gently as he could. He wasn't even entirely sure what that injury meant, but the lower lids of Zach's eyes instantly filled with tears.

"My ACL," he repeated grimly.

"I'm so sorry, Zach."

"Okay. But why am I..." He tapped weakly his forehead.

"There was a second hit as you fell from the first. He knocked you out. You have a level five concussion, or at least that's what your coach told the team."

Zach's exhale quivered as he closed his eyes again so he could absorb this information in the privacy of his thoughts.

He knew what this all meant, just like Des had. It seemed like Zach could look down the long, excruciating tunnel of recovery without anyone having to explain it to him. A tear slipped from the corner of Zach's eye, and Liam watched its quick path downwards towards his pillow. Liam twisted his fingers anxiously behind his back, preventing himself from reaching out to comfort Zach. Just like climbing into bed with him had felt off-limits, Liam wasn't sure he had the right to wipe Zach's tears yet, either.

"You weren't there though," Zach said, after another thoughtful pause. "At the game. Were you?"

Liam shook his head. "No. I saw what happened on TV and I knew I wanted to be with you when you woke up."

"You came from campus?" Even more confusion pressed into Zach's features when Liam nodded. He shifted his head, angling towards Liam's side of the bed. "Why?" he breathed.

Liam knew this was his moment. The clench in his chest felt like a plea for atonement. "Because of course, I love you, too."

It had taken Liam a month, but he finally said the words he should have said that night at the stadium. Liam could remember, and almost still feel, the way the wind had whipped around them. The same frigid bite of tears pierced his eyes. The vile words he'd used and the heartsickness they had left him with returned to him. A rushing desperation to erase those false statements from their joint memory consumed him. He would never be able to take back what the intentional pain he'd inflicted. What he'd said and done was burned into both of them like a scar, forever. The best Liam could do was offer new words to act as a healing salve, words that caressed as much as the others had punched.

"I don't know if this will make any difference to you, but you matter to me more than anyone ever has before, and what I did—shit." His hands went to his hips, and he pressed his lips together, collecting himself. "Look, we both know this is not the first time I've fucked up. I've got a record of letting things go too far and saying things I later regret."

Zach listened, motionless against the mattress. His silence

felt like an open-ended invitation to speak.

"I also have a history of running away when things get ugly. I check out, cut myself off from the situation. Hell, I leave the whole damn continent instead of fighting, even if fighting would have been the right thing to do. I warned you, Zach. I'm not a good person."

"Don't," Zach contested with a ragged groan.

"Just let me finish." Liam settled slowly down onto the edge of the bed. "What you were offering to do for me that night, just so we could be together, Zach, it was so big and so important. It was monumental. And I just, I couldn't fathom it. All I could see were all the bad things that could come from it. And why? Just because you met me, and by some fluke of the universe we actually ended up falling for each other? It was too big and too fucking risky. It still is. So, of course, I ran," Liam's head fell to his chest with an overwhelmed shake. "You wanting to come out, knowing full well the social battle you'd have to wage? It felt reckless to me. Dangerous. Like a battle that you couldn't win. But then again, you were the one who told me that love is a kind of warfare."

Zach's eyes rolled before they fluttered closed. "Us and Ovid and weird timing, huh?"

"But maybe Ovid was right all those millennia ago." Liam's voice gentled. "If you truly love someone the way you're supposed to love someone, you have to fight for it, don't you? You have to fight to keep them. Fight to win them back." Liam covered Zach's hand, and Zach's brow pulled together, affected by his touch. "You have to fight against your own fears and insecurities and outside pressures that want to break you apart."

"Philosopher warriors," Zach whispered.

"What?"

Zach said nothing, only opened his eyes to lock on Liam's. Liam was aware of just how much effort and concentration it took for Zach to do so.

"I know I fucked up, but I love you," Liam continued. "And I want to be with you, Zach. So, I'm going to fight for you. And once I have you? I'll fight with you. Whatever you decide to do.

Whatever the risks."

"Good morning, Mr. Sugarman."

A whole team of doctors and nurses appeared in Zach's room, yanking back the privacy curtain with a quick, metallic pull. The sound gave Liam just enough warning to drop Zach's hand and jump away from the bed. No one seemed to care at all that Liam was there, as he stepped out of the way so a nurse could check Zach's IV.

"How are you feeling this morning?" a doctor asked.

Zach's gaze followed Liam across the room, holding strong. He even managed a faint smile. "Best I've felt in weeks."

The doctors and nurses all laughed, assuming he was being sarcastic and charming. But Liam knew. He knew and he soared.

30

"Have you slept?"

"Not really."

"Liam."

Liam looked down at his brother's face on his phone screen. He was using his "dad face" again, looking both testy and disappointed at Liam's lack of self-care. Liam rubbed at the back of his neck, feeling properly sheepish. The movement exposed a pungent odor he realized was his own body. God, what he wouldn't give for just five minutes in a hot shower.

"I know, I know. It's just—"

The elevator doors to the general medicine floor chimed, and Liam bobbed out of the way with a sidestep. This was a dance he'd been doing all afternoon, and he had perfected the choreography.

If his wait the previous night in the ER had felt like a vigil, the following day had been a stakeout. From his bench by the elevator, Liam hovered around the ward all afternoon, waiting for one more chance to speak with Zach. He'd watched various doctors come and go from his room, some in white coats, some in scrubs, others in fancy slacks, or sensible heels.

Zach's parents had been with him all day. Coach Williams and Des and few other teammates had said their goodbyes before heading back to campus around lunch. Des had caught Liam's eye on his way out, and they'd shared covert nods.

Later, Liam had watched as Zach was rolled out of his room by a porter and taken down the opposite end of the hall. When he'd come back his neck brace had been gone, the head of his adjustable bed propped up high. The sedatives had worn off, and Zach had lost that woozy edge to his appearance. He'd looked like Zach again, and Liam's chest had expanded with relief at the sight.

Liam looked back down at his phone. "I just need to speak with him again before I come home, and then I promise, I'll sleep for a week." Then, with an impertinent grin, he added, "And miss all my classes."

"Haha," Eben said with a wooden expression. "I take it your first chat went well? Was he alert enough to even know what was going on?"

"Mostly. I think. I mean, part of why I want to stay is to make sure he actually remembers it happening," Liam admitted. He bit at his lip and wondered if the heat in his cheeks came through on FaceTime. "But yeah. It was good. Really good."

His eyes flitted over towards the half-opened door to Zach's room. The chief neurologist and her associate had gone into his room about twenty minutes ago. Liam didn't know if a chat that long meant good news or bad.

"Look, Ebbie, my friend who drove me down here left this morning, so I don't exactly have a way to get home. I guess I could just hop on a bus or take an Uber."

His brother groaned but in a way that made Liam hide a grin. "You can't Uber back to Chicago, Liam. Fuck's sake. Do you have your ID?" Liam nodded. "I'll book you a flight, then."

"You don't have to do that. I can call mom."

"Don't call mom. She'll freak out, wondering why you're in Indianapolis anyway. Trust me, it's not worth it." Liam watched Eben prop his phone on his open laptop and begin typing.

"Guess I created some drama that required a babysitter this

semester after all, huh?" Liam asked guiltily.

"I'm not being your babysitter right now, Liam. I'm just being a good big brother."

"You always have been." Eben's eyes stayed firmly on his open web browser, but his mouth pressed into a soft grin.

Movement by Zach's room caught Liam's attention as the doctors, along with Zach's parents, exited. Zach's mother was smiling as she wrapped a long teal-colored scarf around her neck. His father shook the doctors' hands as they walked down the corridor together. It had to be good news.

"You seriously are the best, but do you think you can make the flight for tomorrow?"

Eben rubbed at his eyes with a tired exhale. "I'll book you a hotel room too, shall I?"

—

Even with the door partially open, Liam knocked anyway. Zach wasn't going to answer or anything, but Liam wanted to give Zach fair warning that he was there. After a moment, he let himself in.

The lights were dimmed, the shades drawn, giving the room the feeling of unnaturally early twilight. Zach's face was angled away but he turned towards Liam when he entered. The movement looked awkward, like the muscles of his neck were fighting the motion, tight and cramped. Any evidence of distress melted away when he saw Liam. He broke into a smile of such quiet joy that Liam could hardly breathe for a moment. It felt like a lifetime since Zach had looked at him like that, radiating something shy and cautious, but boundless, too.

"You stayed," Zach said breathlessly.

"Is that okay?"

"Of course."

"Where are your parents?"

"They're at a hotel. I'm supposed to be resting."

Liam gave him an unapologetic look as he meandered through the room, inspecting it like an apartment he might rent. The TV was turned to the sports news channel with the volume low. Liam pointed up at it. "Watching all your coverage, huh? Typical egomaniac."

Zach snorted softly. "They've been speculating all day how long I'll be out of commission. A bit weird considering I didn't even know myself until just now."

"And?" Liam asked, trying not to sound overly eager.

"Six months. That's what the surgeon says, assuming all future head scans stay clear, of course. My neurologist isn't thrilled. She'd prefer that I take up knitting for the rest of my life, but I should be cleared to practice again by late summer. I'll have to be careful. Another hit like that and my career would be a short one, but at least I can still have a career."

It was the best news possible in this horrible situation. Relief compelled Liam closer, ready to hold Zach in modified celebration. But Liam just clasped his elbows with his palms, white-knuckled. He was still unsure that he'd done enough to prove himself worthy of being with Zach. Maybe now that Zach wasn't high on sedatives, he wouldn't be so amenable to Liam's apologies, after all.

"Will you come here already?" Zach demanded as he deciphered the conflict on Liam's face. Zach extended his hand and pulled Liam down next to him on the bed.

There, back in the arms of the person who had shown Liam more tenderness than all of humanity put together, he quickly learned that sometimes forgiveness came not as words, but as an embrace. It came as a sigh that matched his own and said nothing short of "This is where we're meant to be."

Zach's mouth found Liam's lips with magnetic ease, and Liam yielded to Zach's closeness. Even as he melted into Zach's familiar warmth, he was acutely aware of Zach's injuries. There was hardly room for him on the bed between the brace around Zach's leg and the wedge propping it up. Nudging something out of place in his voracity for more Zach would have ruined this perfect moment of reunion.

"You're sure this is okay?" Liam checked, breaking away from their kiss for the space of a breath.

"Yes, I'm sure." Zach dragged him in for another kiss,

promptly shutting down any further worry.

There was so much memory in their kisses but affirmation and mercy, too. Liam never wanted to stop kissing Zach ever again, but he knew there was a limit to how far this exchange could go in a hospital room and surrounded by doctors. They both seemed to find that edge simultaneously. Zach's bicep became the perfect pillow for Liam's head as Liam settled onto it, one hand curled under his chin, the other resting delicately on the flat of Zach's stomach.

"I missed your mouth." Zach pressed his forehead to Liam's.

"Even when it gets me in trouble? Everything I said that night, I didn't mean it."

"I know," Zach replied with ineffable forgiveness. "I know you were just trying to protect me. Doesn't mean it still didn't hurt like a bitch though. It broke me, Liam. For a long time."

It had broken Liam too, but surely that was evident by now. "I know and I'm so sorry, Zach." Liam looked at him, eyes and words sincere. Zach nudged the side of Liam's nose with his. With his silence, Liam's apology was accepted.

"I probably shouldn't have sprung it on you like that anyway."

The calm hand on Zach's stomach turned into a sharply pointed finger. "If you try and make any of this remotely your fault, I'm going to smack you. And you definitely don't need any more injuries right now."

"It's true though." Zach laughed softly as he captured Liam's hand in his. He played with the grip, his fingers sliding in and out of alignment with Liam's before he linked their hands and tucked them to his chest. "I was so caught up in making this grand moment out of telling you I wanted to come out that I didn't stop to think about how it would affect you. When I come out, you'll be dragged into the whole spectacle too. We should have just talked about it. It should have been something we decided on together."

"If, when, and how you come out is your decision, Zach," Liam stated earnestly. "This is your life."

"Our life," Zach corrected. If Liam hadn't been certain that Zach forgave him before, he was then. They shared a soft, lingering kiss before snuggling back into each other and their happy silence.

"You told Des," Liam said. "That's a huge first step."

Zach hummed in agreement. He raked his fingers backward through Liam's hair. His eyes watched the motion tenderly, reacquainting himself with every curl. "So was telling my parents and Coach the night of the Heisman award ceremony."

"What?" Liam propped himself up on his elbow, completely bewildered.

"I told my agent, Drew Carmichael, too. Full disclosure and all. I think he's excited, to be honest. Ready to work the 'gay' angle, though it looks like he might have to wait a year now before he gets to do that." Zach looked down at his knee, and Liam followed the glance, too stunned to do anything else. "I told Rebecca when I was home over break. She was pretty blindsided, but we're ok now. The other seniors and captains on the team have been amazing since I told them right before we left for the semi-final game, but then again, they're my best friends. The plan was to tell the rest of the team after the Championship game, but that hasn't happened yet."

"I'm sorry," Liam looked down at Zach and the unperturbed look on his face. "You did what? You came out to all those people?"

Zach gave him a superior little grin. "Yup."

Liam flopped back to the bed with a stunned laugh. He stared up at the ceiling for a long time in hopes of finding some understanding there. Liam imagined all those delicate conversations Zach had had with friends and loved ones over the past month, bravely speaking his truth after all these years. Eventually, Liam wanted to hear the details of every single one, but right at that moment, he was nearly giddy.

"You did it." Liam breathed, full of wonder. "Even after what I did, you went ahead and did it anyway. Why?"

The sting of remembered trauma coalesced into a furrow on Zach's brow. "I'd already lost you, Liam." His use of the past perfect tense was a beautiful thing. "The least I could do was not lose the self-assurance to be who I really am that I'd found when

I was with you. Even when we were apart, I held onto that."
Zach gave him a bashful grin. "Well, that and the picture."

With a quick scramble and a lift of his hips—delicately, of course, to not to jostle the bed—Liam fished his phone from his back pocket. With a click and swipe of his password, he opened his photo gallery. "This one, you mean?"

It was the photo Zach had taken in secret, a flash of light filling Liam's bedroom like a bolt of lightning. That picture captured a turning point in their affair where circumspection had given way to trust. It was photographic proof of the moment where their attraction turned to affection, and affection had rounded the corner towards love.

"You kept it too."

"Sentimental to a fault, the both of us, huh?" Liam mused.

They looked at Liam's screen for a moment. It was easy to see how their current setup mirrored the shape in the picture, nestled close and soft, the intimacy that had existed between them from day one rekindled.

"Take another one," Zach suggested.

Happily, Liam opened his camera app. He propped his arm up high to capture both of them in the frame and turned his face towards his phone. Just as he tapped the screen to take the shot, Zach hooked his finger under Liam's chin and turned him, kissing him soundly on the lips. The camera clicked.

The image was a bit blurry. Liam's hair was a mess, and Zach's hospital gown wasn't one for the red carpet, but it was probably the best picture Liam had ever taken in his whole life.

"We can use that," Zach said. "When we're ready to come out as a couple."

Liam had never thought of that as being a separate step in Zach's coming out journey, but he liked what that implied: he was now Zachary Sugarman's boyfriend.

"So, you're still going to do it, then?" Liam asked. "Not just friends and family, but all the way out?"

Zach gave him a tender, pleading look that asked for one last line of affirmation from Liam that he was ready for this fight, as he'd promised. Liam made a thoughtful sound, tilting his head back to rest on Zach's shoulder as he considered the picture again. "Slap a filter on it and it'll be perfect."

Zach kissed his hair, not seeming to care about Liam's unwashed state, maybe even enjoying it a bit. "Say what you said to me," Zach murmured, his mouth still hovering against Liam's skull. "Before."

"When before?"

"After I woke up. I want to make sure I never forget the sound of you saying it, and with this head of mine, you never know."

Liam smirked. He was pretty sure he'd happily say those words to Zach every day for the rest of his life.

"I love you, Zach."

Zach let out a holistic, healing sigh. "I love you, too."

31

The strangest thing about Zach's knee injuries was that for all their career-ending implications if not treated properly, he could still walk. In fact, he was encouraged to do so. Movement was slow, though. He found himself lumbering like Frankenstein's monster with one knee completely immobilized in a brace from thigh to shin while the non-displaced kneecap fracture healed. It was like learning how to walk again. The left side of his body adjusted to the robotic swing of a limb instead of a bend and flex. His right side was forced to accommodate the awkwardness with extra work and the assistance of a crutch.

After a few days at home, off the mainline painkillers and constant doting of the hospital staff, Zach almost thought he could handle the bone-deep ache in his knee if it weren't for the other, more mercurial injury he was dealing with. The concussion symptoms seemed to get worse as the days went by. His head hurt constantly, an underlying thrum that could spike to something like a burning inferno at the base of his skull at any moment. God forbid he dared look at the brightness of a TV screen or laptop monitor; he might as well have been staring at a solar eclipse. Writing anything longer than a tweet or a quick text required a new level of concentration that left him both frustrated and exhausted. Reading a book made his head swim, so he didn't even try. A walk across his apartment left the room spinning and his stomach on the verge of emptying its contents all over the floor from vertigo.

Returning to school for the second semester was obviously out of the question. Realizing he wouldn't graduate in the spring was almost as gutting as the realization he wouldn't be able to enter the 2021 draft, either.

The days unfolded in a study of humility and surrender, something Zach was never very good at. He had a winner's heart, but there was no way to beat a concussion. He simply had to live through it and endure. Meanwhile, his mother moved in, taking several weeks off from her real estate business as they waited for his ACL surgery date.

"We have to find the sweet spot," one of his many doctors explained. Perform the surgery too early and we risk an incomplete rehabilitation. Too late and we risk tearing other tendons as Zach's body tries to compensate for the original injury.

Mrs. Sugarman cooked comforting meals that Zach had grown up loving and cleaned him up when nausea took over. He was forced to depend on her in ways he wished he didn't need. As a twenty-two-year-old who had been on the verge of a manhood-defining career, any sense of previously established independence was compromised by having his mother clucking around. And it certainly was a roadblock for his renewed relationship with Liam, too.

The traditional "meet the parents" moment hadn't been traditional at all, coming instead the same day Zach had woken up to the inconceivable scene of Liam asleep at his side. Zach couldn't remember the hit that had felled him or waking up in the ambulance as they drove him off the field. But he would never forget the moment he blinked awake and tried to bring that mess of curls into focus, certain it must be a cruel trick of his injured brain.

A nurse had found them on Zach's hospital bed several

hours later, holding each other, catching up on sleep they'd both desperately needed. She'd woken them gently with a smile and the news that Zach needed to be taken for more scans.

While Liam went to his hotel room for a shower, Zach's parents had returned to the hospital. They'd been so relieved to see their son awake and happy. When Liam walked right into Zach's room a few hours later, his entrance had acted like a proverbial record scratch on the scene.

Liam had frozen in place, looking from Zach to Zach's parents and back to Zach again. Zach's parents had looked unsure of how to handle this situation, too. Everyone seemed to defer to the guy dealing with the traumatic brain injury, which hadn't been ideal.

"So, Mom, Dad, remember that guy I told you about? This is Liam Barnett." Zach said, lamely. "Liam, my parents."

Zach's father cleared his throat with a grumbling bluster. "I thought you two had..." He'd made a splitting motion with his index fingers, pressing them side by side before breaking them apart.

His mother, with a much better read on the situation, had shot her husband a testy eye. "Well, clearly they've..." She'd reversed his hand gesture, bringing her fingers together and twisting them, staying just this side of vulgar. Zach and Liam had tried not to burst out laughing.

Having Liam with him during the in-between times of the day has been amazing. Even with his mother in the guest room, Liam had been sleeping in Zach's bed nearly every night since his return from the hospital. It was the kind of domestic set up Zach had dreamed of, ever since he realized his feelings for Liam were so much more than simple desire.

He had never thought he and Liam would have the chance to be a cohabitating couple. It should have been heaven, but it wasn't. Not under these circumstances. Not when, sometimes just buttoning his shirt required so much concentration that on those days, Liam would toss a sweatshirt at his face and say, "Wear this instead."

Other times, when Liam started to kiss him before bed,

Zach's thoughts and instincts screamed, "Yes. More. Please. I've missed you, and I want you." But his body was unable to build up even the smallest physical reaction, not even for the man who had driven him to the brink time and again. Ignoring the frustration in Zach's eyes, Liam would just make sure the blankets were tucked carefully around Zach's leg and his crutch was nearby before he drifted off to sleep.

There were days where Zach found himself crying for no reason and others where he was aggressively mad, lashing out at anyone who dared to be close by. He knew these were side effects of his concussion, but he couldn't help but feel like he was an emotional basket case and a total asshole. His life was out of his control, and he hated it.

One night, while his mother slept, he and Liam snuggled on the couch under a large blanket. Zach's bandaged leg was propped on the coffee table and pain-free, for the time being. They finally had a moment of genuine normalcy, just binging a baking competition show on Netflix. Liam watched as Zach listened to the commentary from the competitors and judges, all speaking in pleasant variations of English accents. He kept his eyes closed and his head tilted back, only looking to the screen for brief moments to see the grand reveals of the finished products. Even so, by the second episode, the volume got to be too much, and his head started to ache.

"Mind if I turn it down a bit?" he asked.

"Go for it," Liam mumbled, his jaw encumbered by its place on Zach's chest.

Zach searched for the remote but couldn't find it anywhere. His fingers scrambled unhelpfully between the cushions and behind his back. "Where the fuck did you put it, you idiot?" he berated himself in a heated whisper as he twisted dramatically in his increasingly frantic search. Finally, he yanked the blanket off the both of them aggressively, and the remote flew across the room. It had been sitting in his lap all along.

Liam took in Zach's tantrum straight-backed and still. "It's okay, Zach." The saccharine-sweet tone of his voice was too much. Zach couldn't tolerate any more of Liam's pitying kindness.

"I think you should go!" Zach snapped.

"What? Why?"

"This is all bullshit, Liam! You didn't sign up to take care of some invalid—some guy who can't even watch a TV show. Or who is like some octogenarian, who can't even get it up for you." He swatted at his ineffective groin in reprimand. His breath was short, his knee throbbing in time with the pulse in his head.

After a second of stunned quiet, Liam calmly got up off the couch and retrieved the remote. "I'm here to help take care of you, Zach."

"I don't want a nurse. I want a boyfriend."

"Well, lucky you, you've got both." Liam sat back down, handing the remote to Zach, and with it, a modicum of control. "If you think the only reason I'm still here is to get back into your pants then you're dead wrong."

"Why else would you be?" Zach couldn't stop from lashing out. "I'm just some guy from Grindr, right?"

Liam looked at him, his jaw slack, his eyes all fire and hurt. Zach's chaotic subconscious seemed set for retribution. Even though he had forgiven Liam for the events that night on the field, deep down in his injured mind, he'd not forgotten. Zach's emotional pendulum swung to the opposite end of the spectrum as he realized this outburst was just another unwanted display of his injury. He fell against Liam's chest and whispered out a watery apology.

"It's okay. It's okay." Liam cradled Zach's head against him. "I'm exactly where I want to be, okay? Concussion-induced erectile dysfunction and all." Zach snorted and Liam kissed the top of his head. *"Mon amour, tu es insupportable. J'taime.* Do you understand?"

"Not really," Zach sniffled. He needed to start working on his French as well as his Italian if he was going to keep up with his boyfriend. "But yeah."

"Good. Now, press play. I want to know who wins bread week."

—

In his dream, Zach was playing chess with his cousin, Maggie. She lived in Philly and Zach hadn't seen her in years. He was fairly certain she'd recently gotten married. Zach hadn't been able to go, though. He'd had a game. He was warm, so they must have been in Hawaii. He'd never been to Hawaii, but okay. Obviously, Hawaii.

Dreams had been few and far between since the concussion, as his brain needed to rest even in sleep. But this dream was a nice enough one, even though he was awful at chess.

"Checkmate," Maggie grinned, her dark brow rising almost maniacally as she set up the board for another game. Warm wind blew through the tropically decorated space they were staying in, and Zach thought he smelled coffee.

It must have been some sort of reunion because other family members began settling around to watch them play the next match. In the distance, Zach could hear his mother giving orders in the kitchen. That was no surprise.

"The meatloaf is already baked, so take it out in the morning if you're going to eat it that night. I've written the cooking time and temp on the outside of the tinfoil, but I can email you complete directions if that helps."

Monosyllabic, closed-mouth replies came from whomever she was talking to. This unidentified person vacillated between patience and barely contained annoyance. In his dream, Zach's attention was drawn towards that voice in the kitchen, trying to identify its know-it-all cadence.

"Now," his mother continued, "the chicken also needs to be thawed ahead of time. It's raw, so it needs to get cooked all the way to a hundred sixty-five degrees, at least."

"Mrs. Sugarman, I know that, okay? I'm essentially Italian; I know how to feed people."

Finally, the identity of the voice broke through his dream, and so did Zach. The other person in the kitchen was Liam. Zach wasn't in Hawaii; he'd fallen asleep on his couch after a physical therapy appointment that morning. He hadn't been dreaming that conversation at all. It was actually unfolding in his apartment.

"I promise I will not give Zach salmonella poisoning from undercooked chicken."

The fogginess in Zach's brain had little to do with his injury and more to do with the disorienting experience of waking up in the middle of the day to a blossoming fight between his mother and his boyfriend. Zach turned slightly on the couch, trying to make as little noise as possible to avoid drawing attention his way.

Liam and his mother had both tried to claim space for themselves in Zach's recovery. Both were immeasurably important to Zach but for very different reasons. It had been a recipe for disaster and resentment. After nearly three weeks in Evanston, Zach's mother was heading back to Seattle later that day. Maybe it was because the previous day had been the first day since he got home that Zach didn't need pain meds or because he'd simply reached his mothering quota for a lifetime, but Zach was ready for some space.

"Excuse me for wanting to make sure you boys have enough food to eat while I'm gone," his mother said. "I would stay if he'd let me, you know."

"Oh, I know you would," Liam retorted. He was getting testy, Zach could tell. "You'll come back for his surgery in a few weeks, anyway."

"And you'd rather I didn't?" Alone, Zach rolled his eyes. He knew that heavy-handed guilt all too well.

Liam let out a hot sigh. "I didn't say that," he started, but she continued down her self-pitying path.

"No, it's fine. I'll just go ahead and leave my injured son on his own. His only caretaker his friend—boyfriend." She immediately corrected her faux pas. All the belligerence dropped from her voice. "I'm sorry, Liam. Boyfriend. I don't mean to sound small-minded."

Liam was silent for a beat. "It's okay." Zach could imagine the cool way he must have been leaning against the counter, his true opinion not yet revealed.

"You really have been so lovely to Zach, and you do seem to care for him."

"I do. Very much." He said it so quickly that Zach felt the ease of his love, even from across the apartment.

"It's been a lot for his father and me to take in this past month. One minute you think you'll be planning a wedding next spring and he'll be moving somewhere to start his professional career and then—" Her voice broke, followed by the sound of a few covered sniffles. She was crying. It was time for Zach to intervene. But before he could get off the couch, Liam spoke, his voice soft with concern.

"Hey, no, no. Don't. I can only imagine how crazy this has been for you. It's been a crazy time for me, and I'm only, well, the boyfriend."

Zach laid there, frozen. In the kitchen, his mother was crying, and Liam was comforting her. The significance of this moment did not go idly by him; Zach didn't dare interrupt it by getting in the way.

"He didn't think we'd turn him away for being gay, did he?" his mom asked, sounding distressed. "Is that why he didn't tell us before now?"

Her question pierced right through Zach's chest and into his heart. Even on the night he'd come out to his mom and dad, the lights of Time Square an ever-shifting kaleidoscope outside his hotel room, she hadn't dared to ask such a personal question. But at that moment, she sought consolation from that personal fear, not from Zach, but from the man he swore he loved. Zach waited, breathless, for Liam's answer.

"No, I'm sure he didn't. But to be honest, we never talked about it much. Right from the start, he made it very clear that coming out was never an option. Then all of a sudden it was, and he was so determined. It was a stunner for me too." Liam paused. "But if I know Zach, I'm sure not telling you had nothing to do with how you or Mr. Sugarman would react and everything to do with preserving the perfectly sculpted world he'd designed for himself. I think he really had himself convinced he would be fine pretending to be straight forever."

"Until he met you." There was a sweetness to his mother's voice, and Zach heard Liam make a bashful noise. Zach blushed, for Liam's sake. "All those years with Rebecca. He must have been miserable." Liam didn't respond. Zach wondered if he had shrugged away her comment or nodded in grim agreement. "What kind of mother am I to not notice something like this about my only child?"

"The kind who was buying exactly what he was selling to the entire world. God, if I hadn't met him the way I did?" Liam stopped, filling the space with an awkward sound. "Well, let's just say I probably would have bought it too."

There was the sound of the fridge door opening and closing. Zach heard two empty mugs hit the countertop and fresh coffee being poured into them. The drag of a zipper was the sound of his mother unzipping and then closing her purse. This was followed by the crinkle of plastic and the delicate blowing of her nose. Then after that, there was silence again.

"I know you're still getting used to this whole idea of, well, me. But imagine my artsy, European-dwelling parents when I told them I'm shacking up with a football player. And not soccer, but American football. I think they're still trying to get over the shock."

His mother laughed through her tears, a high, unexpectedly girly sound, the likes of which Zach hadn't heard in years. Liam's baritone chuckle joined in while Zach settled back into a comfortable position on the couch, hoping that the amiable silence in the kitchen meant his mom and Liam were hugging.

32

Zach's surgery was scheduled for the first day of February at a hospital in downtown Chicago. The staff there prided themselves on their experience with all of Chicago's professional teams—the Blackhawks, the Bulls, the Bears—so Zach knew he was in good hands.

"Textbook," his surgeon announced to all those in the recovery room, including Zach's parents, Des, and Coach Williams. Liam had decided that he'd had enough of hospitals and the questioning looks he got there, so he had waited at home for news.

Mrs. Sugarman promptly called Liam as soon as the procedure was over to assure him that all was well. "He picked up before I even realized my call had gone through." She gave Zach a knowing smile and smoothed his hair away from his anesthesia-heavy eyes. "I think someone was very eager to hear that everything went well."

Zach was up and walking a few hours later, as per doctor's orders. He went home forty-eight hours later on two crutches. By one week after surgery, he was down to one crutch, and then, two weeks after surgery, he was walking almost normally for the

244 | INGRID STERLING

first time in a month. It felt revolutionary. The ACL repair gave him a steadiness that spread upwards into his head, as well. Everything was clearer: his thoughts, his vision, his emotions. It felt like he'd turned a very permanent corner on his injuries.

Spirits revived, he convinced Liam to skip his last class of the day on a Wednesday afternoon midway through February. It was one of those oxymoronic winter days where the sky was a special kind of blue that only a child's imagination would dare paint, and yet the temperature was so shockingly cold that the air ripped right through one's lungs. Zach got behind the wheel of his Jeep and took his man for a spin down Lake Shore Drive. They blasted music, pressing the upper limits of the legal speed with the windows rolled down, embracing the cold. Zach's eyes flitted from the road to the way the wind caught in Liam's curls. Liam reached for his hand across the gear shifter and pressed a kiss to their laced fingers. For the first time since Indianapolis, there was hope on Zach's horizon, and he drove towards it.

They hadn't slept together again since their breakup—not for Zach's lack of wanting to, of course. While his mind supplied him with ample memories of their fiery chemistry, his injuries prevented him from performing. It was as embarrassing as it was infuriating.

With the sun long since set and emboldened by his recent recoveries, Zach reached for Liam the moment they arrived back at Zach's apartment with a rashly whispered, "Come here." He pulled Liam close by the pale blue fabric of his sweater, and Zach's hips fell against the corridor wall. Zach was desperate for Liam's touch. It had been too long since they'd been intimate, and he was ready, mind and body. He was also in no mood for being subtle, so he grabbed one of Liam's hands and flattened it against the front of his own jeans. Zach's erection was hard won after weeks of physically being unable. He'd never make fun of Viagra ads again.

"What are you doing?" Liam murmured.

"What does it feel like I'm doing?"

Liam inhaled sharply. "Are you even allowed to do this again? You're supposed to keep your heart rate down."

Zach hated how much of an authority on concussion care Liam had become. Despite his clinical concern, however, Zach felt a surge of pleasure, unmuted and delicious, as Liam's fingers curled against the fabric of Zach's fly.

"It's been over a month. And I may have tried things out this morning."

Liam snapped to attention. "You what?"

"In the shower. When I, you know, got up." He was overtly pleased at his innuendo.

"Of all the days for me to have an 8 a.m. class. That's so not fair." Liam's body relaxed back against him, though Liam was but anything but soft.

"I promise, my head won't explode."

"I don't know. This morning was just a bit of solo play," Liam teased, his voice carrying shades of filthy flirtation and actual worry. He shrugged as he cocked his head gently in the direction of the bedroom and pulled Zach away from the wall by the waistband of his pants. "I'm fully prepared to blow your mind."

They came back together like muscle memory. Liam's hands on Zach's body were so beautifully familiar that Zach was able to focus one hundred percent on sensation instead of mundane things like zippers or undergarments. Zach pulled the comforter back from the sheets so they could slide into his bed, skin to skin. With a languid exactness, Liam sat back and spread Zach's legs before ducking beneath the covers. With the show hidden from view, Zach closed his eyes, his hands resting on the mound of Liam's head as Liam's mouth, warmer than warm and lush, found him.

"So good," he murmured.

Yet, there was something lacking. Zach hadn't had sex since the end of November, and it should be rocking his world, but it wasn't. Not quite.

It wasn't the first time he'd worried that their relationship would forever be compartmentalized into "before" and "after." Their beautiful, electric affair had been railroaded by his injuries. Perhaps too many celibate days had passed for them to ever go back to the life-changing romance they'd had.

"Harder, babe. Come on," Zach begged, but nothing changed—not Liam's pace, not his pressure. It was vanilla of the worst order, not only careful but pitying. Zach couldn't stand it. He pushed up from the pillows onto his elbows. "I'm not going to break if you suck my dick, Liam, so just do it!"

So maybe Zach didn't have that.

So maybe Zach didn't have that irrational anger under control, after all. Liam tossed the sheets off over his shoulders. Liam's lips were a wet pink, his hair a debauched mess around his face. His hands fell to his lap with supplication.

"I need to tell you something," Liam admitted. Zach's gut turned cold. Blood draining from his cheeks. Those words were nothing if not ominous. "No, no, no, sweetheart." Liam read the panic on Zach's face like a cipher. He crawled forward to catch Zach's face between his hands. "Not that. Well, yes, that, but not what you're thinking, okay?" Zach looked Liam briefly in the eye. "It happened on New Year's Eve."

The idea of Liam being with someone else while they were split up didn't feel much better. With all arousal stripped from the room, Zach felt exposed in his nakedness. He pulled a pillow over his lap, hugging it close to his body. "Guy or girl?"

"Does it matter?"

"I don't know yet. Guy or girl?"

Liam took a second to process the anger in Zach's voice before admitting, "Guy."

Zach's jaw clenched. If Liam had been worried about raising his heart rate, he hadn't done a great job avoiding it. "Did you use protection?"

Liam looked back to his lap, guilt-ridden.

"Jesus, Liam! What happened to safety first, huh?" Zach retreated even farther away across the mattress.

"We only gave each other blow jobs. It's not like you and I used protection for those either."

"Yeah, but you and me, we were..."

"Not that first night in Rome, we weren't."

Liam had a valid point, and Zach's indignation petered out.

They'd never truly been exclusive, due to the complex, secret nature of their tryst. Into the silence that followed, Zach realized how many impossible things had needed to happen for them to even be sitting there on his bed, having this fight. "Why didn't you tell me?"

"Because I was a mess without you. I quite literally made myself sick after being with him. And then I finally had you back. You've already forgiven me for so much, and I was freaked out that I'd lose you again if I told you. And I can't, Zach. I can't lose you, like, ever. This is it for me, and god, I sound needy as fuck." Liam's fingers played softly with the skin of his neck as he averted his eyes skyward. He was so small in that moment of confession, his shoulders narrow and rounded, his arms pale and thin. But then, Liam had always been that way. Zach remembered seeing him that first night in the doorway to his ratty Roman flat. Physically, Liam could have been an easy and thoughtless conquest if that was all Zach had been looking for. But instead, Liam had been the one with the power play, showing Zach a path previously unknowable. Zach had been following that path ever since. He pulled Liam next to him. They fixed the blankets around them, all safe and calm for now.

"I'll go get tested," Liam offered. "Tomorrow. I mean, the chances are minuscule, but still, I'll go to student health. First thing."

Zach considered Liam's plan and the date with a scoff. "Happy fucking Valentine's Day. Take a number and have some blood work."

Liam looked at him like he'd forgotten what the following day was. He lifted his shoulder carefully. "Well, maybe it could be a happy holiday, after all. I mean, I assume you've been given every bit of testing known to man with all your hospital visits."

Zach nodded.

"And if you're clean and I'm clean then we wouldn't need..." His eyes drifted lower over Zach's body, and the inference was crystal clear. "I've never been with someone like that before." Liam's words were a barely-there whisper.

Zach flushed. He'd wanted to cross that final boundary of

intimacy with Liam so desperately the night before Thanksgiving, another "first" amongst all the other firsts Liam had given him. But he'd never imagined this could be a first for Liam, too. An only.

"I couldn't ask you this when I was with Rebecca, but just so we're clear," Zach stated. "I will not share you. Not again."

Liam gave an unsteady nod, his eyelids hovering. He looked a bit turned on by Zach's directness. Zach tucked that observation away for future reference as Liam reached for his phone. Zach watched Liam delete both his Grindr and Tinder apps from over his shoulder.

"Bye, bye, Ovid quote." Zach said as a prompt window on Liam's phone showed "Delete profile. Are you sure?" Liam pressed "yes" and the app icon disappeared from his home screen. "Please tell me you have that profile pic saved somewhere, though."

Liam tossed his phone to the floor before straddling Zach's hips. "Yes," he hissed against Zach's lips. "I'll send it to you. But now I want you to show me what you did in the shower."

—

After Liam left for class the next day, Zach made a phone call to Drew Carmichael, his agent-turned-professional consultant now that Zach wouldn't be entering the draft that year. Zach was sick of keeping what he felt for Liam behind closed doors or only among family and friends. Love is love is love, and theirs was beautiful.

"You're ready for the final stop on your coming out tour, huh?" Drew said over speaker phone from his office in New York.

"Yes," Zach stated, though he wished Drew wouldn't call it that.

"I'll talk to some people and let you know when I can get a date and a time confirmed for a press conference. You're going to make history, Zach."

After they ended their conversation, Zach knew exactly who he needed to call next. He didn't bother texting her. This person deserved a phone call, and she picked up right away.

"Hello?" Rebecca's voice was light and chipper. It wasn't the voice of the girl whose heart he'd used for so many years.

"Hey, how are you?" Zach asked. He started pacing around his apartment, suddenly feeling awkward and nervous.

"Fine, yeah. What's up?"

"You don't still have those keys to my apartment do you?" Zach winced at the implications.

Rebecca was silent for a moment. "I do. I can bring them right down if you want." Her offer meant she was at her boyfriend's place, just a few floors up. It seemed two could play at the "moving on" game.

"That would be great."

"Ok. There in a sec." The line went dead. Zach placed his phone down on his kitchen counter and let out a heavy breath.

He had met Rebecca when she still had braces, before she'd learned how to control her lion's mane of curls or the power she held in a well-fit V-neck sweater. He'd been her friend before he had been her boyfriend.

"You're different from the other guys," she'd said, and he'd already known why that was true. The first time he'd tried to kiss her, she'd given him her cheek but then blushed so sweetly under the Friday night lights he'd found he didn't even care.

He'd watched her face narrow over the years, her teenage roundness mold into womanly curves. He'd been witness to her blossoming in college, becoming a popular and natural leader of her sorority and sincere in her faith. She'd been his constant, so much a part of the fixtures that he'd wondered, through his anesthetic haze after his ACL surgery, why she wasn't there. She was always there for the big things.

Rebecca had been safe, easy, and guiltless in Zach's narcissistic story-making. She'd played both the romantic lead and the antagonist depending on the day or his mood. She'd only ever known the version of himself that he'd wanted her to know, the part that hoped she'd remain ever faithful, devoted to him till death they did part.

That felt like a different lifetime now.

Zach had owed Rebecca the truth from the beginning, so when he decided to come out to her during winter break, he vowed not to placate her with clichés or platitudes. The weight of their history deserved that much. He would not sugar coat it or try to hide any shameful corner from her: not about knowing he was gay even when they first got together, not about the other men he cheated on her with, not about Liam and the way meeting him had changed everything.

He hadn't been sure their friendship would survive the truth. There had been uncountable tears from both of them, slammed car doors, uncharacteristic curses, and days of silence where he assumed she had gone off to pray for his sinful soul.

When she texted him on New Year's Day, it felt like a resolution. "Just tell me there were times where it wasn't all lies."

Countless memories coalesced into the full arc of their story, beginning to end. He called her immediately and together, with happier tears and plenty of laughs, they remembered it all.

Standing in his doorway, her eyes sparkled with genuine happiness at seeing him, yet there was a tinge of awkwardness on her face, too. No matter the reasons their relationship had ended, an ex was still an ex, and they were finding their footing as friends.

"Look at you, all up and about," she said.

"I'm officially not a quadruped anymore. Or a tripod for that matter. Come in." Suddenly remembering his manners, he opened the door wider for her to enter. When she hesitated, he added, "He's not here."

Rebecca looked like she wanted to say something about how it wouldn't matter if he were, but they both knew that wasn't quite true. "You started going stir-crazy yet?"

"A bit." He closed the door behind her. "But it's better now that I'm more mobile and my head's not a total loose cannon. I even went for a drive yesterday."

"Speaking of. Here." She dangled the keys from the painted nail of her pointer finger. There was one for the front of the building, one for the apartment, and one for his storage unit in the basement. "Probably should have given them back to you a long time ago."

"It's okay." Zach pocketed them. His timing could not be more conspicuous. A set of keys might not be the flashiest first Valentine's Day present, but it sure felt romantic to Zach. "I'm glad you could come by today, actually. I wanted to tell you something. I'll be holding a press conference soon."

Instead of a variation on the "You're sure?" response that his parents, Des, and Coach Williams had given him, Rebecca asked simply, "When?"

"Next week, probably. I figured I should give you a heads-up since I'm sure the press will get in touch with you after. An interview with the scorned ex-girlfriend will probably be a hot commodity."

"Is that all I am, then? Collateral damage?"

Zach shrugged. "It's probably what they'll make you out to be."

Rebecca gave a resigned sigh and dropped onto his couch. She sprawled against the cushions familiarly and casually. "My period was late this month."

Though Zach had never slept with a woman, he knew exactly what those words meant. He dropped heavily onto the couch next to her.

"Don't worry," she said before he could even ask. "It showed up eventually, but I was in a complete panic for a week because Seth had told me I couldn't get pregnant if he pulled out before he...you know." She gestured and blushed.

Zach quickly cursed her Catholic middle school sex-ed classes but tried to keep his voice tempered. "Becca, please tell me you know that's not how it works at all."

"I know that now."

Zach wanted to scream, overly protective of the girl who had been by his side for so much of his life. Seth didn't give two shits about her if he was happy feeding her those kinds of lies. From the ashamed and dismayed look on her face, it was clear she'd reached the same conclusion.

"I spent that whole week praying that I wouldn't be pregnant, but I was sure God wasn't listening to me anymore."

"Why would you think that?"

"Because I haven't been to Mass or confession since I started sneaking around with Seth. All those times I told you I was going last semester?" She shook her head. "I wasn't."

Zach knew all too well the kind of little white lies he'd told when he was desperate to deceive. He didn't hold hers against her. Instead, he winked. "I figured as much."

"But it was weird because I haven't felt like less of a believer because I'm not a virgin anymore. I didn't feel full of sin when I realized that, if I had to, my best option might actually be a termination, even though I don't believe in abortion. I was all over the place, really, but it made me realize, it's time for me to break up with the man upstairs."

Zach's jaw fell open. Rebecca's faith in God had always been unflagging, one her most consistent traits. Her leaving the Catholic church was almost as monumental a decision as Zach deciding to come out. "Seriously?"

"I mean I should break-up with Seth." She pointed at the apartment ceiling where, several stories up, her baller boyfriend lived. She smiled wide, pleased by her own joke, as Zach relaxed. "And once I do, I think it's time to re-prioritize things. I need to re-examine my faith. Its tenants of service still mean a lot to me, but I don't want the doctrines to control me anymore. I want to spend this last semester with my friends, my sorority sisters. The people I've loved the longest." She looked at Zach, sweet and hopeful. "Maybe I'll even go abroad after graduation. Explore the world, meet new people. Your trip to Italy sure worked out for your love life, didn't it?"

That's when Zach saw, under the dark rings beneath her eyes that she'd tried to mask with foundation, another layer of Rebecca's growth, gained, not from a broken heart, but from a disappointed one. Zach laughed sharply and pulled her into a one-armed hug. This was the moment when exes became friends, where those who had met as kids became grownups.

—

Liam still had the Band-Aid plastered to the inside of his elbow when he arrived that evening. He flung his coat off and met Zach with a bruising kiss.

"I take it everything came back okay," Zach asked, as he followed Liam's beeline march towards the bedroom.

Liam shucked off his boots and tossed them over his shoulder. "No, I'm laced with venereal disease, and I've lured you into your bedroom to make you my next victim." He grabbed at the back of his collar with both hands and pulled his shirt off. He shook out his curls, grinning like a man about to have the lay of his life. "They want to check me again in six months to be sure, but yes, all clear."

If kisses could feel like starlight, then these did. More smiles than anything else, their lips met, greedy and giddy. Seconds before toppling onto his bed, Zach remembered his gift.

"Wait, I got you something. It's on the dresser." He hadn't wrapped them, as he was sure Liam would have found that garish. But the keys looked out of place enough for Liam to know they were for him.

"Are these...?" Liam gave him a crooked smile.

"Happy Valentine's Day. Now you can come and go as much as you please. But could we focus more on the coming part right now?"

With a growl, Liam lunged for him, tackling him to the bed with as much ferocity as he could while still being careful with Zach's knee. There was no talk about who would top first because the night was long and neither of them had anywhere else to be. But eventually, Zach found himself on his side with Liam's body spooned against his. Liam gasped softly as Zach adjusted his hips, moving in with one slick and natural movement.

Liam managed a frail "Fuck," before all words were lost. Zach was completely blinded by the beauty of Liam's body around him with nothing between them to subdue the heat.

He remembered holding Liam like that during their first night in Rome. Liam had pressed his back to Zach's chest and their hips had moved in what Zach realized later was only a pale mockery of the real act. Being with Liam this way was the joining of so much more than bodies. Even the word "love" felt woefully insufficient. And yet, trapped by the constraints of the only spoken language they both shared, Liam used that word again. But that night, trembling in Zach's arms, the words from Liam's lips weren't, "I love this, Zach," but "I love you."

33

"I feel like I'm going to puke."

Liam's hands froze around the knot at Zach's throat, stalled while tying a knot far more complicated than the double Windsor Zach had done for himself. "Wait, seriously?"

Even though Zach had been doing well, only suffering mild headaches if he pushed himself too far, Liam immediately scanned his eyes and checked his pupils. Zach appreciated Liam's continued concern. He found it pretty darn adorable. "My brain is fine, Liam. I'm just nervous."

Liam finished his work on the tie and rested his hands on Zach's lapel. There in the ersatz green room, set up in what was usually the players' lounge, he and Liam were safely surrounded by people who already knew the truth. His parents, Coach Williams, Eben, and Mackenzie, at Liam's request.

Des, Ruiz, Jackson, Rick, and the rest of his fellow senior teammates were also there, having insisted on joining Zach on stage. It was their idea to flank him from behind during the press conference, much like they did on the field. They would create an impressive lineup of solidarity, a gesture that touched Zach more than he'd ever be able to express.

Press from all the major networks, as well as both national and local papers, had been filtering in for the last half-hour, creating an anticipatory buzz of humanity in the room down the hall. Drew had planned the event down to the minute. Keeping the nature of the press conference a secret, he had guaranteed that it was huge and that they would want to be there.

When the time came, Zach would go into the media room where he'd given countless post-game interviews over the years. There would be a long table draped in Northwestern purple with four mics lined up on it. After Coach Williams, Zach's neurologist, and his orthopedic surgeon gave a quick update on his treatment and general prognosis, he'd join them and give his statement.

After it was all said and done, he would be the first out college quarterback at a Division I school. The first out Heisman winner. The first out potential #1 draft pick. The first out National Championship winner. It was a lot of firsts, and history loomed large.

Liam's fingers curled into the fabric over Zach's chest. "You could always just post something online, you know."

"I'm not going to come out via Tweet."

"Instagram?" He gave Zach a tepid look.

Zach knew Liam was nervous, too. His sympathetic anxiety was probably worse in a way. Liam wasn't the one who had been imagining this moment for months. He wasn't the one with a speech folded into the inside pocket of his blazer, typed up the night before, and rehearsed in front of the mirror twice that morning. Liam had no control over the situation or how the world would react.

"I need to do this."

"I know," Liam acquiesced. "You sure you don't want me to be out there? I could stand in the back." Drew had thought it best for Zach's parents and Liam to watch through a closed-circuit TV in the green room in hopes of focusing on football rather than on the specifics of Zach's personal life.

"I'd be too distracted by your beautiful face to get the words out."

"Flattery, Mr. Sugarman," Liam tutted with a wag of his finger. He gave Zach a swift kiss and trailed away to refill his paper coffee cup.

Zach checked his phone. 10:57 a.m., three minutes. His stomach flipped. He'd had a restless night's sleep the night before. His heart had been pounding so loudly in his ears as he lay awake that he'd tested his pulse several times to make sure he wasn't having some sort of cardiac event. That same stress thumbed through his veins now. His hands were freezing cold even though he'd already sweated through his undershirt.

The vibe of the room was similar to that of a locker room before a big game. Everyone present was filled with a grim determination to get this right. When Drew opened the door, the noise from the media room burst into the green room, and Zach's stomach doubled-over again.

"We're ready," he announced.

The next thing Zach knew, Coach Williams put his hand on Zach's shoulder, Des clapped him on the back, his parents hugged him, and Liam mouthed "Love you," with thinned lips. Then Zach was walking down the hall and into his press conference.

The last time the media at large had seen Zach was when he'd been loaded into an ambulance somewhere near the thirty-five-yard line. The shutters on dozens of cameras clicked, their flashes popping from every direction, capturing the first glimpse of him walking again on his own two feet. He managed to give them a quick wave of acknowledgment and what he hoped came across as a smile. He pulled out his papers, glad to see that his hands were steady even if his next exhale wasn't. He glanced over his shoulder to see Des and Ruiz on his left, Jackson and Rick on his right. Their hands were clasped at their backs like soldiers at parade rest. Des gave him a quiet nod.

"Thanks to all of you for being here this morning."

The voice that came booming out the audio system sounded like Zach's, but it felt disembodied. He focused on the printed words in front of him and began again.

"Before I get started, I'd like to offer some thank yous. First, to Drew Carmichael for his help in organizing this event today. To ESPN for setting time aside in their schedule to broadcast this press conference live. I'd like to thank the staff of Ryan Field for letting us use the space and being so accommodating in what is usually their off-season. I also want to thank Coach Williams and Drs. Wexly and Freiberg for their updates on my health and rehab. I quite literally wouldn't be here talking to you all today if it weren't for their expertise and the excellent care I've received from them both."

He'd been encouraged to include that opening by his dad. While he'd found it a bit formulaic, he knew it was the proper thing, nonetheless.

Liam had offered to read through the rest of his statement, that morning. He'd been fresh from the shower, his hair still damp. The air in Zach's apartment had been tinged with the scent of Liam's shampoo, the one that he ordered online and whose instructions were in French only. Zach had turned him down and thrown two ties on the bed, asking for Liam's opinion as a way of changing the subject.

He would have valued Liam's thoughts on his statement, but Zach felt overly protective of the words he planned to say. His dad, Drew, and even the Northwestern Athletic Director had all asked to see copies of his speech, but Zach hadn't felt comfortable sharing it. He knew this announcement would send shock waves in the sports world. Snippets of it would be replayed on TV and online, and they would be posted, quoted, critiqued, analyzed, and hopefully, praised. So, Zach wanted the words to be his and his alone, undiluted by the opinion of others, even those he loved and respected. He wanted to own his coming out story, one hundred percent.

With a quick shift in his seat, Zach launched back in. "I certainly didn't think I'd be coming to talk to you like this today. And I definitely didn't think my season would end the way it did." He stopped, giving a well-rehearsed grin. "Well, no, that's not true. I always knew the 2020-2021 season would end in a Northwestern National Championship, I just figured I'd be conscious for it."

There was a bubbling of polite laughter. This was the kind of Zachary Sugarman they'd all come here for, the sweet and well-spoken young man.

"As Coach Williams and my doctors informed you, I suffered a level five concussion, a non-displaced fracture of my left patella, and a complete rupture of my left ACL during the Championship game. Sounds pretty terrible, I know, but the good news is that all current indicators suggest I will make a full recovery and be able to return to training within six months. The bad news, however, is that due to my injuries, I will not be able to participate in any pre-draft activities this year. So, after consulting with my coaches and family, I have decided to not enter the 2021 draft."

Bombshell number one was officially deployed.

"Because of this, I need to offer another thank you, this time to the governing board of the National Collegiate Athletic Association, who, due to the lateness and severity of my injuries, has offered me a retroactive medical redshirt for this season. This means," he paused, smiling shyly. "I guess I'm going to be a Northwestern Wildcat for one more year."

The sea of cameras flared back to life. There was a surge of chatter and pleased sounds across the room. Zach thought there might even have been some applause from where the student editor for The Daily Northwestern was seated. They thought this was it. This was his big announcement. On any other day, it would have been headline news. The Heisman winner whose name has been first on the lips of every NFL scout as their first-choice draft pick was staying in school? It was huge, as Drew had promised.

Coach Williams, who had been as tickled as anyone when their request for another year of eligibility at the college level had been granted, gave Zach a smile. It was one that, from a distance, looked struck with his own dumb luck, but from where Zach sat, he could see that it carried a strain around his eyes that encouraged Zach to go on.

As the noise settled, Zach did too. He smoothed his papers against the table with his palm, finding he didn't really need them anymore.

"You know, people say that football is life. But someone recently reminded me that this," he gestured at the room, "football, is always going to end." He looked to the main camera, hoping that Liam caught his use of those stolen and slightly shuffled words. "It could have ended that Monday night in Indianapolis. It could end next season with another bad hit to the head. It could end in fifteen years, after a couple of Super Bowl rings and an invite into the NFL Hall of Fame."

He kept all thoughts of his career ending after his announcement to himself.

"Regardless of the 'when,' someday, football will end for me. But the man I am and the life I want to lead will continue on, hopefully for many years, even after my career as quarterback comes to a finish."

The world seemed to slow around him. There was peace in his veins. "Ever since I was fourteen years old, I've known two things about myself." He enunciated the words with no effort. They were laced with the final euphoria of truth.

"I knew I wanted to play football at the highest levels of college and pro ball, and that I'm gay."

The silence that followed was, as they say, deafening and deeply profound.

"Good, you are all still listening then." He laughed softly, even when no one else did. "I'm gay, and I'm going to say that again because I've spent so much of my life trying to hide that from everyone around me, I can count the number of times I've said that out loud on two hands. I come here today with the full support of my parents, my coaches, my teammates, including these guys," he jerked a thumb over his shoulder, "who are more like brothers than friends, and a guy who—well, let's just say I'm happy he likes Ovid as much as I do."

A vision of Liam rolling his eyes at Zach's silly comment flashed through his mind and he felt calm.

"I realize how lucky that makes me. Not everyone in my shoes gets the kind of support I have. This is why in addition to all my thanks, I owe some apologies as well. Firstly, to my ex-girlfriend, Rebecca, who was always a solid partner to me. I am lucky that my coming out has allowed us to turn a corner in our relationship and become even better friends than we were before. I want to apologize to the Northwestern Football family, who maybe feels blindsided by my announcement today. I hope this act will allow for discussions and open conversations and the chance to find middle ground. But mostly," Zach steadied himself with a breath. "I want to apologize to those of you out there who are listening and see yourself in me. I want to sincerely apologize to all the other Zachary Sugarmans who are fighting the same battle I did for so long, unable to reconcile their sexuality with the sport they love. To those who can see soldiers come home and kiss their partners of the same gender but aren't allowed the same dignity because they dream of making a career throwing, kicking, or shooting a ball. To those who feel they have to hide who they are from this machismo-obsessed sports world because they didn't know they could be both gay and an all-star because no one had shown them a way before now. I'm sorry because I should have done this sooner. For your sake and mine."

He pinched at his nose, his throat tight. Des's hand fell to his shoulder and squeezed tight. Coach Williams clasped his forearm kindly. Their gestures of support did little to help Zach maintain his composure. He closed his eyes and sighed, the breath amplified by the microphone. He felt raw and exposed, but he could sense the heightened emotional state of the room. Every person present seemed fully committed to this vulnerable and honest moment. He pressed on.

"Some of you out there listening or watching might be pitying me right now. Thinking that I'm some delinquent or a sinner and that I've thrown away any kind of career I might have had. But the truth is, this is the most liberating day of my life. Because what happens next is entirely out of my hands. It's all up to you now."

He turned his attention to the press in the room.

"It's up to you and how you spin this in the media. Am I brave, or am I reckless? Am I a trailblazer for future generations, or am

I an idiot for not keeping quiet? It's up to the team owners, the coaches, the players, and the fans of the NFL. How much will you let my sexuality dictate how you run your team or whether you cheer for me?

"And I get it, I might be a hard sell to certain markets. I'm fully aware that there are plenty of people who are never going to be okay with who I am or who I love. But if you're sitting there disgusted by all of this, disgusted by me, let me ask you, what does this change about me as a player? How does me being gay change one game? One award? One win? One play? One pass? I'll tell you." His voice barely rose to a whisper. "It doesn't."

Silence lingered in the room. It was like when an entire stadium went quiet around Zach as he threw a long pass down field and everyone waited for the ball to connect with its receiver. Eventually, he had to let go. He'd certainly done that now.

Bringing himself back down to reality, he spoke once more into the mic before pushing himself away from the table. "I'll leave all questions to Mr. Carmichael."

—

"'Words can't explain how proud I am to call my man @ SugarmanSugarrush24 my brother and teammate. And to all the haters, it's 2021. Get the fuck over it. Hashtag loveislove' Nice tweet, Des. Very classy," Liam said as he read from his Twitter feed.

Des grinned at him, self-satisfied. "Well, it's true. Our man was a badass out there today."

The mood in the lounge after the press conference could not have been more different than how it had felt beforehand. Everyone was lighthearted, full of pride and relief. People had their phones out, scanning articles and video responses from various news outlets to see how it was all being received.

Zach, having collapsed into the closest comfy chair he could find, was completely exhausted. The emotional magnitude of what he'd done had compounded the residual effects of his concussion, and his head was filled with a dull ache.

"And why am I shaking now that it's over?" he asked no one

in particular as he looked down to where his broad hands were quivering.

"It's your adrenaline," Eben answered kindly as he handed Zach a cup of coffee. "Don't worry, it's decaf," he added with a wry smile that looked terrifyingly like Liam's at that moment.

Zach's dad appeared next to Eben. "We'll get something stronger in you later. I've got reservations at our usual place downtown."

"I don't know, Dad. Going out? Tonight?"

His father crouched down so they were eye to eye. It reminded Zach of when he was on the sideline after a tough loss as a kid. "Don't you start hiding from the world now, Zachary. Not after what you've just done. The hardest part is over, so hold your head up. Be proud. I know I am. Okay?"

"Okay," Zach agreed meekly, blinking back tears.

His father stood and placed his hands in his trouser pockets, looking very pleased by this bit of parenting. He then turned to Eben. "You and your—Kelsey, wasn't it? You'll join us for dinner, of course?"

"Delighted," Eben answered, and the two men walked off together.

"Holy shit!" Mackenzie exclaimed with glee. She then covered her expletive-tainted lips with her hand. There were parents and professors present, after all. "Sorry. It's just—'Zach Sugarman' is trending number one nationwide." She tapped at her phone. "And there is this hashtag: 'westillwant24.' They look like football fan accounts. No, wait." She looked closer at the screen. "Wait, this one has one of those official Twitter checks. There are players using this hashtag, too."

"Of course there are." Drew smiled smugly, emitting the air of one who knew exactly what would happen. Zach didn't know how much his parents were paying to keep him on retainer, but it was totally not enough. Drew pulled a ringing phone out of his pocket, clearly pleased as he examined the number. "And this would be Nike."

"What?" Zach gasped.

"You didn't think you'd be getting these kinds of calls?"

"I can't even be sponsored if I'm still in school."

Drew lifted the phone to his ear, pressing a slick look in Zach's direction. "Oh. They'll wait." He went out into the hallway, addressing whoever was on the other end with a let's-get-down-to-business greeting.

"Ellen made a post about you," his mother said with tears in her eyes.

"And Colin Kaepernick, Jason Collins, and Megan Rapinoe, too. Damn, dude," Des added with a wide grin.

It was all happening so fast, but in this day and age of digital globalization, of course, news like Zach's would spread instantly. He reached into his pocket for his phone, wanting to see it all for himself. Then, as if materializing out of nothing, Liam was next to him, his fingers delicate but halting on his wrist.

"Don't," he cautioned, offering an apologetic look to Zach's indignant one. "Not everything's as positive."

"I knew it wouldn't be." Zach clicked on his phone, but only got a second's glance at his home screen to see it lambasted with notifications before Liam had his hand around his wrist again. It was firmer this time.

"I know you're not always keen on letting me try to protect you, but let us be your filter. Just for a while longer. Please?" With another wave of fatigue and appreciation for Liam's concern, Zach relented, dropping his phone into Liam's waiting palm.

It was impossible for Zach not to notice how the people gathered in this room today were the perfect cross-section of his and Liam's lives. If this were a hint about their future, then it would be a beautiful one. The flutist and the running back. The lawyer and the classicist. The mother and the coach.

And there, by his side, with his shoulder pressed steadily against his, knowing that silence was all Zach needed for the time being, was Liam, the man who was his inspiration and perpetual reward. Zach eyed Liam in profile: his delicate but strong jawline, the elegant arch of his nose, the curve of his pale brows. On that first night in Rome, those features had merely created libido-driven intrigue for Zach. Now the sight of Liam filled him with boundless affection. Yet his beauty continued to catch Zach by surprise.

"You've really gone and done it now, haven't you, Sugarman." Liam smiled softly when he caught Zach looking.

Zach took Liam's hand, lacing his fingers with Liam's. He was instantly reminded of the night at the bar overlooking Chicago where this very same touch had felt outlawed. Later, Zach wanted to walk out of the stadium holding Liam's hand, and he didn't care who saw him.

"The world hasn't ended yet."

In fact, Zach was pretty sure his world was just beginning.

About the Author

The name "Ingrid" comes from a character in a long-abandoned story. The name "Sterling" pays homage to her father's boyhood dreams.

The girl who would become Ingrid, was born in New England. She still considers herself a Yankee through and through, even though she has spent time in the midwest and now lives south of the Mason Dixon.

She began writing as a child, continued through high school, and started college as an English major, before switching to music performance.

After establishing her professional music career, Ingrid wrote in secret, circulating her work in fandom communities, as a means to escape. It was a hobby that she kept to herself and only a very few select people in her life. It wasn't until her late thirtys that she decided to take the plunge, jumping from her classical music world, to that of publishing.

Ingrid writes about love, with love, because #loveislove. The most fascinating thing for her to explore in her writing is how two people can find each other, overcome any obstacles life or society throws at them, and still choose love, in the end.

She strives to make her words sing. The rhythm and pacing of the prose is as important to her as her complicated, imperfect characters and her guaranteed happily-ever-afters.

Ingrid is published by Literary Wanderlust. She lives in a beautiful house with her husband, two children, and four cats.

CPSIA information can be obtained
at www.ICGtesting.com
Printed in the USA
BVHW081915220321
603177BV00006B/267